SURREAL

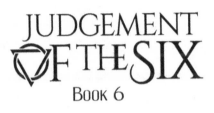

JUDGEMENT OF THE SIX

Book 6

MELISSA HAAG

(SUR)REAL

My sisters hate their gifts, but they don't know how lucky they are. They have a home and family. I have nothing. But, I am Courage, and I know my purpose. I exist for one reason only: to complete the Judgement.

Olivia is blind, yet sees. And what she sees, she keeps to herself. Her father conspires for control while Olivia does her own plotting with forces that only she understands. Now, time is running out, and choices that will impact the world must be made.

For Ednah Walters,
I'm glad you were able to read the conclusion since you were with me
for so much of the journey. You will be missed, dear friend.

For my editors and proofreaders,
Thank you for all the time you put into reviewing my words. Your
group effort helps my stories shine.

For my readers,
Thank you for sticking with the Judgements. I can't wait to hear what
you think of this, the end to their epic story. And, I hope you'll
consider delving into the next world I create, no matter what it is.
Thank you for your trust and support. It's meant the world to me!

PROLOGUE

OLIVIA...

I CONCENTRATED ON WRITING A LETTER, a hard task to complete, considering I was blind to the real world. Swirls of grey outlined the shape of the desk before me as the Others tried to help.

"Trace the letter b on the paper," I said softly.

A tiny swirl started in the center of my vision. I moved the pen I held toward that spot.

"Show me the tip of my pen, too, so I know where to aim." With care, I traced a 'b' on the paper under my pen. "Is it lining up well?"

A horrible wailing moan pierced the air. It wasn't a sound of agreement, but a warning.

"Who's coming?"

"Blaaaake..." The word was more of a long moan.

Hurrying, I put the paper in the desk's drawer and opened the braille book I'd set to the side. My door opened just as I set my fingers to the page. The Others' ghostly grey forms swirled around Blake in an agitated display. They liked Blake.

"Olivia," Blake said. An unsuspecting listener might think he said it in greeting. I knew better.

"Good morning, Father."

He remained in the doorway, observing me for a moment.

"I feel as if you're hiding something from me...what are you doing?" Suspicion and accusation collided in his tone.

"I apologize. This book is an action thriller about—"

"I don't care. Come. You'll spend the day in the Family building."

"Yes, Father," I said, suppressing the dread I wanted to feel.

As soon as I stood, the Others moved away from Blake to swirl around the objects in the room, creating a grey, visual display of my surroundings so I could move unencumbered.

Blake led the way from the room, and I followed.

"You've always been closed off, Olivia, which I appreciate. However, you've been behaving out of character lately. I don't like it, and I don't trust it."

"I apologize, Father. I've been dwelling on the problems with my sisters, trying to find a way to help."

He cocked his head and inhaled deeply as we continued to walk. He wouldn't detect a lie, though. I always told the truth. He stopped to open a door and held it for me.

The cool breeze stole my breath as I stepped outside.

"The families will help you stop dwelling on problems that are not your concern," he said, continuing down the sidewalk.

Looking further ahead, I watched as the Others danced along the large building that loomed before us. Thousands of them filled the air. I couldn't remember a time without them. They were always with me.

When Blake and I approached the front of the building, a woman opened the door. I wasn't sure who it was, though. I just knew it wasn't one of the nice ones. They were never allowed out because they would run if given the chance.

"I will see you at dinner," Blake said abruptly, turning and leaving me to walk the rest of the way now that someone was waiting for me.

"Good morning," I said softly to whoever waited.

"Olivia."

The single word was enough to recognize Marie. I stepped inside and waited for her to lead the way to the central meeting room. A child ran past us. It—I couldn't tell male or female at such a young age—slammed into my leg with a toy as it ran past. I didn't flinch though I knew I'd wear a bruise in a few hours.

Marie said nothing about the incident, but I knew she'd heard. Ahead, the chatter of childish voices drew my attention, along with the lower murmurs of their mothers as they watched their young playing.

When we reached the central room, the children and women quieted for only a moment then resumed. Marie left me, and I made my way to a chair set along the wall. The Others raced with the children, keeping up with their play so I could see what went on around me. A child ran up and pulled my hair before running away.

I turned to look at the mothers.

"I won't tolerate any abuse."

A few laughed but didn't answer. Another child ran up to me. Its hand darted out toward my face, a slap or a scratch intended. I swatted the hand, and the child giggled before

3

running off. It was a game to them. The blind girl who could see.

It had been like this from the moment I came to live with them.

My earliest memory of Blake seemed to have set the tone for my life, and the tone was very reminiscent of a death march. I couldn't have been more than four the first time I'd noticed him. A woman I couldn't recall had been holding my hand and leading me from a building where doctors liked to watch me play. Back then, I hadn't yet spoken any human words, though I'd understood them. I'd been listening to the Others since as long as I could remember, and the grownups around me had assumed I was deaf and blind because I emulated the language of the Others. I could only guess that my parents hadn't liked my moaning wails.

While leaving that building so long ago, I'd been wailing to the Others around me, watching them dance and swirl, when a large chunk of them had broken off to dance around a single person. They'd moved so fast and accurately that I recalled seeing every detail of the man's face in their swirling shades of greys. Stopping, I'd watched the man across the street continue to walk, unaware of the storm around him.

"Come on, Olivia."

The woman had given me a gentle tug, and I'd wailed louder and pointed, drawing the man's attention.

"No, honey, it's not nice to point." But it had been too late. He'd seen me. More than that, he'd caught my scent, and something about it made him cross the street and follow us at a distance.

The woman and I had walked to a parking garage, and I remembered what had happened next with complete clarity.

Blake had called out to the woman, asking something. She'd paused and turned. Blake had moved super-fast and had her head between his hands while I watched. He'd twisted sharply, and the woman had fallen to the ground.

I remembered how I'd trembled in fear. Then, a voice had come to me, and the Others around me had slowed, almost blinding me.

"Child, you are not alone. Go to him. Have courage."

I'd tipped my head up, trying to see the man again.

"Lift your arms to him."

A child came running up to me, pulling me from the past. I avoided another blow and stayed in the present, waiting for the hours to pass.

Marie came to sit with me as many of the families left to fix lunch. She didn't offer me food, and I didn't ask for any. She wasn't my friend. None of the women in this room ever would be.

It was my fault that I was enduring the families. Blake knew I didn't care for the family building. He knew how I was treated. And, he used it as a punishment for not behaving as he expected. I was a tool to the Urbat, a disposable asset. I needed to behave accordingly.

My fate could have been graver. Instead of treating me like a daughter, Blake could have treated me like a human, or worse, a werewolf. I'd heard tales from the women of how the Urbat population had grown. I'd even met a few pure werewolf females.

Long ago, before I'd even been born, Blake had met the controller, Charlene. Back then, both the Urbat and the werewolves had been struggling. The last war between the two races had left their numbers decimated, the werewolves more so than the Urbat. After that war, the Urbat leaders had passed down one directive. Keep the werewolf population low so they wouldn't be a threat again.

The best way to do that was to keep the female population low. Blake and his crew had been out hunting a Mated pair they'd heard about when they came across another rumor. A human female was living with a werewolf pack.

By the time they'd reached the werewolf settlement, the woman had been fully entrenched in the pack and committed to the leader. But the best part was that years of obscurity had seemed to erase knowledge of the Urbat from the werewolves. Blake and his men had stood in their midst and the werewolves hadn't even known.

It was a defining moment for Blake. He'd looked around at what the controller was doing and followed her example with the Urbat. He'd forced his men out into the human world. They'd adapted or faced punishment. In reward for their obedience, they had been allowed to capture, not kill, the werewolf females if the females hadn't established a connection to the leaders of their kind. The Urbat mated with the captured females but did not take them as Mates. That increased the Urbat population while bringing the werewolf population low. Half-breed werewolf children were raised to hate the werewolves and sent to infiltrate the werewolf community.

The werewolf women never lived long. Like wild animals forced into cages, their spirits faded until they gave up. I could think of only one who still survived and was older than me. However, I hadn't seen her since she'd become pregnant again.

Most of the Urbat women were half-breeds. As long as they showed strong Urbat traits, they were welcomed and treated very well. If they didn't...well, Blake couldn't allow the werewolf population to grow.

WHEN THE TIME finally came for Marie to walk me to Blake's private rooms, I didn't hide an ounce of my relief. My quick steps soon outpaced Marie, and I opened the entrance door to Blake's building myself.

The hall was quiet as the Others skimmed along the walls to guide me. Hints of grilled chicken flavored the air, and my stomach growled. I didn't try to hide any of my reactions. He'd be pleased that he could provide food for me when I was so hungry. Blake in a good mood meant I could return to my room sooner.

"Good evening, Father," I said as I walked into the dining room.

"Olivia."

He stood and pulled out a chair for me. The courtesy was an illusion, a way for him to get closer to me so he could decide if I had been appropriately punished for my small slip. I sat and waited. After a moment, he moved away.

"Were you sufficiently distracted from your thoughts today?"

"Yes, Father."

"Good. Leave your sisters to me. I have several men searching for the fighter. I have no doubt they will find her before the dreamer and the rest do."

I reached for my napkin to distract myself from thoughts of my incomplete letter. The Others moved around the room, outlining everything, so I could see the covered plate before me.

After settling the napkin on my lap, I turned toward Blake. He was watching me, waiting for my acknowledgement.

"Of course they will. They were very close with Gabby."

A growl escaped him at the reminder of just how close he'd been.

"Joshua is lucky he's dead. I should have killed him myself for his incompetence with her."

He reached across the table and lifted the lid off my plate. I inhaled deeply, showing my appreciation.

"Eat," he said.

I picked up my fork and knife and carefully cut a small piece from the chicken breast on my plate as I considered his frustrated tone.

Blake had also entrenched himself in the human world, creating a network of contacts and playing the market to build an empire. It was through sheer luck that he'd found the provider. I knew very little about her, other than Blake had kept her isolated from me.

His mood had been high with both of us under his thumb, and everything had been going well until one of his spies had reported an Elder had found the locator, Gabby. Blake could do nothing while she'd lived with the Elder, fearing that he would give away his hand too early.

So, he'd planned and waited, putting the oldest half-breed he'd had in place. Joshua was supposed to make it possible for an Urbat to Claim Gabby. Instead, some unknown werewolf had shown up at Gabby's residence, preventing all challengers from getting close to the girl.

Blake had lost the locator, who was his key to finding the two missing Judgements. Not only that, the provider had escaped just this spring. They had all been at the werewolf

Compound just weeks ago when the dreamer had shown up and Claimed Joshua. From there, Blake's plans had completely fallen apart. Except for me.

"You're very quiet," Blake said.

I swallowed my bite of peas and gave him a small smile.

"I'm lost in my thoughts and looking forward to returning to my room. The book," I said, as if to clarify why.

"Ah, yes. I suppose you'll need a new one soon. Do you have one in mind?"

"I have no particular title in mind, but I do like the suspenseful ones."

"Very good. I'll order something new for you."

"Thank you, Father."

We ate in silence for the rest of the meal. Blake didn't believe in small talk. At least, not with me. My basic needs were met. My time suitably occupied. There was nothing more to say. As usual, he finished before I did. With food still on my plate, I set my fork aside and thanked him for the meal. He stood and pulled out my chair for me, extending manners as a well-practiced pretense, then walked me to my room.

I read for thirty minutes before I pulled the letter out from the drawer. With the help of the Others, I painstakingly continued to write the brief message to the fighter.

The grey mists around me slowed and brightened, and I looked up to see the Lady beside my desk. Where the Others were shades of grey, she was light, almost white.

Dear one, are you certain you want Slith to occupy one of the Urbat?

"He'll be able to find her?" I asked softly.

Yes.

"Then this is worth the risk and the price."

ONE OF BLAKE'S men poked his head in.

"There's a problem."

I continued eating as if the man wasn't there.

"What problem?" Blake asked, setting his fork aside.

"They've found the fighter."

It had been days since I sent the letter. Plenty of time for her to receive and listen to what I'd written. I struggled to contain every hint of my regret.

"And?" Blake asked.

"Not our men. The locator, the controller, the provider, and the dreamer."

Though they knew the names of the ones already found, the Urbat refused to use them. They only ever used my name.

I lifted my napkin just as Blake picked up his plate and heaved it against the wall. The bits of broken china and food bounced off the material I held in front of my face. Calmly, I set the napkin aside. I didn't touch my food again.

"Olivia, back to your room."

"Yes, Father."

IT TOOK over another week before I felt the next shift in our world.

I was just stepping into Blake's office when the swirling grey around me changed suddenly, and I stumbled in the abrupt stillness. Without their movement, I couldn't see the real world.

Have courage, the whisper of the Lady's words drifted through the veil. *It will all end soon.*

"Olivia, what are you doing?" Blake asked impatiently. His voice didn't change the calm of grey around me like it usually did. It was as if my companions were frozen.

"Father, I can't see," I said, keeping my tone respectful.

"You haven't been able to see your entire life. It's never prevented you from walking before."

"I think something is happening," I said instead of acknowledging his words.

"What do you mean? Your sisters?"

I nodded, and he made a sound of impatience.

"Tell me."

"There's nothing to tell. I only have a feeling." I bowed my head as if ashamed. "I'm sorry, Father."

"I don't need apologies; I need information." His shoes scuffed against the floor as he moved to his desk. The shadows of my world remained still. They'd never done that before.

"It's something big. World changing," I said with quiet realization.

"Without you, it can't be world changing. Now, don't just stand there. Sit." His barked order echoed in his office.

Holding out my arms, I tried to recall the layout of his office and made my way to the chair before his desk.

I'm here. The words were a hissed sigh, and with them, I saw a slight movement to my left. I turned and watched Slith drift toward me. His shadow molded into the shape of a chair. Taking small steps, I walked toward him then reached for the back of the chair.

The television, a familiar, gentle voice said. *Tell him to turn it on.*

"Father, I think you should turn on the television."

His anger grew.

"Something is changing. I can feel it," I said again.

A shuffle of noise came from before me then the room filled with voices.

"You're coming forward with some astounding information I know our viewers won't believe. A new species exists among us."

"Not new," another voice said. "We are as old as humans. Here since the beginning."

"And what are you?"

"The most popular term is werewolf."

Shock hit me hard. The werewolves were exposing their existence?

"You can't expect us to believe something like that without proof."

"Of course not. You might want to move back."

I wanted to ask what Blake was seeing but kept quiet.

Blake swore loudly and started yelling for his lieutenants. The conversation on the television continued as he shouted out orders.

"Are you dangerous? How many of you are there? Was that dog attack earlier this year one of you? Why are you coming forward now?" the reporter asked.

"There are two Urbat close to the station. I'm sending them in," Blake said.

"I've come forward because we are all in danger. We are not the only species hiding within the human population. There is another species, Urbat, who are very similar to us in appearance but not in nature. They would see the human population devastated."

Blake made another strangled noise.

"Start rounding up the women and children. I want this place cleaned out in thirty minutes."

Everyone who he'd called in left the room to start the evacuation.

"Urbat," the reporter said. "Why do they want our population devastated?"

"Because your numbers are a threat to their goal. They want to rule. The population, the planet, everything."

"What are we supposed to do?"

"Our time here is over. The Urbat are coming for us because we've shared what they didn't want us to. Find Blake Torrin, their leader. Cut off his connections. He's everywhere and has enough money to do much damage."

Blake roared his anger.

It is time, the lady whispered.

I gathered my courage and made my move.

CHAPTER ONE

HENRY...

I FLIPPED OVER THE NEXT CARD ON THE DECK AND GRINNED AT Liam while still keeping an eye on Mom, who stared out the window. She was trying not to show it, but she was worried.

For the last two days, like the rest of our kind, we'd done as the Elders asked. We'd kept inside and not changed to our fur.

When the boys slept, we all watched the news and monitored what was happening around the country. Chaos continued to spread through the masses. Opposing factions heavily debated the existence of werewolves while seeking evidence to prove their views. Frequently, reports aired with images showing captured people in various stages of shifting due to varying forms of torture. It was hard to tell if those held were Urbat or werewolf, but Mom and Dad's fear grew. As did the fear of the humans around the world.

Amidst reports of captured wolf-shifters, the news recounted the numerous mutilated human bodies being discovered in homes or dumped along roadsides. Agencies pleaded with the public to report suspected wolf-shifters rather than trying to identify them on their own. But, it didn't help. The death toll for the humans rose as neighbor judged neighbor.

Because of the volatile state of the country, Dad had gone alone to the grocery store about three hours ago. Given that we had no car and were supposed to do things with human speed and strength, three hours didn't seem unreasonable, though.

"Boys, let's clean up and get ready for lunch," Mom said suddenly.

"Is Uncle Gregory bringing back pizza?" Aden asked.

"No. We're going somewhere."

The scent of her half-lie tickled my nose. Paul and I shared a look as we helped the cubs pick up the cards.

"Where are we going?" Liam asked.

"I'm not sure, sweetie. I think Uncle Gregory is going to surprise us all. As soon as you're ready, we're going to meet him."

I could tell we were doing more than meeting him, though. While we cleaned up, Mom repacked our hiking bags. They once again contained the only supplies we'd brought with us when coming here.

The moment the boys had the cards back in the box, Mom stood ready with their jackets by the door. Aden and Liam skipped toward her, unaware of the growing tension in the room. She helped the boys into their winter wear, and Paul and I quickly put our own jackets on before shrugging on the packs. Although snow covered the ground, our jackets weren't for our benefit. We needed them to look more human.

"Paul, you lead the way," she said, opening the door.

Mom picked up Liam, and I picked up Aden. At a brisk

pace, we left the house and started down the sidewalk. The town Mom and Dad had selected wasn't that big, and the house we'd rented was only a few blocks away from the outlying woods. We weren't heading toward the woods, though. We were heading toward downtown.

When we turned the corner, we found Dad jogging toward us. A human speed jog, but we were warned not to run at all. Something was happening.

"Dad?" I asked.

He caught up to us, ruffled Aden's hair with a smile then looked at me.

"I'd like the two of you to run ahead." He nodded down the road to the west. "Your mom and I will be behind you. We just need to clean up."

It's what he always said when they hung back to cover our trail, a necessary precaution so the scattered Urbat didn't stumble across our scents. This time, however, didn't feel like a precaution. I met Dad's eyes, and he gave a slow nod. They'd found us. I wasn't sure that was any better than the humans suspecting us.

"All right," Paul said, picking up Liam. "You're with me, bud."

I scooped up Aden and followed Paul at a human run. Grey's message touched my mind before we reached the crosswalk.

Your dad was spotted by an Urbat several hours ago. He tried losing him and covering his scent trails, but it didn't work. You need to leave the area. Three are coming from the south and west. Two from the north and east. Head northwest. Gabby is watching, and we'll guide you.

Paul changed direction, turning at the next block, and I knew Grey was talking to him, too.

Tell Gabby thanks, and tell Michelle that we'll keep her brothers safe, I sent back.

Keep yourselves safe, too.

We reached the forest, no problem, and ran like we were meant to run, weaving through the towering trees.

"We're not getting pizza, are we?" I heard Liam say to Paul.

"Not tonight, bud. We need to play the quiet game again."

Aden laid his head on my shoulder and wrapped his arms around my neck. I worried about the cubs. Humans were so fragile, something Paul and I had learned from Gabby long ago. She'd been our friend and source of human information for years. So much had changed since our first meeting. She'd Claimed Clay, other human potential mates had been found, another species of werewolves had been brought to our attention, and Paul and I finally got to leave the Compound. Not quite the way either of us had hoped, however.

I continued to follow my brother through the trees until Paul slowed in front of me. Neither of us spoke nor let the boys down. Hidden within the sparse lower branches of the spruces, we listened.

"I have to go potty," Aden whispered into my ear.

Paul nodded at me, and I set Aden on his feet.

"You can go right here." The little guy pulled his pants down to his ankles and relieved himself in an impressive arc into the snow. I chuckled, the first real humor I'd felt in days.

Keep moving, Grey's message cut through my humor. *Jim is on his way.*

I shared a look with Paul then hurried to help Aden tug his pants up. If they were sending Jim, it couldn't be too bad. Had they sent an Elder, I would have worried. Scooping Aden into my arms, I took off running again with Paul.

Mom and Dad caught up to us in minutes and took the cubs from us while still running. Without them in our arms, Paul and I could run faster. Together, we moved as a pack, staying close and leaving no trace of our passing. No trace but our scents.

We ran tirelessly for over an hour before Dad stopped. He and Mom set the boys to their feet without speaking. Liam and Aden, glad for a chance to stretch their little legs, walked to where Paul and I stood.

"Jim is close," Dad said softly. "They are closer."

"Why did we stop then?" I asked.

Dad pointed up. I tipped my head back and saw an old hunting stand in one of the tall pines near us.

"Keep the tree safe. Keep the cubs safe," he said.

I understood his reasoning. It would be easier to defend a tree that couldn't move than a child who might try to run in fear.

"I'm scared," Aden whispered, looking up at Mom.

She squatted down in front of him as Paul and I discarded our packs at the base of the tree.

"Try not to be. Remember what I said about our noses? We smell everything. Push your fear aside, and you'll be able to hide better."

She hugged the little boy then kissed his cheek.

"I don't want to hide in the tree," he said.

"You won't be alone. Paul and Henry will be with you."

"Mom," I said.

"Second line, Henry. Just in case. Take them now." She stood and gave me a no-nonsense look.

I picked up Aden and, with only one free arm, scrambled up the trunk and onto the stand. Paul and Liam were right behind us. There wasn't much room. Just enough for the four of us to fit if we didn't move around much.

Paul sat against the trunk and had Liam and Aden sit on his lap. He wrapped his arms around them and began telling a story in a quiet voice that still carried through the trees. The sound didn't matter. Our scent trails would lead the Urbat to our location.

While Paul spoke softly to the cubs, I watched the expanse of barren trees and pines to the south where Mom and Dad stared. In the distance, three wolves raced toward us, their dark shapes easily visible against the white. They were too big for normal wolves, and too focused on my parents. However, three to two wasn't terrible odds. I'd seen my Dad help Thomas settle the disputes that usually occurred at Introductions. He was strong and fought crazy well. But this was different. The Urbat weren't just ticked off because they couldn't meet a female first. They wanted the boys at any cost, and my parents were outnumbered. If I went down to help...

"Stay there, boys," Dad said as if reading my mind.

I glanced at Paul, but he remained focused on the cubs.

A faint howl echoed through the trees. Mom and Dad tensed, and I watched the wolves close the distance. The first two went straight for Dad. The third went for Mom. In all the time growing up at the Compound, I'd not once seen either of my parents move like they did now. Those disputes had been nothing to Dad.

As the two leapt toward him, he jumped up, twisting in mid-air to evade both attacks.

Mom met the one coming at her head-on with tooth and

claws. Paul and I had gotten in plenty of trouble in our lives, enough to question if we'd live to see another day, but I'd never heard Mom growl like she did at that moment. Her face shifted as she opened her mouth and sunk her teeth deeply into the mutt's scruff as the two attacking Dad landed and pivoted. Dad was already on his feet, too, waiting for them.

Mom shook her head savagely, and the scent of blood tickled my nose.

Dad met the second attack with arms extended as if he was welcoming them with a hug. However, his hands closed around their throats. Instead of stopping them, with a heave and twist of his wrists, he spun them away from him.

Paul continued to whisper to the boys, trying his best to drown out the sounds of the snarls and yips. Because of the action and the noise, I almost missed the two coming in from the east.

"Dad, two more," I yelled.

He thrust his claws into the throat of one and spun to face the other. The one he'd wounded staggered backwards toward Mom, who hadn't yet given up her hold on her opponent. Heavily bleeding, the mutt turned and saw Mom. Dad remained focused on his second challenger and the oncoming attackers, unaware that the one he'd injured wasn't out of the fight.

"Mom, watch out," I called.

The one she was fighting reached around and gripped her, not allowing her to turn.

The two newcomers were almost on my parents. I glanced at Paul. His gaze met mine, and he nodded. We needed to protect the boys, but we both knew we didn't stand a chance without our parents.

I jumped from the platform and landed just behind the one reaching for Mom. Shifting, I launched myself at his back. My teeth sank deeply into his neck. He tried to shake me, but already wounded, his weak attempts only furthered his downfall. In seconds, he collapsed to his knees and took his last breath, gurgling from his damaged throat. Blood coated my tongue as I released him and looked around.

The other two had joined the fight, and Dad struggled to keep all three of them away from us. Mom finished off the one who'd held her, and when one of them dodged around Dad, I was ready. So was Mom. She growled low and stepped in front of me, meeting his claw-sweeping attack with a wicked one of her own.

I circled around them, having no problem attacking him from behind. It wasn't cowardly; it was smart. I leapt onto his back and sunk my teeth deep like I had with the first one. This mutt, however, wasn't already weakened. He shook violently, making my gums ache as I struggled to keep my hold.

Mom relentlessly advanced, each swipe of her claws driving him back further. He roared and dove at her. She grunted and tried to retreat. I focused on my hands, forcing them to become more human. Driving my wickedly long claws into the weaker flesh between his ribs, I did everything in my power to distract him from Mom. He reached for me, giving Mom the opening she needed. She snarled and whipped her hand forward, ripping open his throat.

He dropped to his knees, but I stayed on him until he fell face first. A heartbeat later, I spun to help Dad with the remaining two.

Silence consumed the woods when the last Urbat fell, dead. The air reeked of blood.

Dad turned and hugged me hard.

"You're still my cub. Next time, stay in the tree."

I hugged him back.

"Gregory," Mom said softly behind me.

I felt Dad jerk in my arms a moment before he tore away from me.

"Mary..."

I turned in time to see Mom start to fall, her hands pressed against her stomach. Dad caught and held her as he sat on the ground.

"Where'd they get you, Mary?"

He pulled her arm away for only a second before setting it back down. The glimpse had been enough. How? When? I'd been with her.

"Mom?" I said.

They stared at each other, neither speaking for a moment, then she tore her sad eyes from Dad's and looked at me. A smile lifted her lips.

"You were amazing. Did I ever tell you, you look so much like your Dad did when I first met him?" She focused on Dad once more. "Handsome. Stubborn and prone to not listening. Take care of them for me, Gregory. They are the best of both of us."

Pain lanced through me at the finality of her words, and I fell to my knees. Paul made a sobbed sound from above.

"Henry, help me," he said. I struggled to my feet and climbed the tree to retrieve Aden. The boy's eyes were wide with fear. Hugging him close, I gave what comfort I could while my life blew apart.

Below us, Mom continued to speak quietly to Dad.

"Our world is changing. Don't waste time with grief. Get

these boys somewhere safe then join the fight. They'll need you."

"We need you," Dad said with quiet tears choking his words.

At the base of the tree, I set Aden down and went to Mom. Her eyes watered when she looked at me again.

"I'm so sorry, Henry. I don't want to leave you boys. I wanted to be there when you found your mates and to see your cubs. Be good to each other." She reached out and gently caressed my cheek. I leaned down and kissed her forehead.

"I love you, Mom," I said, almost choking on the anguish twisting my insides.

"Find a mate and be happy, Henry."

I moved away so Paul could talk to her. Liam and Aden clung to my legs as I stood and watched my father's pain.

"Paul. My sweet Paul. I remember holding you in my arms, so tiny and bald. You and your brother made my life whole and perfect. Take care of yourself and your father for me." She touched his cheek, her hand pale.

Once Paul kissed her, she turned to Dad.

"Gregory, I knew you were meant for me the moment I saw you from the second story window. But my heart wasn't fully yours until you brought back that bed." Dad chuckled slightly, a sad sound. She reached up and smoothed her fingers through his dark hair.

"I regret nothing," she whispered. "Every moment of my life with you has been the adventure I craved before I met you. I'll still love you, even after I'm gone."

Dad bent down and kissed her softly on the lips.

A hole opened in my chest as I watched them. I never

wanted to love like that. The pain would be too great once it was gone.

JIM...

TREES WHIPPED PAST ME. I didn't slow for roads or houses. There was no point hiding what I was. The humans already knew of our existence. If I was spotted and followed, all the better. The boys couldn't fall into Urbat hands. The other Elders hadn't yet seen what I had. Losing Ethan had almost broken Isabelle. Losing the boys would break Michelle. And she couldn't be broken. None of them could. Bethi had been clear. A judgement needed to be made this cycle if werewolves had any hope of surviving. Save the boys; save our race.

Gregory's anguish interrupted my thoughts. The sensation wrapped around my mind before his words did.

It's Mary, he sent. *She's been hurt. Ripped open and bleeding badly.*

How badly? I sent back.

Gutted.

The word caused my stride to stumble.

The Urbat? I sent.

Dead.

Are you close to a hospital?

More grief swelled over our link before he answered.

Even if it wasn't past that, you know we couldn't take her there. Not with these kinds of wounds and the world knowing what we are.

I focused on Mary's link and could feel her pain. Mary wasn't just another member in my Dad's pack. She was my second mom. She'd watched over me just as closely as my own

Mom. I pushed myself to go faster. My legs and lungs burned with the effort.

I'm almost there, I sent Mary. I raced across the fields, already knowing I wouldn't make it in time.

I am so proud of you, Jim. You will do well as an Elder. Protect my boys. Remind them how much I love them. And tell your mom I love her, too. She was the best thing that happened to me. Without her, I wouldn't have found Gregory. Tell her and Michelle, I regret nothing.

I could feel her link thinning.

Hang in there, Mary. I'm so close.

Save them all, Jim.

Her link vanished from my mind as if it had never existed. In the multitude of connections, the tiny void shouldn't have felt so consumingly vast.

I howled my grief. An answering howl came not far away, joined by a second and third.

When I cleared the remaining trees, I found Gregory on the ground, holding Mary. He howled again, a loud, anguish-filled sound that echoed in the trees and pierced my heart. The loss of a Mate...his pain became my own.

I was too late, I sent Winifred, shifting and falling to my knees just beyond their grieving circle. *Mary is gone.*

The cubs turned and saw me. With tears in their eyes, they flew at me. I opened my arms and caught them in a hug, holding them closely as they cried. Mary's sacrifice hadn't been for nothing. She'd kept the boys safe. It didn't ease my grief, though.

The children? Winifred sent.

Unharmed. As are Gregory, Paul, and Henry.

The three remained by Mary. Gregory held her while her sons touched her arm or leg. Aden wiped his wet nose on my shoulder and burrowed closer. Liam hugged close to my other arm, trembling and quiet, so like how he'd been the first time I'd met him.

"Uncle Jim," Aden whimpered, clinging to my neck. "Is Aunt Mary dead?"

"She is."

The little boy pulled away from me and nodded solemnly. His little chest expanded with a deep breath. Slipping from my hold, he stood and walked to Henry's side. The young man looked up from Mary and gave Aden a weak smile.

Aden laid his tiny hand on the young man's arm.

"Mimi says that mommy and daddy went someplace special where they're waiting for us. Aunt Mary is there, too. You'll see her again someday."

Henry nodded, silent tears tracking down his cheeks, and hugged Aden.

There are more Urbat headed your way, Winifred sent.

Before I could relay the message to Gregory, he kissed Mary and gently laid her on the ground.

"I will love you after I'm gone, too," he said softly. He rose and came to me, laying a hand on my shoulder while Liam still hugged me.

"She told me not to waste time grieving. I'm telling you the same."

I stood with Liam, glanced at Henry, who held Aden, then back at Gregory.

"There are more coming. We need to travel fast," I said.

"Skin or fur?"

"Skin for now."

Gregory took Liam from me, and Paul went to their packs and threw me a pair of pants and a shirt to put on. Dead leaves crunched under my bare feet as I dressed. As soon as I finished, I took Aden, and Paul and Henry took the packs.

Hurry, Jim, Winifred sent. *They are coming from the west and north-east.*

"Stay close. Stay quiet," I warned the group.

CHAPTER TWO

OLIVIA...

I SAT IN THE BACKSEAT AND LISTENED TO FRANK'S IMPATIENT tapping on the steering wheel. We'd been driving for hours since our last break near dawn, and I needed to use the bathroom.

"Can we stop?" I asked.

He growled angrily.

"Bathroom or food?"

"Both." If I only asked for a bathroom, he would find somewhere to pull over and make me go on the side of the road...with him watching.

In silence, I waited for his answer. It took a few minutes.

"There's a station up ahead," he said. Anger laced his words.

I felt the vehicle slow.

"Don't try anything when we get in there."

"Do I ever? I know where my loyalties are."

When the car stopped, I remained in the back until I heard

my door open. He tapped impatiently on the frame as I unbuckled and slid out. The shadows of the Others zipped around us, painting my world grey so I could see my way toward the gas station door.

I pulled the sunglasses from my pocket and placed them on my face.

"Take 'em off," Frank said from behind me.

"We're not supposed to call attention to ourselves. And, my eyes will do that," I said.

He growled and opened the door. As I stepped past, he leaned in.

"He's not here to know," he whispered.

I kept moving, not allowing any worry or fear to surface.

In the bathroom, I exhaled shakily and splashed water on my face. Frank was dangerously close to losing control. Since the moment Blake had called him back into the office and told him to drive me west, Frank's resentment had grown. Why would Blake tell him, a pure and strong Urbat, to listen to a weak, blind Judgement? Frank's failure to obtain the provider had cost him much within the Urbat ranks. He'd lost Blake's respect and was desperate to get it back. That's why he'd been ideal to drive me across the country. However, his desperation wasn't keeping him in line as planned.

After quickly using the facilities and washing, I opened the door. My sense of smell wasn't anything compared to either the werewolves or the Urbat, but it was better than most humans. Even without the shadows dancing around Frank's body, I knew he was standing right outside.

"I'm sorry I took so long." My quiet apology was sincere. If Frank lost any more of his composure, I would suffer.

Frank didn't immediately answer or move. I hesitated,

listening. Although the shadows gave me basic outlines, there was much I still couldn't see. Things I needed my other senses for...like the faint sound of Blake's voice.

"You called him?" I said in surprise and concern, not bothering to suppress either emotion.

Frank disconnected the call on Blake's recorded message.

"Yeah, and he isn't answering. It's your turn."

"He was clear when we left. He doesn't want to hear from either of us until we get there. If I try contacting him and he asks why, what am I supposed to say?"

Frank stepped close.

"Something is wrong. I can feel it."

My pulse jumped in panic, and I looked around as if suspecting whatever he sensed was within the gas station.

"Not here. With Blake," he said.

One of the shadows started swirling crazily around the person behind the register.

"We have the attendant's attention," I said softly, facing Frank. "We should make our purchases and go back to the car."

"Do you know how close I am to not giving a shit about what Blake says?" Frank asked with menace.

"Yes."

I waited, wondering what he'd do.

"Then stop acting like you're Blake. I don't listen to you."

He turned and headed toward the register. I followed slowly and stood by the exit as he tossed several bags of something onto the counter. He didn't waste time with idle chat, although the woman behind the register tried.

As soon as he'd paid, he strode toward me and pushed the door open.

"Hurry up."

Neither of us said anything more until we were both in the car. Something landed in my lap before I had a chance to buckle.

"Get ahold of Blake," he said. "I need to know where we're going."

"You've already guessed where we're going, just like me," I said, calmly.

He hit the steering wheel. "Then tell me why."

"Do you honestly think Blake confides in me? Blake tells me what to do, and I listen. I know what will happen if I don't."

A brush of sound was the only warning I had before his hand closed over my throat. The shadows, which had been swirling outside the car, moved inside, churning around Frank in a wild frenzy. Frank leaned over the back of his seat until he and I were almost nose to nose. His pungent hot breath bathed my face as he spoke.

"Call him."

My heart hammered in my chest and fear pooled in my stomach, but not for the obvious reason.

"I can't," I rasped. "If I do, we'll both be in trouble."

The shadows wailed in excitement around us.

"We're running out of time, Frank. I can feel it."

To punctuate my words, the swirls outside the car started to take shape. A person walked toward our vehicle. Something hit the window hard.

"I'm calling the police," a voice said.

Frank's hand abruptly left my throat, and his door opened. The woman scrambled backward but didn't make it far. Her scream was brief. The shadows converged on her body before Frank even released her. They always did that when someone died near me.

As she fell, she twitched and jerked with their attempts to inhabit her. They couldn't. But that didn't stop them from trying.

The door closed again, and I could smell the tang of copper —of blood—that Frank brought back in with him. The engine started, and the car jolted in reverse. I swallowed painfully and buckled. Outside the window, the shadows continued to try to possess the woman. Any observer would think her movements death-twitches.

The car jerked to a stop then lurched forward slowly. The synthesized beeps gave away Frank's attempt to reach Blake yet again. The sound of the pre-recorded voice caused Frank to hit the steering wheel and swear. A moment later, a loud clunk came from the front. He'd likely thrown the phone.

"I need to know what the fuck he's thinking," Frank seethed. "What are we supposed to do when we get there? And what about when we're done? Does he really think they're going to let me walk away just because you're there?" The car sped up.

"I don't know what he thinks, Frank," I said softly, turning in my seat to stare at the grey tornado spiraling over the woman's body. "But I think we might both die. Sooner than either of us wants."

"Say one more word, and I won't give a shit who's protecting you."

I wisely faced forward and stayed quiet. My throat ached from where Frank had gripped me. I would have bruises. If Blake were here, he would have killed Frank for what he'd just done to me. If Blake were here, he probably would have finished what Frank had started.

Around me, the world suddenly came back to life. Smokey

wisps circled and twirled inside the car and out, defining whatever was closest to me. Frank's seat. The trees just beside the road. Everything floated in an otherwise light void. The Others never bothered with the ground unless I asked. And I never asked unless I was alone.

I shifted in my seat, and something crinkled beside me. My hand brushed over a bag, food that Frank had thrown at me. The idea of eating didn't appeal to me, but I opened the bag anyway, hoping to appease some of Frank's lingering temper. My fingers found a scant number of pretzels at the bottom of the package. It was a good thing I wasn't really hungry.

The tapping on the steering wheel increased as I crunched, so I only ate a few.

"Would you like some?" I said politely.

"No."

"How close are we?" My voice was barely a whisper, but he heard. The tapping stopped.

"Close. A few hours." The tapping resumed.

I set my head back against the seat and tried not to think about what might happen, but it proved too hard to ignore the future we were racing toward. What would happen when we got there? Would they even know who I was? We knew from Joshua that the dreamer had learned her history and our purpose, and she'd been afraid. That had been our last contact with him before everything started to go so very wrong for Blake.

The hum of the tires on the road and Frank's impatient tapping on the steering wheel crawled into my ears and ate at my thoughts with annoying persistence.

When the car started to slow much later, I sat up and looked around. Trees surrounded us on both sides. The Others raced ahead, outlining more trees.

"Are they here?" I asked.

A wailing filled the air, along with Frank's snarled, "No."

"Tell him we're here," Frank said, pulling the car to a stop.

"Have you tried texting him?"

With a snarl, he opened his door. I quickly released my seatbelt and braced myself. My door flew open, and Frank jerked me from the car. My head hit the jamb on the way out, likely intentional. Bitter cold wrapped around me and burned my lungs with each careful breath while the Others swirled around Frank in a frenzy.

Frank's fingers dug into my shoulders as he yanked me toward him. His sour breath bathed my face, and his nose touched mine.

"You are less than worthless," he said, his voice deceptively calm. "You think this is some kind of game?" The flat of his hand cracked across my face, lightning fast. I would have staggered if his fingers hadn't returned to grip my shoulder again.

Face throbbing, I focused on his shape and tried to breathe through the pain.

"Where are your witty comments now?"

"Beating me doesn't change anything," I said slowly. "Blake will continue to ignore us, and you and I will still need to—"

Crack.

My jaw joint crunched slightly, and a small grunt of air left me.

"Have anything else to say?"

I shivered and kept my mouth shut.

"Good girl. Maybe you do have a brain after all."

The Others stilled. Blindly, I turned my head.

"Don't turn away from me," Frank said, gripping my abused jaw cruelly and forcing me to face him.

"I have a brain," I said. "And ears. They're coming."

He swore and released me. "Get in."

He shoved me back toward the car, and I spread my arms wide to catch myself against the frame, not willing to sink onto the seat like he wanted.

"No, Frank," I said, trying to swivel away from his gripping hands. "This is why we're here. To face them. To give them a message."

The bruising pushing stopped.

"What message?" he asked.

Tires crunched on gravel, and I turned my head toward the sound.

"What message?" Frank demanded, stepping closer.

The world exploded with motion again, outlining Frank and the four vehicles pulling to a stop just inside the clearing. Frank's anger wrapped around me, and I opened my mouth to prevent another blow to my head.

"The only message that—"

A door opened. People started getting out of vehicles. Fear and trepidation pooled in my stomach. Anything else I wanted to feel, I kept hidden.

Frank moved to stand beside me. The Others converged upon the newcomers, giving me my first glimpse of the other Judgements and the werewolves protecting them. No one spoke. It gave me a moment to study the group of thirteen. Based on shapes and sizes, there seemed to be six women and seven men.

"My name is Olivia," I said, taking a step forward and

stopping. "I've been sent with a message. Which of you is Emmitt?"

"I am." The owner of the smooth voice stepped forward.

"You're the one who stole my sister, the provider, from Blake." I turned my head slightly to the right toward Frank. "I'm sure you remember Frank."

"What's your message?" Emmitt asked crisply.

"Who leads you?" I asked. "Is it Winifred? Sam? Grey?"

"We lead our people together," a woman said.

"Yet you spoke. So, it's you I need to talk to."

I turned to Frank. "What kind of ground is this?" I asked softly.

"What are you doing?" he demanded.

"What I was told to do."

"You stay here." His fingers wrapped around my wrist.

I sighed. "This will never end, then."

He growled, shoved my hand away and told me to hurry up. Without knowing what kind of terrain I needed to cross, I started forward slowly, testing each step.

"It's gravel and grass with a few divots," Winifred said, moving to meet me halfway.

I lifted a hand, palm out and fingers raised. When she was close enough, I set my fingers on her face. She held still as my fingertips slid over her features. Worry pulled at her brow but couldn't disguise the laugh lines around her eyes or mouth. She had kindness and strength. I hoped it would be enough to keep me alive for another day. I let my relief free.

"He needs to die," I said, clearly.

The words had barely left my mouth when Emmitt, still a step in front of the rest, flew at a snarling Frank. Their growls and the sound of ripping fabric, along with a few soft female gasps, filled the air.

Frank's end came swiftly, and silence once again claimed the clearing as the Others played with his body for a few moments.

"Are you all right?" Winifred asked.

I couldn't remember the last time someone had asked me that and needed a moment to consider the question. The temperature stole my body heat with each passing second, my pulse throbbed in my face despite the frigid air, and my bruised throat ached with every swallow. Yet, I knew this wouldn't be the end of our suffering.

"No," I said honestly. "But it doesn't matter. We need to leave."

"And go where?" a new voice asked.

"I'm not sure. Hopefully somewhere warmer, though."

"I second that," another female voice said.

"I apologize if this sounds rude, but can you all say your names for me so I know who's talking?" I asked. A lifetime of listening left me with a very good memory for voices.

"I'm Bethi."

"I'm Luke, Bethi's Mate."

"Isabelle."

"Carlos."

"Gabby."

"Clay."

"Charlene. Do you want some ice for your face?"

Again, the unexpected show of concern gave me pause. They stood together just beyond Winifred, a united group. A group I needed to join. Would it be enough? I swallowed hard, the pain a useful reminder of what was at stake, before answering.

"No, thank you. It'll be fine."

I turned my head toward the rest.

"Thomas, Charlene's Mate."

"Michelle." Her voice sounded shaky and strained, understandable given her connection with Frank.

"Emmitt, Michelle's Mate."

"I'm Sam. Can you tell us why you came here?"

"This was the most likely place the locator would know well."

"The locator?" Gabby said.

"I don't mean anything insulting by using that term."

"I'm Grey. You look cold. We can talk in the cars."

"Thank you."

Winifred wrapped her hand around mine and gently drew it away from her cheek. A swell of embarrassment pushed its way forward, and I didn't suppress it.

"Sorry," I said. "I forgot I was touching you."

"It's all right. I'll lead you to the SUV."

"Keep us posted," Isabelle said before she and a man moved toward a car.

The rest went back to their vehicles, splitting up the Judgements. Smart.

Winifred led me to the SUV. One of the smaller women walked beside me. It wasn't until she spoke that I knew it was Bethi.

"Please tell me my mom's okay."

Winifred opened the back door. The Others swirled around the seats to guide me. I didn't get in, though. I faced Bethi, who moved anxiously from foot to foot.

"Your mother?" I asked. I wasn't sure if she was speaking of her birth mother or the Lady.

39

"When the news broke about werewolves being real, she called a news station then disappeared."

I didn't envy that she still knew her birth mother. It would only make what needed to be done that much harder.

"Blake didn't take her," I said. "He didn't have time. I promise."

"Good." She let out a shaky exhale and climbed back into the third row of seats. I took a spot in the middle row. Winifred settled in next to me while two men sat in front. The last woman joined Bethi in the back. Before the door even closed, we were moving.

It felt weird that I was finally here, with them.

"Where to, Gabby?" Sam asked.

"South, I guess. There's still not much movement," she answered.

"What about Jim?" Winifred asked.

"He's staying ahead of the Urbat for now. You might want to suggest that he find a car, though. They're definitely tracking him. Others are moving position to the north of him. They aren't coming at him but repositioning, I think."

"Urbat?" I asked, unsure.

"Yes," Winifred said. "How does Blake know where to place his men?"

"He doesn't. His men have phones and send out group texts when they sight one of you or catch your scent trail. By communicating where you are and aren't, they slowly pinpoint you. Sometimes."

"Seriously?" Bethi said from behind me. "A mix of dumb luck and technology is kicking our asses? We need to end this now. We're all together like she wanted." Something tugged on my seat, and her voice moved closer. "Tell me you know how to make the Judgement so this can finally end."

My chest tightened as I realized which Judgement spoke.

"You dream our past lives?" I asked.

"Yep. Every crappy one of them."

"Can you tell me about mine?"

"There's not much to tell. You've always died young."

"That's what I thought." But not this lifetime. This lifetime would hold so much more suffering for me. For all of us.

"She's told me what we are. Hope. Peace. Strength. Fortune. Wisdom." Bethi said the last word with contempt. "I know what the others can do, but I'm not sure what Courage does. In each brief glimpse of your lives, you're always sorta blind."

"Not sort of. I am blind. To this world."

"This world?" she asked.

"Yes. This world. The coveted playground for all the races to rule. It's not the only world, just the most desirable one to inhabit. And, I don't know how to make the final Judgement. The Lady only tells me the things I need to know when I need to know them."

Bethi made a sound of frustration.

"I'm sorry," I said.

"It's not you. It's her and the dreams. I'm so tired of dying."

I couldn't reassure Bethi. Not with what I did know.

"I do know that we need to decide what Judgement to make before the Judgement can be made."

"What do you mean?" she asked through a yawn.

"Will we Judge in favor of the Urbat or the werewolves?"

There was a moment of silence.

"Bethi's sleeping. Perhaps this conversation should wait until we're all together again," Gabby said.

I nodded and turned my head to watch the Others zoom around trees and signs and houses. After years of waiting, everything was starting to fall into place at an alarming speed.

Courage, the Lady whispered from the grey, a reminder of what I would need.

CHAPTER THREE

WINIFRED...

I CONSIDERED THE YOUNG WOMAN FACING ME. HER CHEEK AND some of the tissue around her left eye had already begun to swell. Yet, the swelling didn't draw my attention as much as her eyes. Her pupils consumed her irises, leaving no hint of color. While humans likely found them unsettling, her eyes didn't bother me. However, the way she had appeared at the Compound did.

According to Bethi, Blake felt driven to collect each of these gifted women. Her words had been proven true with each attack our group had suffered, and especially with the most recent attack Mary's family suffered. Yet, somehow Olivia had been allowed to travel across the country to come to us and, as soon as we'd arrived, had asked us to kill the man with her. Why?

Does she seem anxious to you? Sam's message interrupted my study of the young woman beside me.

Yes.

What are you thinking? he sent me.

That I'm suspicious of her purpose here.

"How long were you with Blake?" I asked Olivia.

Her gaze shifted slightly as if focusing on me.

"As long as I can remember. I was young. Maybe three or four."

"That's a very long time. Michelle saw you in a vision. She said you were treated well; your face says otherwise."

"It doesn't matter how I was treated. My purpose is all that matters."

That doesn't sound promising, Sam sent me. I agreed, but didn't say so.

"And, what purpose would that be?" I asked.

"Completing the Judgement."

Her anxiety notched up, but not because she lied. Her words rang with honesty. Yet, as I'd learned with Jim, honest words still held secrets. In this case, though, her anxiety seemed reasonable, given the level Bethi usually displayed when talking about anything relating to the Judgement. Still, what Olivia said disturbed me.

According to Bethi, completing the Judgement was Blake's obsession. Why, then, would he have willingly let go of one of the Judgements? It didn't make sense.

"I don't understand why Blake allowed you to leave," I said.

"He didn't have a choice after the news aired." She took a deep, slow breath. "I understand that you might not trust me because I've been with the Urbat for so long. And, there's little I can say to persuade you otherwise. But, whether you trust me or not, know that I'm here because the Judgement needs to be made."

"We need to head east," Gabby interrupted. "It looks like they're netting again."

"Where's Jim?" I asked.

"West," she said in an unsure, subdued tone. "I don't see how we can get to him without heading east first. It's like the Urbat suddenly realized we were at the Compound."

"Frank killed a woman a few hours ago," Olivia said. "She's probably been found by the humans and linked with the recent news of werewolves. That close to your home would have been enough to make the Urbat suspicious."

The way she delivered that bit of information without any facial cues or changes in her scent worried me. She seemed too detached from the situation given the state of her swelling face and bruised neck. She had to feel something, didn't she? That meant she was hiding her feelings, much like Carlos. Why? What didn't she want us to know?

The sooner you find a vehicle, the better, I sent Jim. *The Urbat discovered we were at the Compound and are netting around us like they are you.*

Already found one, he sent back. *What direction should we head?*

South.

That's a bit vague.

We're not sure where we need to go yet.

Wandering around increases our chances of being found and makes it harder for Gabby to know where to watch. I say we pick someplace and change the location later if we need to.

I sighed. His wisdom was why we knew he would make a good Elder. His impetuousness and lack of humility were why we'd hesitated for so long.

I reached out to Sam and Grey at the same time.

We need to find a safe place to meet up with Jim. Grey, I'll have

Gabby text Michelle with Jim's current location so you and Michelle can coordinate a place. Have Michelle continue working with Gabby via text messages so she knows where to watch.

Keeping conversation in your car quiet? Grey sent us.

Yes, I said, simply.

Don't trust Olivia? Sam sent me.

No. Although her words were true about the deaths, there are too many lives at stake to trust blindly.

I focused my attention back to Olivia.

"Can you tell us more about the Urbat?" I asked.

"What would you like to know?"

Her soft, neutral tone carried no hint about her feelings regarding the Urbat.

"Tell me what they are like."

"Hard. Motivated by the need to dominate everyone and everything."

"Did you like living with them?"

Olivia's lips twitched slightly, almost as if she wanted to smile. The sign of her humor when asking such a question increased my concern.

"Liking where I lived has never mattered. But, no, I did not like living with them."

There was no animosity with the words. Just a calm delivery of truth. Why the almost smile, then?

"Did you have any friends where you were living? Michelle only saw Blake with you in her visions. But, when Blake's complex was raided, the news reported signs of families," I asked.

"Those females who lived there willingly were cruel and cold."

"Willingly? They had women there who weren't willing?"

"Yes. What do you think happened to your female cubs who went missing?" Again, her words were neither accusatory or sarcastic, just spoken as a simple question. But there was nothing simple about it.

"What do you mean?" I asked, a memory from long ago surfacing.

"I don't know much about what happened before Blake found me. I've never been his confidant. Only his prize," she said, her choice of words the first revealing piece of information about her relationship with the Urbat.

"But I do know that your shortage of females is because of the Urbat. They hunted the pregnant, Mated pairs and took any newborn females to raise as Urbat. The werewolf females weren't treated as pureblood mates. Just breeders. And their half-breed male children, like Joshua, were only tolerated if they proved their loyalties to the Urbat. The half-breed female children were kept and allowed true Mates...if one came forward."

The news stunned me. The deaths that had been reported during the early years of the Compound's existence had caused everyone concern. Yet, we'd never attributed them to anything more than the males' struggle to find Mates when females were so scarce. As the Elders, we'd created rules for the Introductions to ensure the males would feel they all had an equal chance at a female. When the reports of deaths had tapered off, we'd thought the problem solved.

"To keep the bloodlines from becoming too clouded, the half-breed males are only allowed pure Urbat mates. Any new female werewolf cubs are designated to pure Urbat males."

"New?"

"Yes."

My chest clenched painfully. I struggled to breathe. The Urbat had continued to murder our Mated pairs and kidnap our young right under my nose?

Our people, those cubs, should have reached out to us. Why didn't they reach out? I sent to Sam.

I had no right to call myself an Elder. I'd failed my people. The constricting pain in my chest intensified. My heart struggled to beat.

Winifred, breathe. You did nothing wrong. It typically takes several months for the newborn's link to find its way to us through their parents' links. Perhaps, without their parents to guide them, they couldn't reach out to us. Without that connection, we would never know.

The pain eased, and I took a calming breath.

"I'm sorry I've upset you," Olivia said quietly.

Again, her scent contradicted her words. She wasn't sorry; she was…nothing.

"Thank you," I said to Olivia. "But it's not your fault. You did not kill and murder my kind."

What does she smell like to you? I sent Sam. He remained silent for several moments.

My first instinct is to say something sweet, like some kind of dessert. But there's something lingering just beneath that. Something off. Almost sour. What does she smell like to you?

Nothing beyond the chemical smell of the shampoo and hand soap she last used, I sent back. *No hint of any emotions, at all.*

Olivia hadn't shifted her gaze from me.

"How many of our women were there?" I asked.

"I'm not sure. I wasn't allowed to see them. How long does Bethi usually sleep?" she asked, abruptly changing the subject.

While I wondered why Olivia was concerned about Bethi's sleep schedule, Luke answered.

"It depends on her dream," he said. He held her to his side, stilling her twitching with a reassuring brush of his hand over her arm.

"Why do you ask?" I asked.

"We need to make a decision quickly. Time is running out." With that, Olivia turned her head and looked out the window. My eyes met Sam's in the mirror.

She sounds a bit like Bethi, he sent me.

She did. But she neither felt nor smelled anything like Bethi at the moment.

"Sam, take the next right," Gabby said, interrupting my thoughts.

"What do you see?" I asked. When I turned to look back at her, she was texting.

Gabby says we should head to Salt Lake City. I've let Jim know.

"There are several Urbat coming in from the east. We'll cross paths if we continue going that direction here. We need to head south, but not too far. There are some waiting to the west, as if those to the east are driving us toward them."

"They know you're watching and will try to anticipate your moves," Olivia said. "Watch the south. There are probably some moving away from the area they want you to go."

"There are," Gabby said. "But I haven't fallen for that in the past and don't plan to now."

Clay made a slight noise, almost a laugh.

"I apologize. I only meant to help," Olivia said.

OLIVIA...

THE STEADY THROB in my cheek helped distract me from the ache in my middle. Winifred's obvious suspicion and Gabby's dislike and mistrust shouldn't have hurt me. I had a lifetime of it, after all. Yet, it did hurt. I belonged nowhere. With no one.

"No, I'm sorry," Gabby said. "I haven't been sleeping well and am a bit touchy about them finding us. A friend died because of me."

"Not because of you," Clay said.

"You need to stop blaming yourself, little one," Luke said. "Isabelle doesn't blame you."

I could feel their connection, a history that brought them together as a closely-knit group. As much as I wished I could have the same, I knew it was better for everyone that I didn't.

"I understand, Gabby. There's no need to apologize."

I continued my study of the grey swirls outside my window and struggled to keep my memories from pulling me into the past while waiting for Winifred to ask more questions about the Urbat.

"Is there anything you can tell us about them that will help us?" Winifred asked after a moment.

I turned away from the window to focus on her shape.

"Help you to do what?" I asked.

"To keep our people safe."

Have courage. Tell her the truth, the Lady whispered from the grey.

I struggled to suppress the overwhelming despair that wanted to consume me.

"I'm sorry, but no one will be safe. Individuals change slowly. Even with time, we often resist change. With this Judgement, we will change the world. If we don't complete the Judgement, the world will burn and everyone will die. If we do complete it, many will still die. There's nothing that will keep anyone safe."

"That's what the Lady told me, too," Bethi said. "About the world burning, I mean."

I turned my head and saw the grey wisps of the Others dancing around her reclined form. She still leaned against her Mate, Luke. I envied her that connection.

"Well, in a past dream," she said. "Not this one, though. We're all together now. Instead of showing me what we need to do, she showed me one of your past lives. Do you know how many times you were left in the woods to die? I wanted to bitch-slap that last mom. She gave birth to you twice. Both times she took one look at you and brought you to the trees. Same damn spot. Your bones were still there from the first time. I had to feel your loneliness, hunger, and fear twice."

Those were the very same emotions I struggled not to feel in this lifetime. My stomach growled, as if my body had heard that brief thought and took it as permission to react.

"I'm sorry," I said, apologizing for the dreams and my stomach.

"When did you last eat?" Winifred asked.

"Several hours ago." I didn't clarify that it only had been a few pretzels and a candy bar the day before that.

Winifred bent to grab something. I listened to a slight rustling before she extended her arm toward me. I held out my hand and felt the smooth wrapper around some type of snack bar.

"Thank you," I said.

"How long was I out this time?" Bethi asked as I unwrapped the food and took a hungry bite.

"Not long," Luke said. "Maybe thirty minutes."

She groaned, and he kissed her temple.

I looked out the window again while I chewed. The budding regret, loneliness, and appeased hunger died quickly under my focus.

"Do we know where we're going yet?" Bethi asked.

"No," Gabby said. "I'm just trying to keep the Urbat from finding us."

"When you find somewhere that looks safe," Bethi said, "we need to stop and talk with the other three Judgements. If what Olivia is saying is true, I want us to make up our minds so we can move on to the Judging part. I'm way past ready to be done with this crap."

A small, neglected part of me cowered at the thought of making the final decision. Yet, I understood better than the rest the need for one. And, the faster, the better.

I swallowed my bite of the snack bar and quietly took another.

CHAPTER FOUR

HENRY...

Dad sat in the back with Aden while Liam and I took up the middle seat. Paul sat in front with Jim, who drove in a tense silence, likely communicating with the other Elders about where we needed to go next. Wherever they wanted us to go, I hoped getting there wouldn't take too long.

Grief still clawed at my insides, threatening to rip apart my composure. I couldn't let that happen. Not with Liam sitting next to me. The way Paul bounced his knee told me he was barely holding it together, too.

How could they just kill Mom like that? A female, no matter what age, mattered. Females were supposed to be protected at all costs. All werewolves knew that. Yet, the males who'd killed her weren't werewolves. My hatred for the Urbat boiled just beneath the surface of my skin, where I felt the change ripple. I swallowed hard, struggling to maintain my hold on the shift.

Liam reached out, his little hand closing around my fingers. He didn't say anything, just leaned against me, seeking comfort. The change receded, and I wrapped my arm around his shoulders and pulled him close.

I wanted to tell him everything would be okay, that the Urbat wouldn't find us again, but I didn't think it would be true. Not anymore. The fact that Jim hadn't tried to reassure us meant he felt the same uncertainty. What hope did we have when the Elders didn't even believe we'd pull through this? I thought of Gabby and hoped the others were doing better than we were. That everything they'd done had served its purpose. Otherwise, what was the point of telling the humans about our existence?

I'm so sorry, Henry. Mom's voice echoed in my mind. *Find a mate and be happy.*

I didn't see how either of those things would be possible now. And, not just because of Mom's death. In the days since the revelation of the existence of werewolves and Urbat, the world had changed drastically. Any smart, unmated female would hide deep in the woods, away from all men. What future could any male offer a female at this point? A life of running and hiding? A life that would end in a tragic death under the branches of an old tree?

Facing the window, I tried to stop thinking about Mom and all the times she'd kissed me or hugged me. The times she'd yelled at me for doing something stupid. The way she'd watched me when she thought I wasn't looking.

Be happy.

The harder I tried not to think about her, the more the memories pushed their way to the surface. Even at her angriest with him, no one could have ever doubted Mom's love for Dad. Or his love for her. Every male craved a mate. The need seemed embedded in our very bones. And, that need warred with fear. Against everything I was raised to think and believe, I hoped I wouldn't find a mate like Mom had told me to.

"I hear you," Jim said, startling me. Had I accidently sent him my thoughts? I still wasn't used to the idea of Jim being an Elder.

"When did you last eat, little man?" he asked, using the mirror to glance not at me but Aden.

"I dunno," the cub said in a subdued tone. His stomach growled loudly, and I realized that was what Jim had heard.

"We'd missed lunch," I said.

"We need to drive a little longer, but I'll stop and get you something as soon as we can. What about you, Liam? Ready for a burger?"

"No, thank you." Liam's sad voice stirred my clawing grief again.

"I know you're sad, buddy, but your Aunt Mary wouldn't want you to be. She loved you, all of you, very much. Seeing you sad would have made her sad."

Jim's words, meant to help, only made me hurt more.

Liam nodded against me, acknowledging Jim but remaining silent. His response, however, reminded me that his and Aden's young lives had a lot more grief in them than mine. Even now. Paul and I both knew their history. Abused and alone, with only Michelle for company, they'd escaped and found Emmitt. They'd only had a few months of peace before everything went to hell for them again.

Mom, Dad, and the rest had tried shielding the cubs from what was happening. But those boys were smart. Their fear told me they understood more than the adults wanted them to.

I tightened my hold on Liam, hugging him close.

"Don't fear what might happen. Fear stops us from living," I said softly. "And Mom wants us all to live."

I put aside my fear of finding a mate and focused on the drive. We'd passed several towns since Jim "acquired" the rusted minivan. Traffic picked up as the sun hovered just over the tree line. If the mutts weren't already tailing us, I doubted they'd be able to pick up our trail anymore.

Jim drove straight through town and turned into the drive-through of a fast food place.

"Listen close, Aden," he said, rolling down his window.

"Hello. My name is Ashley. Can I take your order?"

"Hi, Ashley. I'd like twenty-three cheeseburgers."

A moment of silence greeted his order.

"Did you say twenty-three cheeseburgers?" the woman asked.

Aden giggled from the back.

"Yes, ma'am. You better make that twenty-six. I'm pretty hungry. Four teas. Sweet, if you have it. And twelve regular fries."

"Um…that's going to take us a few minutes."

"Then, I better order two ice cream cones to hold us over while we wait."

"Uh, okay."

Paul shook his head, grinning slightly. I couldn't help but grin, too. No doubt Jim's order had sent the kitchen into a state of panic.

She gave him his total, and when he pulled ahead to pay, she had the two cones ready. He turned in his seat and held up the first cone for Paul's inspection.

"I don't know…" Jim said. "Liam's not that hungry, and this seems like a lot." He opened his mouth and devoured the top of the cone in a single bite before handing it back to an open-mouthed Liam.

"What about you, Aden? You hungry?"

"Yes!"

Jim chuckled and handed the cone back without taking any.

The fear that had flooded the vehicle dissipated enough that the scent of Dad's sorrow became clear. My humor fled, and I turned in my seat to look back at him as he helped Aden turn his cone.

"I'm fine, Henry," Dad said softly, without looking up at me. "Not all sorrow is bad."

I didn't see how that could be true, but didn't argue. Jim pulled ahead to a spot to wait for the food and started teasing Liam about eating the rest of his cone.

"Do we know where we're going yet?" I asked.

"Nah," he said. "We're going to wing it for a bit. A road trip, right Liam?"

The boy nodded and crunched into the top part of his cone.

Seriously, I sent Jim. *Where are we going?*

We're headed toward Salt Lake. Big city so we can disappear until we're ready.

Jim's gaze shifted from Liam to me.

I am sorry about your mom.

I know. I didn't blame Jim for arriving too late. The blame lay with the Urbat and their crazy-ass leader, Blake. The same lunatic who'd held Michelle and her brothers for years.

When we find Blake, we'll make him pay for what happened.

That we will, Jim sent back grimly.

JIM...

WINIFRED'S THOUGHTS cut into my contemplation of what I would like to do to Blake for everything he'd done to Michelle, the rest of the girls, and all the males in this car.

Why have you stopped moving? She sent me.

Aden is starving and everyone needed a minute to think of something other than death.

I understand, but you need to keep moving. Gabby says there are several Urbat nearby. I'm worried.

We're in the car at a fast food place. Lots of exhaust to cover up our scent. As soon as we get our order, we're heading south like we agreed. How are things looking for you? How are Mom and Michelle?

Everyone's fine. You just worry about keeping your group safe, and we'll keep everyone here safe.

Someone tapped on my window. I turned toward a woman and teen boy who carried several bags of food and a cardboard tray of drinks. With a grin I didn't feel, I rolled down the window.

"Thank you. The little guy in back was about to starve." I winked at the woman so she'd know I was joking and started accepting the bags and handing them off to Paul.

"We're sorry about the wait," the woman said, handing over the drink tray.

"Don't worry about it. Thanks for the food."

Jim! Get out of there now.

The fear and command in Winifred's message had me shoving the drinks toward Paul and grabbing the wheel. I slammed the vehicle into reverse and twisted in my seat to see behind me. However, my foot never descended onto the gas pedal.

A group of seven males, directly behind us, stopped me. They'd made little attempt to blend. Ragged, dirty clothes covered them, but the threadbare material would have never kept a normal human warm.

The woman still beside the window made a small noise, also seeing the mongrels that held my attention.

The lead man smiled slowly, showing his elongated canines.

They've found us, I sent Winifred as I slammed down on the gas.

The tires squealed, and we shot backward. The woman screamed, she and the boy still not moving.

"Run," I yelled to them.

The mutts scattered, jumping out of my way. They didn't go far though. With snarls and curses, some partially shifted.

I cranked the wheel as I reversed, listening to claws screech against metal. Aden whimpered. Shouting erupted from the nearby humans, spilling from the restaurant.

Slamming on the breaks, I shifted to drive. The glass behind Gregory shattered and curled forward in a webbed sheet. Furred hands reached for Aden.

Gregory's gaze met mine in the rearview mirror. Angry knowing lit his eyes. He growled, and his own claws erupted.

We needed to get out of here, but people ran in every direction. My foot hesitated on the pedal. Save their lives or those of the cubs. I glanced in the mirror again. Gregory swiped at the mutts then used his nails to cut Aden's seatbelt.

"Henry," he called, throwing the boy forward. The cub's eyes were wide and panicked.

I gunned it forward as Henry caught Aden and curled protectively around both cubs. A man yelled and dove out of my way, and I jerked the wheel to the right, avoiding the back end of the nearest car trying to escape the chaos.

Cackling laughter exploded from the back. I looked up at

the mirror in time to see arms grip Gregory's shoulders.

Don't stop, he sent me. *Keep them all safe.*

With a heave, several of the mutts pulled Gregory from the back as we swerved out of the parking lot and onto the main road.

"Dad!" Paul yelled from beside me, proof he'd witnessed what had just happened.

I checked the mirror again as I wove in and out of traffic. Gregory fought five of them in the middle of the road. Two sprinted after us, their paws eating up the distance.

"Keep hold of those cubs," I said to Henry.

Giving the van more gas, I ignored the distant wailing sirens, the sound of Paul begging me to turn around, and Liam and Aden's soft whimpers. Cars honked and veered out of my way. One of the mutts jumped on top of the roof of an old beetle, using it as a springboard to launch himself at us. He just missed the back end of our van, his claws scraping briefly on metal then nothing as he fell to the road and rolled in a heap of fur.

The second mutt trailed us persistently to the edge of town. Then he veered off the road and disappeared into the sparse trees separating one business from another. The sound of a helicopter overhead sent my heart racing.

The south is clear, Winifred sent, interrupting my thoughts. *Head south.*

They shifted in the open, calling attention to all of us. There's a helicopter in the air now. I'm not sure if it's following us or trying to track the Urbat. The back window is broken out. We're too easy to identify from the ground and air. I need to change vehicles.

Do what needs to be done.

I turned onto the next street I found and parked the car.

"Everyone out," I said.

"Are we going back?" Paul asked, opening his door and moving to grab Aden from the middle.

I grabbed their bags from the back and tossed them each one without answering.

"You know we can't," Henry said.

Both boys—men—looked down at the cubs.

"We need to move, now," I said, my eyes on the sky while I listened to the approaching sirens and closed the back of the van. "Cut through this yard to the next block over. No fur. As soon as we're on the next block, hold hands with the cubs and walk like nothing's happened."

They listened then responded immediately. One block over, a helicopter flew overhead, speeding in the direction we'd been headed.

"Don't hurry," I said softly.

We continued walking, cutting another block west. A car idled on the sidewalk.

"This one?" Paul asked.

"No. It'll be reported missing too quickly."

Three houses down, I saw a paper still on the front stoop. After we passed the house, I told the boys to keep walking and ducked in between yards, circling around to break into the garage. The older car looked brand new. It didn't take me long to start it up and quickly back out of the garage. Hopefully, the owner wouldn't notice it missing for a long while.

Catching up with the boys, I pulled over so they could pile in. Liam helped Aden buckle as I pulled away from the curb.

"Are we going back for Uncle Gregory?" Liam asked.

"No, buddy. He doesn't want us to," I said.

Is he still alive? Henry sent me. I allowed myself to focus on

61

where Gregory's link should be in my mind. Its presence was only a small relief. We'd left him surrounded by Urbat and exposed to humans. If the first group didn't kill him, the other would likely take him and—I couldn't finish that thought.

Where should we meet you? I sent Gregory. I waited several long minutes before I understood there would be no response.

He's alive, but not answering, I sent back to Henry.

We can't risk going back for him.

No, we can't.

His maturity saddened me. Too much, too young. Paul sat in the front. He'd said nothing since getting in. Soft traces of anger laced his scent. Mostly, though, I smelled his grief.

"I'm sorry, Paul."

"It's not your fault. It's not anyone's but the mutt who wants power at any cost. He won't win."

I agreed with his last, growled sentiment.

The distant sound of the helicopter grew louder before fading again. We headed out of town, my thoughts on Mary and Gregory and the boys they'd left behind.

Blake wouldn't win. We would make sure of that. But at what cost? Would there be any werewolves left in the end?

We're in a new vehicle. I sent to Winifred. *Does it seem like anyone is following us?*

After a moment, she answered.

Gabby said that no one seems to be following you.

There was a moment of silence where I could feel her worry and sorrow.

Who did you leave behind?

Gregory.

How many will we lose before this ends? she sent, echoing my thoughts.

CHAPTER FIVE

OLIVIA...

THE TENSE SILENCE REMAINED AFTER GABBY'S ANNOUNCEMENT that Jim was clear of the Urbat but that Gregory was no longer with them. Whoever Jim and Gregory were, they seemed pretty important given the group's reaction.

"I'm sorry for your loss," I said softly to Winifred, masking the pity and sorrow I wanted to feel.

"Thank you," Winifred said. "Gabby, if it's safe, can you find us a place where we can stop for the night?"

"Sure," Gabby said. "There's a town a ways to the south that looks good. Maybe another hour or two. I'll text Michelle."

"Good," Winifred said.

I could feel her gaze on me. I wasn't unaware of their vague conversations about where we were going and understood that Winifred, and probably the rest, didn't trust me. Not that I blamed them. Blake had hurt so many in his reach for power and control and would continue to do so until the end. That I'd lived with him for most of my life but couldn't tell these people anything significant about his plans hadn't endeared me to anyone. Yet, their feelings toward me changed nothing.

"Blake needs to be stopped," I said, looking out the window. "Soon."

"How do we do that?" Winifred asked.

"Complete the Judgement. The dreamer has the answer to that, even if she hasn't dreamed it yet."

"That's just fucking ducky," Bethi mumbled.

No one said anything more, and I hesitated to again bring up the need to decide the direction of our Judgement first. Blake had pushed them all so much already. If I did the same, they would trust me even less. And, I needed their trust.

For the next two hours, we traveled in silence. It was something that I was very used to, but a small part of me had hoped it would be different when I joined my sisters.

Bethi slept frequently, usually waking with a curse. Luke would murmur assurances to her; she would calm then sleep again. I didn't envy her gift. I didn't envy any of our gifts. But, I did envy Bethi's connection with Luke. And Gabby's with Clay. Although those two never spoke, he would turn often to look back at her. What would it be like to have someone honestly care about me, not just because of the role I would play in the Judgement?

Courage, the echo of the Lady's whisper brought my attention to the Others. I forced my mind away from thoughts of caring mates and waited for our next stop.

When the vehicle finally parked, Bethi woke up.

"About time," she said, reaching for the door.

I sat still, waiting for the rest to leave first. The grey swirls outlined the door and the people as they hopped out of the car but not the floorboard or the ground. I would have to try to judge the distance for myself. Before I could move to get out, another person came to stand beside the door. Based on the angle of her face, she was watching me.

"Can I help you?" a female voice asked. It took a moment to place it with a name.

"Thank you, Charlene. I think I can manage, though."

I gripped the side of the door, just in case, and slowly stepped out. My toes hit the ground an inch sooner than I anticipated, and the door saved me from stumbling. Still, Charlene reached out to steady me. Her offer hadn't been an empty, polite gesture after all but one of true caring.

"Thank you," I said.

"It's no problem. Can I walk with you?" she asked.

"Sure. Is this a paved parking lot?"

"It is." She wrapped her arm through mine, and we slowly walked to the entrance of a building. Despite my best efforts, I couldn't stop myself from enjoying the simple contact.

"You're different from the rest of us," Charlene said. "Not just your eyes. When I touch the other girls, things happen. Michelle sees a white room filled with images of the future. Bethi sleeps. Gabby sees her sparks better. And each time, it seems to drain me. But not with you. What happens when I touch you?"

I checked the swirls.

"Nothing. Well, you do make me feel more confident that I won't trip or run into something."

She chuckled.

"Why are you different?"

"Probably because my purpose is different," I said honestly.

"What's your purpose?" she asked.

"I'd rather wait until we're all together to talk about it."

"Fair enough. Michelle and Emmitt are getting room keys. Would you mind staying in a room with Winifred?"

Winifred. Their unspoken leader. I understood what they all were thinking. Keeping me close would ensure their safety if I turned out to be a threat.

"I wouldn't mind at all," I answered.

We approached the rest of the group who waited just outside the entrance door. Three people stood slightly apart from the majority. The largest of the three staying protectively close to a smaller person. Charlene steered us toward them.

The smaller person moved a lot. Just little bits of movement that the Others picked up with their swirling presences.

"I don't know who I'm with if I don't hear your voices," I said when we stopped.

"It's Winifred, Carlos, and Isabelle," Isabelle said. "I have to say, you are a relief. You're almost like Carlos. A pleasant void of emotion. Not even Winifred has managed to cap it off that well."

I turned my head slightly toward Carlos, the larger person. Keeping everything hidden took years of practice and usually stemmed from some kind of desperate need.

"You must have had a very strong motivation for keeping what you feel hidden," I said to him.

"Winifred told us about werewolves living with you," he said, not acknowledging my comment. "Females taken when they were cubs. Did you know a Sophia?"

It surprised me to hear the name of the oldest female werewolf who had still lived at Blake's complex, but I kept that surprise carefully bottled away.

"I did. I wasn't allowed to see the werewolf women. But she was pregnant and felt better when she walked. I ran into her twice. She was very close to giving birth before all of this happened."

"Pregnant." Pain filled his voice with that one word.

Isabelle staggered slightly, as if hit, and gripped Carlos.

"I'm sorry," he said immediately.

"What was that?" she asked. "What happened?"

"Just something from the past."

"Who was she to you?" I asked Carlos.

The entrance door opened and two more joined the main group who listened to us. Everyone waited for his answer.

"She was my sister."

Charlene gasped. Isabelle wrapped her arms around Carlos. Another man came over. Everyone started asking questions. Why hadn't Carlos told anyone? How long had he known he had a sister? What happened to her? Did I know how to find her?

"She died," Carlos said. "I felt her link disappear just after we left New York."

"Link?" Sam said. "You're not an Elder. Links only happen with Mated pairs and Elders."

"And twins," Winifred said, her voice soft and filled with pain.

As much as I truly felt sorry for Carlos and Sophia, I knew more grief would come to all of us if we didn't hurry.

"Perhaps we can discuss this inside?" I said.

"Yes," Winifred agreed.

Michelle started handing out keys.

"Everyone should meet in our room," Charlene said, her hand on Carlos's arm. "I'll order all of us something to eat since we missed dinner."

That statement almost made me cringe. Not because I

wasn't hungry—the snack bar Winifred had given me was long since digested—but because every minute we wasted meant more suffering. How long had it been since Blake called Frank back into his office? Two days and seven hours? A little more maybe. I purposely tried not to think about it or what would happen when my time was up.

"Could I speak to the Judgements alone, first?" I asked.

The Others showed how Winifred and Charlene exchanged looks.

"Why do we have to go through this every time?" Bethi said irritably. "Talking to people alone shouldn't be this big of a deal. Yes, Olivia. We'll all talk privately."

Bethi moved to my side and took my arm. She also plucked something from Winifred's hand.

"What?" she said. "I just spent the last two hours being burned and skinned alive. Are you going to do something worse? If not, let's just get our shit done."

Although I appreciated her sentiment, her angry tone worried me. Luke, too, apparently.

"Bethi, luv—"

"Don't worry about it," Isabelle said. "Come here you little crack head. Time for your next fix."

Bethi immediately released me and walked to Isabelle. The woman put a hand on Bethi's arm. A moment later, Bethi sighed.

"Thanks. I needed that."

"I could tell," Isabelle said. "Let's go inside and hurry up this talk so Carlos and I can spar."

Isabelle nudged Bethi forward. I carefully followed, relieved when Charlene once again looped her arm through mine.

"Thank you," I said.

"I don't want you to fall."

We made our way down the hallway, and Bethi opened a door, stepping aside so we could enter. Winifred continued walking down the hall with the rest of the group.

"You know they'll still hear us, right?" Bethi said, closing the door.

Charlene led me to the bed and sat beside me. Bethi sprawled out on the opposite mattress. Gabby and Michelle sat on the edge of the other bed, facing me and Charlene. Isabelle paced near the door.

"Yes," I said, acknowledging Bethi. "It's not that I don't want them to hear. I don't want them to distract us."

"From what?" Gabby asked.

"From deciding. I don't think the Lady will share how to complete the Judgement until we know which race we're going to Judge in favor of. And we need to complete the Judgement as quickly as possible. We're running out of time."

"The only logical choice is the werewolves," Charlene said.

"What's going to keep the werewolves from taking over just like the Urbat want to do?" Bethi asked.

"Thomas. The Elders."

"Bullshit," Bethi said. "They want what's best for the werewolves, not for everyone. Look, I love Luke. I think he's amazing, and I trust him. But that doesn't mean I trust his whole race. Don't forget I have lifetimes of history floating around in my head. There's a reason humans were given the initial Judgement."

"Yes," I said. "They were weak and needed protecting. They aren't weak anymore, and the three races are far out of balance. We cannot rule in favor of the humans again."

"And we can't rule in favor of the Urbat," Michelle said.

"That would be suicide for the other two races, giving them what they want."

"So, we're saying it has to be the werewolves, then," Gabby said.

Bethi snorted and rolled to her side.

"I disagree. I don't think the power of humanity outweighs that of the werewolves. And even if it did, fine. Let them have more power. They need it to keep everything furry from going on a killing spree."

"I'll admit I'm on the fence," Isabelle said. "I know Bethi just acknowledged that all those past lives in her head are clouding her view of the present, but I've seen the power in the werewolves. What would stop them from going on a human killing spree if we named them captain of this sinking ship?"

"Please listen," I said. "We cannot Judge in favor of the humans. The balance is already too far in their favor. A balance must be maintained, or the world will burn."

Bethi exhaled heavily. "That's what the Lady told me, too. Showed me even."

"And she will keep showing you death and devastation until you understand."

"Fuck that. Fine. Werewolves. Now what?"

"Just like that?" Isabelle asked.

"No," I said. "I think we all need to truly believe in our choice. I know we cannot Judge for the Urbat or humans. I don't know what it will mean for this world to Judge in favor of the werewolves. It worries me, but not as much as what will happen if we try to Judge in favor of the other two."

There was a long moment of silence.

"I honestly had expected you to want us to choose the Urbat

after hearing you call Blake Father," Michelle said. "How did they find you?"

I thought back to my earliest memory. To that moment in the parking garage when Blake approached the woman and me.

"I was young. Maybe four years old. I'd just left a doctor's office and saw Blake across the street. He stood out from the other people. I don't know if it was the way I looked or my scent, but he followed us into the parking garage. The woman with me stopped by her car when he called out. He killed her and took me."

"He killed your mother?" Charlene asked in shock.

"I don't know if that was my mom. I don't really remember her. Just him. For a long time, I thought him finding me was by chance," I said. "But I'm not sure anymore."

"What do you mean?" Bethi asked.

"You've said that I've died early in every life, right?" I said.

"Yes. Every time. Most of them you're not even a year old."

"I think the Lady let the one person who would keep me alive, find me."

"Holy shit," Bethi said softly. "I didn't really like her before. I like her even less now. She has to be the sickest person on the planet to push this kind of shit on us."

"I think she's that desperate. How many times have we been born this cycle?" I asked.

Bethi was quiet a moment. "Just once."

"She planned this. All of this. Strength, being born first, to fortify the werewolves by giving them sons and a home to protect any future potential mates. One of your Elders finding Gabby before the Urbat could. Gabby, who would have made it so easy to find the rest of us. And, sending me to live with the

Urbat so I could tell the rest of you that, as the race they are right now, there is nothing redeemable about them. She knows the Judgement needs to be made, and I think she's helping influence us to make the right choice the best way she can."

"If she wants to help us, she should just off Blake and make the Judgement herself."

I shook my head and thought of the shadow world. "There are rules."

"What do you mean?"

I hesitated, not sure what to tell them now. What wouldn't send them running or cause them to dismiss everything I say? I watched the Others swirl around the women in the room, creating my grey view of our world.

"Would you believe me if I told you there aren't just three races?" I asked.

"Yep," Bethi said. "Too much crap has come true to not believe something at this point."

Michelle and Gabby made sounds of agreement.

"There are three races here, but this world touches another where a different race lives. I don't know what they are. I call them the Others. They kind of float around us, always moving, surrounding people and things. Like brushing up against them. That's how I can see some things. They outline this world for me. When they stop moving, I'm truly blind."

"I thought you said they always moved," Bethi said.

"There have been times they've stopped. When something really big happens. Like when you revealed the existence of Urbat and werewolves to the world."

I focused on Bethi's shape. "They are the reason we need to maintain balance here. If we don't, they get to live here."

"Based on all this world burning crap the Taupe Lady keeps

telling me, I'm guessing these 'Others' are pretty bad."

"Yes and no. They want what we have. Real bodies. A way to interact with our surroundings. I think the Lady is one of them. She can control them. Sort of. And they tend to listen to her."

"This is making my brain hurt. If she's one of them and they want to live here, why would she want us to maintain the balance? And, that wouldn't make sense anyway. She showed me how we were created. All of us were in her belly, and she touched different women to put us inside them. That was the very first cycle."

"I can't pretend to know our history. That's for you. I can only tell you about the world I see. The Others are around us. Everywhere. All the time. Whenever someone dies, they try to get inside the body. But they can't without permission. They can hear me and understand me. They know we're trying to keep the balance so they can't have our world, but it doesn't seem to upset them. They help me see when I ask them."

"Well, I know I'm not the only one creeped out by the idea of an unseen race moving around us in this room. Tone it down, Michelle," Isabelle said.

"Sorry," Michelle answered.

"I feel like we've gotten off topic," Gabby said. "I thought we just needed to decide which race to Judge in favor of."

"We do," I said. "I wanted you to understand why you truly need to believe in your choice and what waits for this world if we fail this Judgement."

"Yeah, we get it," Isabelle said. "Invisible people who will make the world burn. I think we're all onboard with Judging for the werewolves. Now what?"

"Now we wait for Bethi to dream the rest," I said.

CHAPTER SIX

HENRY...

HEADLIGHTS LIT THE INSIDE OF THE CAR BRIEFLY BEFORE THE OTHER car passed us.

It hurt. All of it. Losing Mom and now Dad. Liam shook next to me. I kept my arm around him, trying my best to help him feel safe again. Aden had cried himself to sleep hours ago and currently leaned against me in oblivious peace. At least, it smelled like peace. I hoped the cub continued to have good dreams.

Liam's scent remained far from peaceful. Worry, grief, and confusion melded together to create a toxic soup that I wanted to choke on with each inhale.

"I'm sorry you didn't get anything to eat, Liam," I said.

"I'm sorry they took Uncle Gregory," he said.

"I know. Me, too. But we can't stay sad about it for too long."

He tipped his head up to look at me.

"Why not?"

"We have things to do. Being sad will distract us."

"What do we have to do?" he asked.

"Get you back to Mimi safe and sound. I'm not going to lie; those bad guys are going to keep trying to find us. But Uncle Jim, Paul, and I are going to do everything we can to keep that from happening. You can help us by staying focused. What did Aunt Mary tell you about what you feel?"

"It all has a smell."

"That's right. And little kids, like you, usually smell happy. Sure, they sometimes smell angry or sad, but never for long. The bad guys looking for us are going to use their noses to try to find the saddest, most scared kids they can. So don't be sad. Don't be scared."

Liam nodded and looked out the window. I hated having to tell him all that. Cubs weren't supposed to worry about their scents or people using them to track. But, we needed to do everything we could to keep the cubs safe.

Slowly, Liam's scent changed. It stayed far from happy, but the grief and worry eased up considerably. I caught Jim's gaze in the mirror. He nodded at me and returned his focus to the road.

"Have you ever been on a vacation?" I asked Liam.

He shook his head.

"Me, neither. I think when we get to Emmitt and your sister, we'll tell them we want a vacation. Where should we go?"

"The place where they make the mouse pancakes."

His immediate answer surprised me.

"You mean Disney World?" I asked.

"Yep. I want to see that mouse." He lowered his voice and looked up at me. "Uncle Jim isn't so good at making that shape. Dad isn't any better."

Jim burst out laughing, and I grinned.

"Then, we need to go there."

"Yep. Aden would like that, too. I think it would help his smell."

"I think you're right. What do you say, Paul?"

"I'm always up for mingling with some princesses," he said.

He didn't sound up for it. He sounded ready to fight. I knew my brother well enough, though, to know his issue wasn't with a vacation.

Tell him to cut it out, I sent Jim.

He just wants blood. Like we all do.

I know. But, I just told a cub to hide his emotions. Paul needs to do the same, or he'll be the princess when we finally get to Disney.

Jim snorted, but otherwise remained silent.

"Hey, Liam," Paul said suddenly. "Do you think Henry could get in free if we dressed him up like Merida?"

Liam snorted.

"I'm disturbed that you know who Merida is," I said.

"Nope. You should be more disturbed that you know who I was talking about," Paul said.

Liam's mood lightened further over the next few minutes with Paul and me quietly bantering about who would make the best princess.

"Gabby is telling me it's clear, and this tank needs gas," Jim interrupted. "I'm pulling into the next station."

Any hint of humor left Liam's expression, and I could tell by his scent he was struggling to keep his emotions positive. I understood his concern.

How clear? I sent Jim.

She said they are still in the same city. There are a few around here, but nothing close. Grey will keep me posted.

"A gas station is good. Paul made me hungry for some man-food with all his princess talk," I said. Paul snorted, and Liam giggled from behind his hand.

"Perfect," Jim said. "You two princesses can take the cubs to the bathroom and grab some road food. I'll fill the car."

Any update on Dad? I asked silently.

Winifred has been listening to the news. There were reports of the fight but so far there's nothing being said about anyone having been captured. Your Dad's still not answering, but I can feel him.

I almost wished Jim couldn't feel him. That he wasn't answering meant that someone had him and he didn't want us to know who and try to get him. Whether human or Urbat, there was only one reason to keep Dad alive. Information. And he wouldn't ever give any. No matter how they tried to pry it from him.

Jim found a quiet place in the middle of a country community. Pulling up to the vacant pumps, he winked back at Liam.

"Get me some Twinkies, okay?"

Liam grinned and nodded. Paul opened the door for him and stayed close while I woke Aden and took him inside. The clerk called out a friendly hello, only looking away from the TV mounted behind the counter for a moment.

I said hello in return and steered the boys toward the back. They went in together with a promise to be quick and wash with soap. I didn't care about the soap, just the speed.

While Paul stood by the door to wait for them, I started loading up on some food items. Nothing looked good. I doubted anything would for a long time. But, I knew we all needed to eat. So I grabbed things at random and took them up to the counter just as the clerk's show was interrupted with a breaking news update. The reporter talked about a werewolf and Urbat sighting north of us. The screen switched to show a parking lot of a familiar fast food place. Glass and blood smattered the blacktop. My chest ached at the sight and anger boiled in my veins.

"I still don't believe that shit's real," the guy said, not looking away from the screen. "I mean, how could another race possibly exist without a hint of anyone knowing?"

"I don't know," I said calmly. "Where else would all those legends have come from?"

"True," the guy said, turning toward me. "Paying for the gas, too?" he asked.

"Yep." I pulled out my wallet. Mom and Dad had split money between all of us in case we were separated. Thanks to Michelle and her lawyer, there was plenty of it.

While I counted out bills, the reporter on the television went on to ask for help finding the van that fled from the attack. They believed the "family" of one of the "victims" fled in fear and stole another car. My pulse jumped, and I looked up at the TV. The screen showed a house with an open garage and an older woman with a picture of the car we now drove. The clerk looked up at the TV, following my gaze. He frowned and glanced out the window where Jim now filled the car, then he looked back to the TV.

"Shit," he breathed softly.

Our eyes met.

"They killed my mom, took my dad, and are after the rest of us. I'm sorry about this."

Using my speed, I grabbed the back of his head and slammed his face down onto the counter, knocking him out. I checked his pulse before letting him go. He slowly slid to the floor.

I just knocked out the clerk, I sent Jim.

I hope you had a good reason, he sent back.

The TV had a picture of our car and was asking for anyone with any information to call in.

Are there cameras inside?

I glanced at the wall behind the register, my stomach sinking.

Yes.

Hurry up.

Throwing the payment on the counter, I turned toward Paul. He released his hold on the door knob. Liam opened the door and frowned up at Paul.

"Sorry, bud," he said, messing the cub's hair. "You're right. It wasn't funny. Let's get these Twinkies to the big guy."

Neither boy seemed to notice the missing clerk as we walked out. Jim teased Aden about eating all the snack food as we got back into the car.

What now? I sent Jim. *We're clear of Urbat, but what about the humans?*

JIM...

Winifred, we have a problem. Henry just had to knock out a human because we're on the news. They're looking for the car we're driving.

For a moment, she said nothing. I could feel her frustration over the link and waited.

Michelle can contact her lawyer for a car. Head to Casper. There will be a rental waiting for you.

I did a U-turn in the road and started heading north again.

"Did we forget something, Uncle Jim?" Liam asked in a worried voice.

"Nah. Just took a wrong turn, bud," I said. "Can you hand me a Twinkie?"

He threw one my way, and I caught it without looking back. Aden giggled. I heard cellophane crinkle and got ready to catch another one.

"I'll eat them all if you keep throwing them," I warned with a laugh I didn't feel.

The cub didn't throw any more after the second one. I opened the first and took a bite, making a good show of it. The boys smiled and snacked in the back, filling their little bellies during the drive. We stuck to as many backroads as possible. Not that there were many around these parts.

A distance from Casper, I cut the lights and turned off the road onto a little easement a farmer used to access his field. Creeping slowly forward, I drove along the tree line, slipping and sliding over the snow-covered ground. The boys giggled and grunted over the bumps. When the car wouldn't move any further, Paul and Henry got out and pushed us the rest of the way. Nestled in between the trees of the two fields, the car would be hard to see from the road. Especially after we covered it with snow and cleared the tracks.

Once we finished, Paul and Henry carried the boys, and I shouldered the bags for all of them. The jog to town didn't take long. Still, the cubs' cheeks were red with cold by the time we arrived.

If the guy behind the counter wondered how we'd gotten there, he didn't say anything. I provided my ID and signed his sheets of paper then got the keys from him.

As soon as we were in the new car, I turned up the heat for the cubs.

We have the rental and are heading for Salt Lake, I sent Winifred.

Stay on the main roads. If what Olivia says is true, it'll be unlikely they find you. We're at a hotel in Missoula. Grey, Sam, and I will stay up and keep watch on things here.

Gabby sleeping then?

Yes. She needs it. She'll likely wake and check again at some point in the night just to verify Urbat positions, but she said since we'd picked up Olivia, nothing's changed.

Still not sure if you can trust her?

No. She feels different. All these girls have some sort of strong emotions. Bethi's fear. Isabelle is anger. Charlene and Michelle are worry. Gabby has desperation. But Olivia has nothing. She's hiding something. Until I know what, we won't let down our guard. Keep those cubs safe.

Aden stripped out of his winter jacket and fell asleep against Henry. Liam watched out the window for an hour before crashing.

"I need you both to sleep," I said when neither Paul nor Henry tried to rest. "We don't know what's coming next and can't all be exhausted when we face it."

Paul exhaled loudly and closed his eyes. Henry watched me for a few minutes before speaking.

"What's going to happen to us when this is finished?"

"If your dad's not back by then, you can stay with me," I said. Did he honestly think we would forget about them, even if they were adults by human standards?

"Not that," he said. "I mean what's going to happen to all of us when the girls do their magic, whatever it is? Even if the humans are no longer 'in power,' they aren't going to conveniently forget we exist."

"No, they won't. It's not going to be easy, but we've survived worse according to the stories Winifred liked to tell us when we were cubs."

"Come on, Jim. Do you honestly think the humans are just going to roll over and show us their bellies?"

I didn't think that at all. Winifred and the other Elders were so focused on helping the girls and getting the Judgement made that they hadn't discussed what might happen afterwards. Like Henry, I'd thought of little else.

When I'd told Winifred, the cubs were our future, I'd meant it. They were the bridge that would tie our two races together. Growing up with us, they would have no fear or prejudice. But they were only two voices against many, and they wouldn't influence the world yet for several years.

"Honestly? I think it will be chaos. Look at what they're doing already. Human remains are popping up all over the place, dead from humans torturing other humans. They're already obsessed with eliminating both werewolves and Urbat. But if you look at any pivotal point of history for our world, you'll know one thing for certain. Change and acceptance don't ever come easy."

Henry closed his eyes and rested his head back against the seat, an arm around each cub.

As the tires ate up the miles, my mind stayed on Henry's question. I'd heard enough conversation over the last few weeks to know the Judgement Bethi kept talking about was meant to change the ruling race. If I were human like them, I'd want to just stick with what I knew and Judge in favor of the humans.

I mean, it didn't take a genius to know those girls would never Judge in favor of the Urbat. Not after what those bastards had done to Michelle, Isabelle, or the dreams that Bethi kept having about them murdering her in previous lives.

No matter how they Judged, we'd irrevocably changed the world by announcing our existence. I still remembered the fear in Michelle's eyes when she found out what Emmitt and I were and the way Mom talked about how she'd feared our kind in the beginning too. The world would turn into a dangerous place to exist for any race.

At first, I'd questioned the wisdom of revealing ourselves. Then, I'd realized, just as the Elders probably had, we had little choice. Living in the shadows had nearly killed us. Mom's persistence in bringing us into the human world had stopped our extinction, but our numbers hadn't flourished. We needed to change. Not just for the sake of changing, but to make progress.

I fully believed the time for living in the shadows was at an end and hoped all our suffering now wouldn't be for nothing.

Well before the sun rose, Paul opened his eyes and stretched.

"Want me to take over for a while?" he offered.

"Yep." I pulled over to the side of the road. Elder or not, I needed sleep. How long had it been?

Paul and I got out and switched seats. Henry roused in the back but said nothing about the switch.

Paul's driving. I'm taking a quick nap. We only have an hour to go before we reach the city, I sent Winifred.

I'll let you know if I hear anything from Gabby.

I closed my eyes and sunk into an immediate dreamless sleep.

It felt like seconds before the smell of fear swamped the car. I opened my eyes just as the front window shattered from the impact of a large, furred body.

"Don't stop, Paul," I said, grabbing the wheel to keep the car on the road as the pup tried to avoid the next shape hurtling toward us.

The cubs started whimpering, letting me know they were awake.

Winifred, we're under attack. I need to know how many.

There was a moment of silence.

Four. Nothing else is moving toward you.

"Henry, hang on to those cubs. Paul, stop the car."

Paul slammed on the brakes. As the car screeched on the blacktop, I opened my door and launched myself out, already shifting. The momentum carried me into the next shape emerging from the trees. I slammed into the body and raked my claws up the mutt's soft middle, just like they'd done to Mary. Letting him fall, I turned for the next. One ripped at the roof of the car, claws piercing the metal. Another pulled the driver's door clear off its hinges. Paul burst out in his fur, snarling.

Be careful, I sent him, already launching myself at the one on the roof. I knocked the mongrel off and slammed into Paul's attacker, taking them both at once. Claws ready, I gutted the first in a spray of blood. The teeth of the second dug into my shoulder. I shook him off and went for his throat.

A sudden yip filled the air, followed by another growl.

"Send 'em out, pup," a male voice called from the other side of the vehicle. "Or I'll break his other leg."

I hurtled over the car without a second thought. As the air ruffled my fur, I took in the sight of a half-shifted man gripping

Paul in his arms. Still in wolf form, it was easy to see Paul's broken hind leg hanging at a useless, odd angle. The man's gaze shifted from Henry, inside the car, to me. He pulled back his lips in a silent snarl, tossed Paul aside, and jumped to meet me.

He never saw my claws. But, he felt them. With a grunt, the mutt fell to his knees and clutched his middle. His pained sounds weren't the only ones. The other two men were moving, trying to drag themselves into the trees. The fourth had already shifted to his skin. The three who were wounded wouldn't last much longer. Our healing could only do so much.

The back door opened, and Henry climbed out. Behind him, Aden and Liam clung to each other, their little faces pale and their eyes wide.

"I'll grab some clothes from the trunk for both of you," Henry said.

Paul shifted back to his skin in the bloodied snow where he lay. I shifted as well, the cold winter air giving me goosebumps. Kneeling beside Paul, I felt along his leg for the break.

"Want me to try to straighten it?" I asked.

"Yeah. I don't want it to heal funny."

He grunted as I gripped his leg and did my best. Our healing gave us an advantage, but it needed help sometimes. I hoped what I'd done would keep him from walking with a limp in the future.

Henry tossed clothes at us then went to the car again to hold the cubs.

As much as I want to see them suffer, we don't want them communicating our location to anyone, Henry sent me.

I lifted my head to see the one near us trying to use his phone.

"Get dressed," I said.

I stood, leaving my clothes in the snow to approach the dying Urbat. Knocking the device from his fingers, I swiped my claws across his throat on the backswing before moving to finish the other two. I left them where they lay, thankful that the falling snow and the pre-dawn hours had kept the road free of any traffic.

"We need to move," Paul called.

In the distance, I caught oncoming lights and regretted my thankful thought.

"Damn."

I picked up the first body and threw it into the ditch, followed quickly by the second. The blood in the road would be hard to see with the falling snow. A naked man would be easier to spot. Sprinting around the car, I tugged on my pants then lifted Paul into the front seat.

We were back on the road before the car passed us. With any luck, they hadn't noticed anything.

Henry spoke soothingly to the cubs in back while Paul panted beside me.

Winifred, Paul's been hurt. Broken leg. He'll live, but we need a place to hole up so he can rest and heal until you get here. Oh, and you need Michelle to buy the rental. We can't return it.

CHAPTER SEVEN

OLIVIA...

I opened my eyes to the light of the third morning away from Blake and shivered with fear. This was taking too long. I'd need to end it this afternoon. Any longer than that and the Others would demand more than I could afford to give.

"I think that's the first true emotion you've shown," Winifred said from somewhere in the room.

"Is that why you don't trust me?" I asked as I sat up. "Because I hide my emotions?"

"It's hard to trust someone who seems to be hiding so much."

I nodded and eased out of bed. The Others were busy dancing around objects. A few clung to Winifred, like they did when someone was in pain or grieving.

"Why are you upset?" I asked. "Did something happen overnight?"

"Why would you think that?"

"The Others are fascinated with you right now. There are

only a few times they do that. One is when a person is truly, emotionally upset."

She considered me for a moment, her stillness reminding me of Blake whenever I'd upset him.

"The group we mentioned yesterday was attacked while you slept. Four Urbat. All dead. One of the group was hurt. A boy, barely a man by our standards. His leg was broken. The two little human children with them were the target. The Urbat want them so they can control Michelle and the Judgement that Bethi tells us needs to be made."

My stomach churned.

"They didn't get the children, did they?"

"No. They are unharmed. Michelle and Grey are working to find them somewhere safe to stay until we can reach them."

"Blake never spoke to me of my sister when he kept her. But, like her, I sat through many dinners while they pretended I was as stupid as a piece of furniture. I heard what they did to her. How they used her brothers to control her. They can't get them again." I stood and shuffled toward my bag. By touch, I found what I needed to change clothes.

Turning toward Winifred, I said what needed to be said.

"No matter what, you cannot allow them to have her brothers."

The Others spun faster as her shock, and likely outrage, settled in her heart.

"I'm sorry." I closed myself into the bathroom and dressed quickly after washing. She stayed sitting in the same position, the walls not blocking my view of the Others and, thus, her.

Blindly, I reached out and touched the mirror I knew hung above the sink and stared at where my reflection should have been.

"I envy their ignorance," I said softly. "And, I wish our existence wasn't necessary."

Daughter, I am with you always. Take comfort in knowing the time for Judgement is near, the Lady said from the other side.

I stepped back from the mirror and brushed my hair. When it fell straight and tangle free, I picked up my things and opened the door. I kept quiet as I repacked then went to sit on the edge of the bed, not facing Winifred, but not facing away either.

In the silence, I considered what the day had in store for me and let go of the fear and anxiety that wanted to well up. My future remained set. The fate of the world depended on it.

"Are you hungry?" Winifred asked, finally.

"Yes."

"I'll walk you to the breakfast bar downstairs." She stood and offered me her hand. I took it. The gentle curve of her fingers brought on a swell of pity. For myself.

"I wish one of you would have found me," I said honestly.

"I wish we would have, too." She led me out the door.

"Who is ignorant?" she asked as we walked, echoing what I'd said in the bathroom. "Us or the humans?"

"All of you."

"Of what are we ignorant?"

"Reality. But you won't stay ignorant for long, and I am sorry for that."

She remained quiet the rest of the way to the hotel lobby. The smell of toast and the sound of Bethi's voice let me know when we arrived.

"Well, that was a wasted, shit-night," Bethi said angrily. "Not a single useful dream. Just more death." She slouched in her chair and tipped her head back toward the ceiling. "What the hell is the Lady waiting for? We made up our minds, didn't we?"

"If there's doubt in any of us, I don't think we have made up our minds," I said, still moving with Winifred.

"Here's the breakfast bar," Winifred said. She placed my hand on the counter. "I'll help you fix a plate."

"Thank you."

"What do you mean?" Bethi asked. "You think one of us is doubting? Who?"

I shook my head slightly. "Doubt isn't something you can threaten and make go away. We all have doubts. Winifred doubts my intentions. I doubt we'll come to a decision quickly enough. You doubt the Judgement will give you a reprieve. Doubts are more natural than trust. But, that's what we need to do. Trust ourselves, each other, and our decision."

"You sound like a fortune cookie."

I smiled slightly at the bitterness in her tone. We all carried a measure of anger. Bethi just hadn't learned how to hide it yet.

"They have waffles, scrambled eggs, bacon, and muffins," Winifred said in the quiet. "Which would you like?"

"All of them, please." This would be the first meal I might actually eat in its entirety, and I planned to indulge myself.

I followed Winifred as she filled my plate and went to sit at Bethi and Luke's table. Bethi seemed to be sullenly playing with the food on her plate. Luke watched her.

She needs you, the Lady said, her voice a whisper through the veil. *Tell her the truth.*

"It won't be okay," I said, facing Bethi.

She stopped her small movements and lifted her head.

"What?"

"This thing we need to do. It won't be easy. It won't be okay."

"Is this supposed to be some kind of pep talk because if it is, you suck at it."

"Not a pep talk. The truth. Yes, your life sucks, but it could be worse. Ge—"

A sudden jolt of anger pierced my mind.

"Blaaaake..." the Others stopped moving and moaned as one.

"Not yet," I panted, focusing on keeping myself carefully emotionless. "Not yet."

The Others' movement picked up again in a frenzy that made me dizzy and wish that I could block them out by closing my eyes.

My time was almost up.

"Are you all right?" Bethi asked, her tone a toss between screw-you and concern.

"Yes. I'm saying we need to get over it and do what needs to be done," I said, weakly. "Thank you for the food, Winifred, but I don't think I can eat it. We're running out of time and need to leave. Now."

"Winifred!" a voice called urgently.

The echo from the hall made it hard to tell who it belonged to.

"There's movement. Everything's coming our way. We need to leave. Now," the voice said.

Winifred turned toward me.

"What just happened?"

"The beginning of the end." I turned to Bethi and set my hand on hers. "She wants me to remind you that you will get to relive five lifetimes full of love, family, and friends. You have Courage. Use it."

Five. Not six. I understood too well I would have no happy ending.

I stood and went to the door. Within five minutes, I sat in the car with Isabelle, Carlos, and Grey.

"Winifred thought you might want this," Isabelle said, passing back a banana and a water bottle.

"Thank you."

The car moved, and I quickly ate. No one said much during the tense drive south until Isabelle turned in her seat.

"Everyone thinks you're leading them to us," she said.

"Isabelle," Carlos warned.

"I think they're wrong. The Elders with Gabby are communicating silently with Grey to give us directions to avoid the Urbat."

"I know," I said. "Blake spoke about the Elders ability to communicate with all werewolves."

"You sent it, didn't you?"

"Yes." I didn't pretend to misunderstand. That letter had cost me much to get to her.

"I thought you were warning me about them, werewolves, at first. I ran when I saw them. Why didn't you say more?"

"I'm blind. Writing is hard."

She laughed slightly and turned forward.

"Thanks for the warning. It did help," she said.

"Thank you."

"For what?"

"For letting me know it was worth the price I paid to send it."

I turned and looked out the window, watching the Others

dance around the passing trees. After a few minutes, Isabelle reached out and turned on the radio at a low volume. For the next several hours, stories of werewolf sightings, captures, and fights filled the car. The state of the world made me shiver.

"That's the first emotion I felt," Isabelle said.

The reminder had me quickly focusing. Think, but don't feel. I knew better.

"I'm sorry."

"It's okay. It wasn't much," she said.

"Why are you so closed off?" Grey asked, speaking for the first time. "Carlos explained about his sister and protecting her. What about you? Who are you protecting?"

"Myself. Will we be stopping soon?"

Another surge of anger pierced my mind. The Others stilled outside the car.

"Whoa," Isabelle said. "What was that?"

"Not yet," I whispered. I turned away from the window and breathed slowly.

"There's coordinated Urbat movement again," Grey said. "They were still moving toward Missoula, where we'd stayed. Now they're moving south, toward us. What just happened?"

"My hold is slipping, and we're running out of time. Has Bethi dreamed the answer yet?"

There was a moment of silence.

"Not yet. What hold?" he asked.

"If I told you, you might make a rash decision that would jeopardize everything. Bethi needs more time, and I'm trying to give it to her."

"What exactly does that mean?" Isabelle asked.

"You'll see soon enough. I'll let you know when we need to stop."

WINIFRED…

She says we'll need to stop soon, Grey sent me.

Stop? That made no sense.

"How close are they, Gabby?" I asked.

"About thirty miles behind us. I'm not sure if they have our scent or if they just know we're on this road."

"Perhaps it's time to detour. Is there anything close?"

Gabby looked down at my phone, using the map app and her extra sense to guide us.

"Logan, Utah would be ideal. We should get to the exit before they reach us. It's out of the way through a mountain pass. If they aren't following us, but guessing, they'd pass right by."

"And if they aren't guessing?"

"It's a big city. We should be able to hide."

"Do you really think she is leaking our location?" Bethi asked.

The switch in seating arrangement had been a necessary precaution.

"I hope not."

How is Paul? I sent Jim.

In heaven, just like his brother and cubs. Michelle is the best for picking this place for them.

The place she'd selected was a high-end ski resort in the mountains just outside of Salt Lake. When Michelle had seen pine trees decorated with lights, an outdoor year-round heated pool, and suites fit for royalty, or a family who'd just lost everything, she hadn't hesitated.

She doesn't think they will look for you there. Everything else we've used has been cost efficient and low profile.

I don't think they'll look here either. How close are you? Will you meet us here or should we pull out and meet you in the city?

Stay where you are for now. We're being followed by some Urbat and plan to stop in Logan, Utah to correct that. We're only a few minutes from the turn off.

Stay safe.

"Text Michelle and let her know that her brothers are doing well and love the resort she picked for them," I said to Gabby.

"Wish I was at a resort," Bethi grumbled.

"We're going five star when this is done," Luke promised her.

She snorted. "I doubt it. You heard what she said. It won't be okay."

Luke sighed. I could smell his frustration and annoyance. I knew neither were at Bethi. That was the other reason I'd put Olivia with Grey. Bethi had enough of her own negativity. She didn't need Olivia adding to it.

"It will be what it will be, Bethi. You're not facing this alone," I reminded her.

She sighed, and Luke grunted.

"She's out again," he said. "I hope this ghost lady gives her the damn answer soon. I'm going crazy seeing her like this."

"We'll take care of her, Luke."

"Take the next exit, Sam," Gabby said.

Sam turned on his signal. The scent of his worry mingled with Luke's. He glanced in the mirror at Gabby.

I wanted to offer him some comfort, but couldn't. I knew what she meant to him. She was the daughter he'd wanted the first time he'd looked at me. A daughter he was never meant to have.

OLIVIA...

THE VEHICLE VEERED SLIGHTLY to the left. I hoped that meant we were stopping soon. Each passing minute tingled along my skin. Like a clock ticking down, I could feel the final hour drawing to a close. So few minutes left.

When the car increased speed, and I could feel the tilt in the road and hear the engine work, I began to worry. This wasn't an ideal location to stop, but the Others and my hold wouldn't last any longer.

"We need to pull over," I said.

"It won't be safe," Grey said. "We need to go further."

"It won't be safe if you don't stop. Please."

"If we stop here, the Urbat following us will see us. According to Gabby, there are—"

Another stab of anger speared my mind. Isabelle swore, and I reached for the door and fought to push it open against the wind. Carlos braked hard and swerved to the side.

Before the car came to a stop, I fell to my knees on the snowy shoulder. My heart hammered as I ripped the oversized sweater off and pulled it to my chest, leaving my back exposed.

"Now," I told them. "And, take your payment quickly."

I tried to bury the fear, but I knew what was coming. Pain flayed the skin on my back, from shoulder blade to lower rib on my right, along my spine, and shoulder blade to lower rib on my left. I could feel flesh separate as the Others ripped three long, thin strips of skin from me. I screamed at the white-hot agony, though I didn't want to, and fell forward into the snow, a shivering heap.

Outrage and fear consumed me.

Vaguely, I heard one of the men yell something and car doors open. Hands pressed snow onto my back, numbing some pain but creating more. Through my tears, I watched the Others dance away with my skin and disappear into their side of the veil.

"Olivia!" Isabelle's face got right in mine. "Olivia, what just happened? It looked like something invisible just ripped off your skin and disappeared with it."

"Charlene has the strength to lead us." My words were a stuttering slur. "Bethi has the wisdom to guide us. Isabelle's serenity, and Michelle's prosperity keep us safe. And, Gabby is the hope that brings us together." I gulped in a breath of air as the hand on my back pressed more snow onto the wounds.

"I have the courage to be the sacrifice. Courage to do what I must to save not just one race, but all of them." I breathed through the pain. "Blake will now know where we are."

"How?"

The pain made me drift and remember that moment in the garage. The moment I did as the Lady told me and asked Blake to pick me up. I remembered him grunting in disbelief before he did as I'd asked. My little hands had settled on the shoulder of his suit jacket as he started walking out of the parking garage.

"Now, bite him," she had said.

I'd tensed, knowing what she'd asked was wrong. Children shouldn't bite.

"He won't be angry. I promise."

Leaning my head against his shoulder, I'd put my arms around his neck and held him tightly.

"Good girl," he'd said.

Trembling, I'd opened my mouth and bit him hard. He'd grunted and stopped walking. He'd pulled me away from him and held me out to stare at me. For a long time, he'd said nothing. I remembered the rush of emotions spinning through my head, though. Feelings I hadn't understood at the time. Anger and lust had battled with suspicion until an overwhelming sense of resolution had filled me.

"That was probably for the best. I'll be able to keep you safer this way. Come on. Time to take you to the pack."

I inhaled shakily and focused on the present and the current emotions swirling in my head. I hadn't shielded him from the pain. He'd felt it. Felt my agony. And he continued to rage and fear for me. I was his tool. He couldn't afford to lose me, too, like he had the rest.

"Blake will know because of me. I Claimed him. He can sense me. There will be no hiding from him now. Tell Bethi to hurry."

I closed my eyes and let the black take me.

CHAPTER EIGHT

OLIVIA...

MY HEAD LAY ON SOMEONE'S LEG. FINGERS STROKED MY HAIR. Nothing touched my back, thankfully. The slight vibration under me assured me that we were once again in a vehicle and moving. Not that it would do any good.

"She needs to dream," I said through pain-clenched teeth.

"Can you tell us what happened?" Winifred said. "Grey swears it looked like something removed the skin from your back."

I wanted to snort. Now I could travel in the main vehicle? The time for secrets was at an end. And, my patience was at an end, too.

"I told you. There's a fourth race. I see them. I talk to them. They help me in return for a piece of my flesh. What don't you get?"

"What help did they just give you?" she asked.

"I asked them to control Blake for three days. Three days for three strips of flesh."

Not nearly enough time. Had I been sure I could have endured more and still have been useful for the Judgement, I would have tried. Even now, I could feel Blake in my head, his anger at war with moments of soothing calm.

"Holy fuck," Bethi said.

"Is it true that you Claimed Blake?" Winifred asked.

"Yes."

"Why?" Her complete disgust and confusion annoyed me. Hadn't she listened?

"Because I needed to live this time. Please, just leave me alone."

No one spoke, and I drifted for the next several minutes.

"They're just behind us now," Gabby said, breaking into the peace-filled blanket of oblivion that had slowly begun to wrap around me.

"Where the hell is the city? This looks like Hicksville," Bethi said.

Their conversation jolted me further into awareness.

"City? No. We can't be by a city. We need a wasteland."

"Well, that's what this looks like," Bethi said.

I struggled to sit up and grunted at the pain lancing through my back. Winifred's hand on my arm helped me. That's when I noticed I wore my sweater again. Weird that I couldn't feel it on the wounds.

"I butterfly bandaged the gashes once we got the bleeding to stop," she said. "I didn't think we had time for stitches."

Her words held little meaning as I stared at the nothingness around us. The Others outlined an occasional home within the distant whiteness. The rural area gave me hope.

"How close are they?" I asked. Blake didn't feel close. He still felt like he waited on the east coast, where I'd put him.

"Not far."

"I'm not asking you, Gabby," I said, not unkindly.

The groans and moans of the Others filled the car. I listened closely, turning my head to watch the swirls of grey behind us.

"So many," I whispered, more to myself than anyone in the car. "Please tell me you've dreamt something, Bethi."

"Yeah. I died hung upside-down, throat slit. I'm not even sure which of us that was anymore. Not you. But one of us."

She has the answer, the Lady whispered.

My anger almost slipped. I felt Blake's emotions pull back. He'd felt it.

"What else about the dream, Bethi? Think. I said this wouldn't be easy. The answer won't be clear. What else was in your dream? She says you have the answer. Use your head."

"You know what? Screw you. My throat still hurts." The girl curled into her Mate's side.

"Of course. Very insensitive of me to forget your pain." Who was this bitter person I was becoming?

Facing ahead and careful not to lean against the seat, I exhaled slowly and forced myself to focus on my breathing and not the anger and frustration that wanted to well up.

"How long until they reach us?" I asked.

"A few minutes," Gabby said. The Others confirmed her answer.

"If they kill any of us, the Judgement won't be made. Do you understand, Bethi? What happened to me will happen to all of us when the time of the Judgement comes. The veil holding the Others back will disappear. They will flood this world and wear every human, werewolf, or Urbat like a pretty body coat. If you think having your throat slit hurts, wait until you're skinned alive by the Others. They feed off your pain and agony. Even now, more swarm around you than any of the rest of us."

"That's enough," Winifred said sharply.

I could hear Bethi's ragged breathing and feel Luke's angry gaze.

"No, Winifred. It's not. The world will burn in their wild abandon, and Bethi will relive everyone's pain because we will still be born again."

Bethi began to softly sob behind me.

"There is no end for us. Not even at the end." And that was the cruelest truth of our sorry lives. "We cannot die this time."

"We're almost there. I can see humans ahead," Gabby said.

"We need to stop. We'll risk them," I said.

"If what you just said is true, the humans are at risk no matter what," Winifred said.

I sat in suppressed anger and struggled to think what I could do to prevent us from being injured. I could call Blake now, but he wouldn't believe any lie I told him, not with the Judgements right here listening.

Use Peace.

"This fight has to be Isabelle's," I said. "She needs to use her power to kill them all."

"She can't," Winifred said. "It almost killed her last time."

"The Lady said—"

The bite of my seatbelt robbed me of air as the vehicle braked suddenly. Loud bangs filled the interior. The Others were in such a frenzy, I struggled to see what was happening. I focused on my other senses. Growls just outside. The splintering sound of glass. Tires screeching on asphalt. As soon as the vehicle came to a stop, I unbuckled and reached for a door. A hand over mine stopped me.

"Wait here," Winifred said. The growls grew louder, a sign the door had opened, and something brushed past me. The coppery scent of blood burst into the air.

"Get out of the way, Luke," Bethi said. Their steps and the whisper of clothes said they'd left the vehicle, too.

I turned my head, ignoring the pain in my back in my search to see if I was alone. Fixated on the fight, the dancing grey of the Others had left the vehicle, so it was hard to tell.

"Move it, albino!" a rough voice yelled nearby. An Urbat, given the pet name.

I reached forward, releasing my hold on my fear, and got out of the car.

Bits and pieces of the scene flared to life as the Others danced within the chaos. Beast attacking beast. Some falling. Some moving on to the next. One moved faster than all the rest and killed more quickly.

"Where are the Judgements?" I asked.

Some of the Others focused their swirls around a group of people who stood in the center of a protective circle. One stood apart in the pandemonium, kicking and punching, moving with a fluid grace that seemed at odds with the killing going on around her.

"Shields!" Isabelle yelled. Something tugged at my chest. I put a hand over it, but felt nothing. The tug came again, harder. All my fear left me, weakening me to the point that my knees gave out. I fell to the snow and closed myself off.

No one touched me. The fighting continued around me as if I really wasn't part of that world. I stood on shaky legs and moved forward.

"You can't hurt them," I yelled. "The Judgement is too close."

Something knocked into me, and I fell onto the snow.

"Stay down!" a voice snarled at me.

Ignoring the warning, I pushed myself to my hands and knees.

Do not fear. There is Hope, the Lady whispered.

GABBY...

OLIVIA FELL BESIDE THE SUV, one of the Urbat having pushed her over. Isabelle pulled hard again, knocking the dick to his knees, and stealing some of the fear I'd tried to keep bottled. It wasn't easy when there were so many of them. Just like that night we'd lost Ethan.

I closed myself off from the guilt and concentrated on the sparks flooding my mind. I knew what would happen with too many of Isabelle's pulls and couldn't afford to pass out now. Everyone needed me.

Within the confines of the protective circle, I watched Bethi gut another dog in front of me. She yelled angrily and turned toward the next attacker, Luke protecting her right and Clay protecting her left. Grey, Emmitt, and Thomas stood on the other side of the circle with Sam beside Clay. Winifred moved around us, keeping away the majority. Further away, Isabelle and Carlos fought in the sea of Urbat, for our protection.

"More coming from Grey's side," I called out. Winifred moved to that section, leaving Bethi and Luke more exposed. The Urbat pressed in, trying to take advantage. Bethi moved quickly, ending that attempt.

The sparks continued to reposition in a flurry of movement. And, not just the Urbat numbers gathered in force on the other side of the mountain range. The fighting at the outskirts of Logan had called the attention of humans, too. Traffic no longer passed us. Cars had stopped miles away, up the pass. The soft yellow-green of their sparks pooled around us much like our immediate protective circle.

The Urbat on the other side of the mountain range began to move.

Seeing the movement of the fight around me and tracking the movement of the sparks converging on us created a dull ache between my eyes. I blinked slowly. Exhaustion pulled at me. The naps I'd been living on since leaving the Compound before Thanksgiving had begun taking their toll long ago.

"More coming over the mountains!" I yelled. In less than fifteen minutes, we'd be hopelessly outnumbered.

Without meaning to, my fear slipped. Blake knew we had either Claimed or Mated with werewolves, and he had proven that he would remove that obstacle without hesitation. I glanced at Clay then returned my focus to the sparks in my mind. So many yellow-green sparks. Enough to outnumber the blue-grey of the Urbat now surrounding us. What would they do if they knew the future that faced them if we couldn't complete this Judgement. Their fear of the werewolves would dim in the light of their fear for the things that hurt Olivia.

"Shields!" Isabelle called again.

I wished she could pull the fear from the humans. With their help, we could survive this.

Isabelle's pull touched the center of my chest, and I quickly tossed my fear to the side, focusing on the sparks.

They moved. Not all of them, but at least half of the humans within the Logan mountain range started toward us.

"Humans," I yelled. "They're coming!"

I didn't know whether to panic or cheer. The way they moved seemed like they were controlled by something. I turned to look at Charlene.

"Are you controlling them?" I asked.

"No," she said, focusing on the Urbat trying to get to Thomas. Some of them flew backward as if hit by an invisible force. Without a doubt, that was her. I didn't care what she did as long as it helped keep us all safe.

Clay twisted in front of me, dodging a swipe of a clawed hand and coming back around with a swing of his own.

The first of the humans reached us. I couldn't see them, but did witness the light of their sparks abruptly extinguish. More came. And more. A few of the Urbat focused on them. Not enough to give the werewolves a break, though.

Not a single human spark lasted more than a moment once it met with an Urbat...until the first loud bang. One of the partially shifted Urbat yipped.

"The police are here and have guns," Michelle called out.

"I'll make sure they don't shoot at us," Charlene added.

The odds were far from even, but the humans with guns did distract the Urbat enough that—

Clay grunted, the sound oddly concerning in the din of all the other sounds. I looked his way and caught him stagger a single step back toward me. He immediately snarled and lunged forward at the half-shifted dog grinning at him. The grin didn't last long. Blood sprayed when Clay's claws sunk into the man's throat and, with a fisted hand, pulled out his windpipe.

The Urbat clutched his neck, gurgling his last breaths. Clay didn't make any move to fight the other Urbat pushing their way toward us, though. I watched in horror as one knee gave out, and he sank to the ground. Everything slowed when he turned slightly, and I saw the red blossoming on the front of his shirt.

Flashes of Ethan's death filled my mind.

"Help me!" I screamed, breaking formation and rushing toward him.

A wall of bodies surrounded me. I didn't look away from Clay. He sat heavily on the ground, one hand bracing his weight and keeping him from laying back completely.

"Don't do this," I said, shaking. "Don't die. Don't leave me." I took off my jacket and pressed it to his stomach.

"Shh...it's okay," he said.

He reached up and smoothed his bloody fingers over my cheek.

"No, it's not. I saw Ethan." I remembered Isabelle's reaction to Ethan's death. Fate had been smart to make her Peace and not me. Everyone would die when Clay did.

"Sweetheart," he said, brushing the tears streaming from my cheeks. "Lift the jacket and look. It's not the same as Ethan."

He pulled back the jacket and showed me the long gashes that had ripped open his stomach. It wasn't a bloody hole, but it wasn't good either. I could see intestine.

"Fuck. Shit. Fuck."

He collapsed all the way to the ground. A spray of blood painted his face. I looked up, searching for help. A strangled gasp escaped me. Carnage lay around us. Human men. All dead. Clay lay in the center with me kneeling at his side.

Around us, with the help of the remaining humans, the rest of the group still fought a losing battle against Urbat. I focused on the sparks crossing the mountains. They were almost here.

"Isabelle, you have to end this," I yelled.

She glanced at me and saw Clay on the ground, my jacket once again pressed to his stomach. Rage filled her features.

"Shields!" she screamed.

I felt the tug, but gave nothing. The Urbat fell to their knees with her inhale and completely collapsed with her exhale. Blood seeped from their noses and their sparks faded in the darkness of my mind.

The humans had remained standing, though, oddly unaffected by Isabelle.

"Thank you for your help," Charlene said. "Once you return to your homes, you'll feel happy that you helped defeat the Urbat and protect innocent women."

None of them moved. I didn't care. I stared down at Clay's pale face. He'd closed his eyes.

"We need to get him to a hospital," I said.

"You know we can't," Winifred said.

I choked on a sob.

"I'll be fine," Clay whispered.

I looked away from him to Olivia. I didn't know what I wanted from her. Help? Hope? Answers? She stood from her place on the snow and came toward me.

"Gabby, now you. Release them," Olivia said.

For a second, I thought she said him. Then I realized she was talking about the humans still standing there, not doing anything but staring at me.

Me? I looked at them again in shock. I'd called them.

"I don't know how." Yet, even as I said it, I knew I did. I focused on my fear for them, instead of myself and Clay, and touched their sparks with that fear. Those closest turned and ran away.

OLIVIA...

THE OTHERS PLAYED with the bodies of the dead, making them lurch and twitch on the ground as the rest of the group surrounded Gabby and Clay. I let my fear and anxiety pour from me.

"Show me Gabby's phone," I said. A few of the Others raced back to the vehicle we'd abandoned.

I turned and followed. Inside the vehicle, I felt along the seats until my fingers touched an object on the back seat. Her phone still had buttons, making it easier to dial Blake's number. He picked up on the first ring.

"Father," I said.

"Olivia. Stay there. They are coming for you."

"If they do, we risk everything."

Snow crunched behind me, and I held up my hand for silence.

"What do you mean?" he asked.

"They are starting to trust me. They know they cannot Judge in favor of the humans. With me here, the Dreamer is piecing together the answer to the final Judgement. A day, two at most, and she will know. Sending your men forced Gabby to call the humans to her. This close to the end, their powers will only evolve with each attack, risking not only our men, but the Judgements when they fight against us."

"And they just let you call to tell me this? Do you think I'm a fool?"

I could feel his growing anger.

"No, Father. They are caring for one of the men, Gabby's

Mate, who was injured during the attack. Gabby left her phone in one of the vehicles, which is where I am. You know I'm not lying."

He was quiet a moment.

"What are you suggesting I do, then? Nothing?"

"Use me to follow them at a distance until the Dreamer has the answer. I'll find a way to let you know. I need to go before they notice me."

"Stay in touch."

He ended the call. I turned and handed the phone to whoever stood behind me. The Others continued to play with the bodies of the dead as someone carried Clay to a vehicle.

"You're playing a dangerous game," Winifred said, accepting the phone.

"A game I've been playing since I bit Blake's neck. The only game that might keep us safe and buy us the time we need for Bethi to find the answers."

"What happens when she does?" Winifred asked.

"We tell Blake and meet him somewhere far from any humans. Then, we will pass our Judgement."

CHAPTER NINE

JIM...

EVERYONE IS STILL ALIVE, WINIFRED SENT ME.

I exhaled slowly. Paul and Henry did the same. The cubs continued to watch their cartoons, completely unaware of the danger the rest of their family had just faced.

Michelle is making arrangements for Salt Lake, she continued. *The group needs to rest. I want you to meet us there.*

Aden giggled at the cartoon, his head resting on Paul's shoulder where he reclined on the bed with his leg slightly elevated. Liam sat by Henry on the floor. The cub didn't notice when Henry looked back at me, impatience reflected in his gaze. It wasn't due to Aden but our situation. Being away from the pack while they'd fought hadn't sat well with Henry.

I want to leave Paul and the cubs here. I think it is the safest place for them.

She was quiet for a moment.

Agreed. I don't think Blake will be actively searching for the cubs now.

Why? What happened?

It's a long story, but Olivia is playing both sides, it seems.

I frowned, wondering on which side her true loyalties lay.

We'll need to be careful, I sent Winifred.

Yes. I'll have Michelle send you the information for our new destination.

My phone beeped a few minutes later with the new hotel address, located just outside of Salt Lake.

I cleared my throat to gain the attention of the room. The cubs immediately turned to me.

"I have some good news and some bad news," I said with a playful wink. "The good news is that you two get to stay here and watch cartoons and order room service until Santa brings you some presents. The bad news is that you need to make sure Paul stays in bed."

Aden cheered and jumped on Paul. The boy grunted in pain but didn't complain. Another few days and the bone would be knit solid again.

"That means you and Henry are leaving?" Liam asked. He still sat on the floor.

"Yep. We're going to go pick up Mimi, Dad, Grandma, Grandpa, and Nana Wini. Maybe even do some holiday shopping, too. Is there something you want from Uncle Jim?" I asked with a teasing grin.

The cub stood and came to me, his serious expression unaffected by the promise of presents. I picked him up without him needing to ask. His little arms wrapped around my neck as he hugged me.

"Races on our porch like we did this summer."

He was telling me to come back. He was too smart. My heart ached a little, and I hugged him tighter in return.

"Aden and I are going to kick you and your dad's butts."

Aden whooped. Liam nodded and pulled away, signaling he was ready to be let down. I set him down and watched him return to his cartoons.

It didn't take Henry and me long to pack a bag and say our goodbyes. Both cubs were back to watching cartoons already, their small bodies tucked against Paul's sides. I worried I was making the wrong choice, but I worried more what would happen to them if they came with us.

Keep them safe, I sent Paul, pausing for one last look before closing the door.

Always.

HENRY...

I INHALED DEEPLY as we left the lobby and stepped out into the cold. Nothing unusual scented the air. No Urbat. Nothing but the white snow drifting down from the grey mid-day sky as we walked to the new rental in the parking lot. There was no trace of the previous, destroyed car.

Jim unlocked the doors, and I got into the comfortable, leather passenger seat, glad we were finally moving again.

"Michelle's going to run out of money at the rate we're going," I commented as I closed the door.

Jim snorted.

"I doubt that. Her gift likes to pop up just when we need it. Winifred feels bad about using her like that, but if it helps the pack..." Jim shrugged and turned the key. The engine purred to life, and he eased forward out of the parking lot.

Although his words could come across as indifferent, I knew better. He loved Michelle like I loved Paul.

"So why didn't you leave me behind, too?" I asked. "Two are better than one for protection."

"Given what just happened to the rest of the group, I think we'll need you more than Paul will. Winifred believes Blake will leave the cubs alone now."

"Why?"

"Because the new girl, Olivia, is feeding him information."

Anger swelled inside me. My mom gave her life to keep the boys from the Urbat and Blake, and the new girl was giving him information? Was she the reason they'd found us?

"Calm down," Jim said. "We don't know whose side she's really on. Until we do, we play it safe and we play it smart."

"What does that mean?" I asked, frustrated.

"Be nice, but don't trust."

The supposed hour drive took twice that long because of the snow, road conditions, and other cars. Jim didn't say much, and I spent the time thinking of Mom, Dad, and the upcoming holiday we'd always celebrated with the Cole family since as long as I could remember. All the laughter and family. It wouldn't be the same ever again.

"Do you think there's a chance they'll let Dad go when they get what they want?" I asked.

Jim remained quiet for a moment, but I knew he'd heard.

"I think you want the truth from me, no matter how harsh. Am I right?"

"Yes." I needed someone to say what I already knew so I could stop feeling guilty for thinking it.

"Since the Urbat want all werewolves dead, I don't think they'll be letting him go no matter what the outcome of this

Judgement thing. That's if they're the ones who have him. There's a possibility the humans have him, too. But, I don't think that'll change anything. I don't think he's coming back. And he knows that."

My throat grew tight with grief, and anger formed a throbbing mass in my chest.

"I've been talking to him," Jim went on to say. "Just sending, not receiving. Telling him you're both okay. Sharing the little things he's missing. Giving him something to think about. Something better than what they're probably giving him."

"Thank you. For talking to him and for telling me the truth. I figured as much."

Neither of us spoke the rest of the way to the hotel. There wasn't anything more to say. I focused on what Jim had shared and the future. Jim thought the girls would Judge in favor of the humans, but I wasn't as sure. They all had werewolf Mates and neither Mom nor Gabby were too keen on their own kind. Whether they Judged in our favor or not, my plans wouldn't change. Paul would be healed by then, hopefully, and we could start hunting for Dad. My chest tightened at the thought of having to wait, but I wasn't some young cub who didn't understand the needs of the many outweighed the needs of the one.

Plus, I knew enough about links to understand that I'd need an Elder to locate Dad. I glanced at Jim. Once the Judgement was made and the cubs were safe, I knew he'd help. Every member of our race mattered to all the Elders. Especially Jim.

Jim pulled into the parking lot, cut the engine, and grabbed the bag from the back seat.

"They're a few minutes out yet," he said, giving me the bag. "Go get us checked in, and I'll run to get some supplies."

"All right."

He jogged down the dusted sidewalks, and I strode toward the lobby doors. This place had nothing on the prior place. The tree that waited just inside seemed pathetic compared to the twenty-foot fresh pine in the resort's lobby.

I went to the desk and gave the lawyer's name and my ID. After answering a few questions and signing a form, the guy handed over several key cards.

Instead of picking a room and dumping the bag, I took a seat on one of the sofas and impatiently watched the door.

Getting pizzas, Jim sent me. *Everything okay?*

I almost snorted. When he said supplies, I was thinking bandages. I should have known better. Jim being an Elder still didn't fully make sense to me.

Yep. Waiting in the lobby, watching for the rest.

Winifred said they're only a few blocks away now. I'm just around the corner. You see anything odd, yell.

Will do.

I leaned forward, focused and yet wondering what this new girl who worked with Blake looked like. It wasn't hard to spot the group when they pulled in. The missing side window of the SUV and shattered windshield of Uncle Thomas's car gave them away.

Leaving my bag behind, I stepped out into the snow again. Grey was the first one out of his car. He came to me and wrapped me in a big hug. I closed my eyes and exhaled, trying not to let his grief influence my own. Grey and Thomas had both been like second fathers to me.

"I'm so sorry," he said.

"Don't be. Mom did what she promised to do. She wouldn't have had it any other way."

A softly sniffling Michelle touched my back. Grey released me, and I turned to face her. Her red eyes and wet cheeks conveyed her pain as much as her scent.

"It wasn't supposed to be like that, Henry," she said, hugging me.

"I know. Don't blame yourself. Blame Blake. I do."

When she pulled back, Charlene waited behind her. She didn't say anything, just pulled me into her arms. She hugged me like my mom would have. One hand on the back of my head, smoothing over my hair like Mom had done whenever I'd been hurt. I closed my eyes and returned the hug, letting myself soak up the comfort for just a moment. I could feel them all around me. My pack. My second family. Who would we lose next? The thought stirred my grief.

"All this death and pain…" Charlene said.

"It's our reality," a new voice said. "Our future."

My gut clenched at the sound. It was her. I released Charlene and turned to find the source.

My gaze locked onto the prettiest pale-haired woman I'd ever seen. She stood tall at the back of the group. An ugly bruise marred her cheek and another tinted the skin of her neck. I barely noticed either of those, though, as I stared into her eyes. Black eyes, like her pupils had swallowed her irises. I shuddered but couldn't look away, held under some kind of spell.

She didn't move. My stomach started doing all sorts of crazy shit, and it took a moment to realize I was feeling the pull. If Mom were there, she would have been cheering. Thoughts of Mom smothered the persistent tug in my gut.

I shuddered and stepped toward the new girl, angry and ready to fight. Jim's words stopped me. Be nice.

"You must be Olivia," I said.

"I am."

"You're the one feeding Blake information?"

"Yes."

I inhaled deeply, her sweet scent making my mouth water. The pull didn't stop the anger, though. Not at her or Blake.

"Good," I said. "I'm supposed to want a Mate above all else. But I don't. I want Blake's death more."

She reached up and placed her cold hand on my cheek.

"There's nothing I want more, too."

I set my hand over hers and removed her touch.

"I won't be the one," I said. "I refuse to ever feel that loss again."

She opened her mouth to say something more, but Winifred interrupted.

"Where's Jim?"

I stepped back from Olivia and focused on Winifred, who stood just behind her.

"Getting everyone something to eat. I have the room keys." I handed them over, and she immediately gave one to Sam.

"Get Clay to his room. I'll be in to see if it's something I can repair."

It wasn't until she said those words that I noticed Clay. He leaned heavily on Thomas and had one arm pressed around his gut.

"Like Mom?" I asked, staring at him.

"No, I'll live," Clay said. "I'm sorry about your mom."

I nodded and watched the pair walk inside.

"What can I help carry?" I asked Winifred, who'd already taken Olivia's arm.

"Anything Grey can't."

The rest of the group trailed after Winifred. It was then that I noticed Bethi's limp and Luke's support as well as Isabelle's swelling eye and Carlos's bloody arm.

Guiltily, I met Grey's eyes.

"I should have noticed."

"It's hard to see other people's injuries when you're hurt, too. Come on, son, I'll teach you how to be a bellboy."

He clapped me on the back and led me toward the rear of the SUV. As I picked up the first of several bags, I caught sight of Jim further down the sidewalk. A towering stack of pizza boxes blocked his face from view. If that wasn't enough to give away his identity, I easily recognized the walk.

Grey followed my gaze and chuckled.

"He'll eat half those," he said.

I nodded and picked up another bag.

"I felt the pull for her."

"I know. We witnessed it, and acknowledge your interest."

"I don't want it acknowledged."

He stopped picking up a bag to look at me.

"Why? It seemed real to me."

"Because I want Blake's death more than I want her teeth on my neck. Then, I want to find my dad."

Grey nodded slowly.

"I understand."

"So what happens now? With Olivia and me."

"That's up to the two of you."

That meant they wouldn't try to force anything.

"Good."

Grey sighed and shook his head.

JIM...

NOTHING SMELLED BETTER than pizza in vast quantities. Well, not true. Any food in vast quantities smelled amazing. My stomach growled again, and I pushed aside the thought of stopping for another slice.

Stop thinking about eating that pizza, and get over here to help me talk some sense into Henry.

I looked around the boxes and saw Grey and Henry still in the parking lot.

Why? I sent back. *What's he doing now?*

As soon as he saw Olivia, he felt the pull. We noted his interest, but he's telling me he doesn't want it.

Instead of relief, joy, or pride—emotions the rest of the Elders probably felt—pity wormed its way into my head. This was the worst possible time to find a Mate.

His mom just died, Grey.

I know. That's what I'm trying to tell him, but he doesn't believe his grief is the problem. He believes it's the girl.

Maybe he's right then. I've never known a truly interested male to walk away.

You didn't see them together. He didn't notice anything but her. And there was plenty more to notice. Hurry up with those pizzas so you can help Winifred stitch up Clay. His guts keep poking out. It might help control your appetite long enough for the rest of us to eat our fill.

Nothing can control my appetite. Believe me...Mom tried.

I stepped up next to the SUV and purposely bumped into Henry.

"Take a slice out of this top box and feed me a bite, will you?"

The lid hit the top of my head. It disappeared at the same time Henry groaned.

"This is really good. I could eat a whole box myself," he said.

Does that sound like a man overwhelmed by the pull? I sent Grey as he led the way inside.

The stink of chlorine overpowered the beautiful scent of baked cheese and meat. I sniffed, trying to get the good smell back. Didn't work. My eyes watered, and I breathed through my mouth to ease the burn in my sinuses.

"Set the pizzas in here," Mom called.

I followed the sound of her voice, taking a few blind steps into the hotel room.

"I got those," Emmitt said, taking half the stack from me.

With the top half gone, I glanced around the room. Clay lay on one of the beds, towels shoved under him to catch any bloody runoff from the gashes across his middle. Gabby sat near the headboard, cradling his head in her lap and stroking his hair while Winifred stitched him. No doubt it hurt, but the man looked like he didn't mind the extra attention he'd gained because of his injuries.

Michelle sat on the bed, out of the way, next to Dad. Mom stood beside Winifred, handing her whatever supplies she needed from her homemade first aid kit.

"Want a piece of pizza while you're pampered?" I asked Clay.

His beard twitched, and he shook his head slightly.

"Set the rest over here," Emmitt said, motioning to the dresser next to the table, which he already had covered with pizza boxes.

Grey, still in the hall with Henry and the bags, nudged me aside. I half-turned to tell Henry to grab two boxes for us to take to our room but froze. Words escaped me.

Just inside the door, only a few feet away, stood a white-haired goddess. Her black eyes pinned me, staring into my soul as if determining my worth. And, I desperately wanted to be worthy.

The pizza boxes fell to the floor at the first wild tug in my gut. I inhaled, long and loud. She smelled like Winifred's fresh baked chocolate chip cookies. I couldn't think of a better smell on the planet no matter the quantity.

I took a step toward her, wanting to inhale every ounce of her scent. Realization kicked me between the eyes. Mate.

No. It couldn't. I couldn't. I'd taken the oath.

Pain exploded in my chest, making it impossible to breathe. The pain didn't dull my awe and need. After Emmitt found Michelle, I'd been sure I would never have a chance. Fate didn't work like that. Not twice in one family. But there was no denying what I felt as I stared at Olivia. She was my fated Mate. And I wanted her with every fiber of my being.

The pain clenched harder, like a physical fist around my heart.

I staggered back a step, and another, then collapsed to my knees.

"Jim, no!" Winifred yelled.

Mom started to cry.

I'd just sentenced myself to death.

CHAPTER TEN

OLIVIA...

HE IS THE ONE, THE LADY WHISPERED.

"An Elder?" I asked softly, trying not to let any hint of what I wanted to feel surface.

Yes. Son of Strength and imbued with strength. You must not fail.

I watched the man fall to his knees with a sinking feeling in my stomach. If Bethi had disliked the Lady before, she'd hate her now. They all would when they finally understood what this meant.

WINIFRED...

I LEFT the needle in Clay and rushed to Jim. Taking his face in my hands, I forced his gaze to mine.

The pain is telling you that you're trying to make the wrong choice, I sent him.

How can you know? She smells right. I have no doubt she's the one.

She might have been before you were an Elder. Not now. She's Claimed Blake, Jim. We need you. You need to stop.

How do I stop wanting her? he sent not just to me, but Sam and Grey too, proving just how unfocused he was right then.

I stroked my fingers along Jim's face, sorrow engulfing me. We never should have made him an Elder. How many different types of losses would our race need to suffer? I thought.

You tell yourself every single second of every single day you can't have her, Sam's voice cut in. *It's what I do. It keeps the pain at bay.*

I looked up and met Sam's gaze, the pull stirring in my stomach like it always did when I looked at him.

It doesn't get easier, but I would have done anything to spare Winifred the pain she felt when she saw me. Even to make sure she didn't have to endure it alone.

The tension in Jim's clenched jaw and corded neck eased fractionally. From the corner of my eye, I saw Charlene lead Olivia from the room and Grey move to finish with Clay.

We need you, Jim. Blake will not leave these girls alone. He's waiting, biding his time. He will try again.

Jim closed his eyes, and his breathing slowed. I knew he was fighting to contain what he was feeling for Olivia. Sam and I shared another look. It wouldn't be easy. Sam hadn't lied. Even after all these years, it was hard to be so near him.

"I'll be fine," Jim said in a rough voice. However, when he opened his eyes, his gaze immediately went to the place where Olivia had stood.

"Come on," I said, lifting him to his feet. "Let's get you some pizza."

"I'm not hungry."

My stomach twisted with worry. Jim was never not hungry. Since the moment Charlene had given birth, he'd needed to be fed often and a lot.

"Then come sit on the bed."

He did as I suggested. Thomas watched him closely, worry etching his features. We both knew the risks. If Jim continued to think of Olivia as his Mate instead of an extended member of the pack he needed to protect, he would die.

JIM...

DAD SAT BESIDE ME. He didn't say anything. He didn't need to. The worry poured off of him like cologne gone bad. As much as I wanted to reassure him, I couldn't. It still felt like I was dying. The pressure inside me had eased enough that I could breathe, but not by much.

I focused on Grey and Clay. Grey worked with quick efficiency, finishing the small, neat stitches needed to close up the first of the three gashes. Clay didn't move at all, but I could see the glint of his brown eyes from beneath his lowered lids. I wondered if he hurt as much as I did.

A hand swiped gently over his brow, and I shifted my attention to Gabby. She didn't look at me, her focus completely on Clay. Her fingers smoothed over the skin of his cheek, again and again, giving him what comfort she could.

I wanted that. A Mate to fuss over me. I should have never taken the oath.

The pain, which had been receding, swelled forward again.

I grunted, and Dad gripped my shoulder.

"We can't take any more loss," Dad said quietly. "You took the oath. Let thoughts of any other life go."

The pack. My people. He was right. I needed to think of them. When I did, breathing got easier.

Olivia would never be my Mate. I needed to come to terms with that.

I'm sorry it's you, Henry sent me, *but I'm really glad it isn't me.*

The thought of the pup trying to pursue her set my teeth on edge, and I fought not to growl.

Me too, I sent back.

Henry turned from the box of pizza and frowned at me.

That doesn't sound like a guy who has given up.

Mom walked back into the room alone. The immediate need to know where she'd left Olivia caused the pain to squeeze to life in my chest. This time I didn't grunt.

Knowing what worked last time, I focused on Paul and the cubs. The people who needed me the most. The pain eased, and I almost grinned. This was a little like lying to Winifred. Just like Sam said. It wasn't about not wanting my Mate, it was about distracting myself from acknowledging it.

"Are you all right?" Mom asked, moving to stand in front of me and fussing about my color and the sweat on my forehead.

"I'm fine, Ma."

She lightly smacked me upside my head.

"Then don't ever pull that shit again."

Even Grey stopped what he was doing to turn and look at her.

The angry light left her eyes, and she immediately burst into tears and hugged me tightly.

"I can't lose anyone else," she sobbed softly.

I held her close, hating myself for not getting to that clearing faster. Mary hadn't just been like a second Mom to me. She'd also been a sister to Mom.

"Come on, Charlene," Dad said, tugging on her arm and loosening her stranglehold on me. "Let's go to another room for a while."

She nodded against me, pressed a kiss to my forehead with a warning to behave for once in my life, then left with Dad. I watched them go and noticed that Winifred and Sam still stood near the door. Both watched me closely.

I exhaled heavily and stood.

"I'll be back," I said.

"Where are you going?"

"Away from the stares. Don't worry; I don't plan on dying today."

I left the room and went back to the lobby.

Outside, I stood in the falling snow. Each time my mind drifted to Olivia, the pain grew worse. When my mind remained with the pack, the pain lessened. The pack depended on Olivia, though. Not just Olivia but all of the women. According to Bethi, they controlled the fate of the world. As an Elder, how could I not think about them and how each individual impacted that fate?

Just like that, the pain eased further.

I didn't let the relief distract me from my train of thought because I suddenly understood that thinking about Olivia was essential. Before I'd arrived, Winifred had hinted that Olivia was playing both sides. We needed to understand why. I couldn't avoid her; the Elders needed to talk to her and discover her intent for the safety of the pack. Anyone associated with Blake—the words Winifred had just said during those first few shocked moments clicked into place, and

I growled. No, not just associated with him. My Mate had Claimed—

The sudden crushing pain devastating my insides brought me to my knees in the snow. I didn't stop, though. I focused my thoughts on Olivia, not only a threat to the pack but a potential Mate to an Elder. That couldn't be a coincidence. Henry had felt something for her, too. Something strong, according to Grey. Yet, nothing compared to what I felt, what fate wanted me to feel. Why me and not Henry? Why an Elder? There had to be a reason, but what?

All the pain, even the slightest amount, disappeared.

I looked up into the falling snow with a heavy heart, having my answer. Almost the same answer I'd given Henry. Be nice, but don't trust. The attraction was so I would pay attention to her—close attention—because as an Elder, I would see something no one else would.

Standing, I took a deep breath and went inside to find Olivia. Now that I'd scented her, nothing could cover up her trail. I followed it down the hall, past the room where Winifred once again stitched Clay, to a door next to the room where my dad spoke softly to my mom.

I knocked and waited. When the door opened, I felt no pain as I studied every inch of her face. Deep bruises covered her cheek and colored the skin around her eye. How had I not noticed that?

"You could use some ice," I said. "I'll be right back. Leave the door open."

I grabbed the bag from the hotel's plastic ice bucket and went to the ice machine without waiting for her answer.

When I returned, Olivia faced the curtained window, as if she could see the parking lot through the material. Her long pale hair hung in a smooth cascade down her back, almost reaching the curve of her butt.

Her stomach growled very faintly, and I did my best to ignore the urge I had to go to her and care for her. Instead, I looked closer. She wore a sweater and leggings. The leggings didn't hide her trim legs, and the sleeves of the sweater showed her bony wrists.

"Here's some ice," I said.

"It's not necessary."

"Why? Is the bruise not real? Do you not feel pain?"

"The bruise is real, and it hurts," she said without turning.

"Then why wouldn't you want ice for it?"

"Because it doesn't matter." A heavy, frustrated breath escaped her, but nothing changed in her scent. Interesting.

"Why doesn't it matter?" I asked.

"The only thing that matters is the Judgement. Why is no one listening?"

"Maybe because they don't trust you. It's hard to believe someone who has Claimed the man responsible for all the misfortune the group has experienced."

With quiet steps, I moved directly behind her.

"I've explained my reason for it."

"Explain it again," I said softly. I didn't miss the way she trembled slightly.

She turned and tipped her face up at me. Her lips drew my attention. An ache grew that had nothing to do with being an Elder. I pushed it aside and gently set the ice against her cheek.

A shaky exhale escaped her.

"I die. Bethi confirmed it. I always die. In order to live long enough to make it possible for us to pass Judgement, I needed to Claim Blake. I was three, maybe four, at the time.

He has kept me alive. That's it, because that's all that was needed."

"Are you telling me that Blake doesn't care about you?" I asked, masking my disbelief.

"No. He does care, but only enough to keep me alive and under his control so that I can complete the purpose he has planned for me."

I understood what she wasn't saying, what she wanted me to know. She didn't care for him. She felt no alliance with him. Was it true? I doubted it.

"You are so beautiful," I said, leaning closer. Her breath tickled my lips a moment before she turned her head away.

"Don't," she said. "You cannot pursue what you feel. Not now."

I tilted my head and studied her. It wasn't quite the rejection I'd anticipated and still left me uncertain about her loyalties.

"The Lady knows you're testing me because you don't trust me. That none of you do. But, she says you need to trust your heart. It knows more than your head."

I snorted. The Lady sounded a lot like Winifred.

"Can you blame me for needing to test you?"

"No. And, I know you're not done yet. That's fine. Just don't try to test me like that. It's too dangerous for all of us. I need to be very careful with all my emotions. Blake is always paying attention."

Because she'd Claimed him. Because they were now linked. Jealousy burst forward, igniting the pain again. I grunted and bent forward slightly, involuntarily leaning my forehead against her shoulder. Her fingers touched the hair at the back of my head, a light feathering touch that disappeared too quickly.

"She says to stop fighting it. Our only priority can be the protection of our world."

The Lady was right. I breathed deeply and straightened away from Olivia. She held the ice to her cheek, still facing me with her sightless eyes.

"Your connection to Blake is a risk to that priority. You need to break it."

Preferably on my neck so I could keep an eye on her. Oddly, the anticipated pain didn't return.

"I can't. As much as Blake pays attention to me, I pay attention to him. He's still on the east coast. When he's ready to make his move, I'll know. I'll feel it."

"He already has men following, according to Winifred. Why would he need to come here?"

"The Urbat are different from the werewolves. You have Elders and pack leaders. We only ever have one."

I frowned at her slip. We. She considered herself one of them?

"What do you mean?" I asked, not acknowledging her slip.

"I mean, if Blake is not here when the power shifts, he risks losing his position in the Urbat. He is the leader. The only leader. He doesn't just want power for the Urbat. He wants it for himself."

She seemed so sure of that. I reached out and held the fingers of her free hand, slowly leading her toward the bed.

"We know very little about the Urbat. Tell me more."

OLIVIA...

THE FEEL of his hand on mine made my pulse jump again. He

needed to stop touching me and standing so close. It was getting harder and harder to control what I felt each time.

Blake's impatience stabbed at me. I tugged my hand free of Jim's, took Gabby's phone, which Winifred had let me keep, from my back pocket, and dialed Blake's number.

"What are you doing?" he barked at me.

"I could feel your impatience, so I called to give you an update."

"No. What are you doing right now?"

"I'm in my hotel room."

"Alone?"

"They have me staying with an Elder. He's kind. He went to get ice to help with the bruising from Frank," I said, carefully choosing my words and purposely trying to distract him from asking too many questions about the present. He would sense any lie.

"Frank touched you?" Blake growled.

"He grew agitated as we drove to the Compound. When we arrived, he hit me because I refused to go against your wishes and call you."

Blake remained very quiet. I could feel his confused mix of emotions. He wouldn't remember giving any orders. But I'd ensured others were in the room when he'd given them. Witnesses who traveled with him while he was possessed. Witnesses who had likely already filled him in on what he'd told me to do.

"The rest of the group are in another room helping care for the one who was injured," I continued. "The dreamer and her Mate aren't present. With luck, she's sleeping somewhere and dreaming the answer we need."

"I felt something before. What was it?"

"One of them surprised me with a simple act of kindness. I don't understand why they are so willing to be nice to me."

"Use it to your advantage. Find out where they plan to go next so we can greet them."

"I will."

The line went dead. I hung up the phone and slipped it back into my pocket before turning to face the man who made my stomach go wild with just the sound of his voice. He stood before me, his arms crossed and his head tilted as he studied me. I wished I could see his face.

"Are you really blind?" he asked, startling me.

Was I that easy for him to read?

"To this world, yes. There is another world that touches ours. I see the creatures in that world. They are like wisps of grey smoke. They like to move and swirl around the objects in this world, giving me sight, sort of. Rough outlines of things."

"What do you see in here?"

I turned my head, looking around at the Others as they played.

"Two beds, a lamp, a desk, a toilet, sink, and shower."

"You can see in the bathroom?"

His surprise almost made me smile. I needed to keep better control around him.

"Yes. They like to move around the objects we interact with. People don't really interact with walls."

"You can see into the next room?"

I turned my head slightly and glanced at the two people who snuggled on the bed not far from us. Across the hall, someone ate on a bed next to someone who slept. Further down, I saw the familiar shape of Winifred slightly bent over another person. Likely still stitching Clay.

"Yes. I can see them all. I'm glad we're on the first floor. It's weird to look down and see people below me."

"I bet it would be. So you can only see some shapes and only in grey?"

"Yes. Except the Lady. She's different. Her smoke has color."

"Why is she different?"

"I think she rules the Others. And maybe even us."

"Why do you think that?"

I laughed, unable to help myself.

"You like the word why," I said.

"Yeah, I drove my mom and Winifred nuts with all my questioning. I'd like to say it was only while growing up, but I still question everything."

"It's a sign of intelligence."

Jim snorted. "They think I just don't grasp what they are trying to tell me."

I liked talking to him. A lot. The sound of his voice soothed me, and I wished I could actually see his face.

"Can I touch you?" The question popped out of my mouth before I thought what it would mean.

"Yes."

My stomach gave a nervous flip. Touching him probably wasn't a smart idea. Yet, I couldn't resist.

I stepped closer to him and lightly set the tips of my fingers to his cheeks, ignoring the burn in my back.

Tiny rough stubble poked my fingers. Whiskers. A tingle started in the pads of my fingers and sparked through my hands and up my arms. I started to pull away, but he caught my hands and took control, sliding my fingers down to his mouth. The first touch of his lips caused my heart to stutter.

"Please let go," I said, firmly.

He did.

Instead of pulling away, I continued what he'd started. I traced the curve of his lower lip then top. He held still, letting me explore the strong line of his jaw, the smooth ridge of his brow, and the slope of his nose. Once I had an understanding of his features, I dropped my hands to my sides.

"Why did you do that?" I asked.

"To see how you'd react."

"Why?"

"Who's the one who likes why now?" he asked.

I could hear the humor in his voice.

CHAPTER ELEVEN

OLIVIA...

I STEPPED AWAY FROM HIM AND SAT ON THE BED NEAREST THE window. He sat across from me and leaned forward, bracing his elbows on his knees as he studied me. I was used to scrutiny. His felt different, though. Any hint of resentment, impatience, and calculation—all a Blake specialty—remained absent from his body language and tone of voice. Even their Elder Winifred had displayed a few of those traits. Not this one.

"Your name's Jim, right?" I asked.

"Did the Lady tell you that?"

"No. I heard Winifred yell it."

He chuckled, a deep, rich sound that made my heart give another odd thump. I fought to control any emotional reaction that wanted to go with the physical one.

"To answer your question about why I placed your fingers on my mouth...it's easy to lie to one of us if you know how, which you've proven you do. But, reactions are harder to fake. I wanted you to touch me to see how you reacted because I still don't understand. Why you? Why us? Why now?"

Panic, sorrow, and fear began to unfurl inside me, and suppressing what I wanted to feel became harder with each question he spoke because I knew the answers to all of them.

Now is not the time, the Lady whispered.

"Your turn," he said. "Why do you think your Lady rules over all of us?"

Relieved he didn't expect me to answer the prior questions, I readily told him what I suspected.

"It's the only thing that's ever made any sense. She's one of them. The Others. She's made of the same kind of substance. I know she's influencing what's happening here, but I'm not entirely sure why. The Others want to be here, in this world. They'll do anything for it. It's why they help me, even though they know we're trying to make a Judgement to correct the imbalance. They know we're trying to stop them from coming here, but it's never really mattered to them. They still help. They still try to possess dead bodies and willingly possess living ones even though it hurts them. Despite their desperation to get here, she's giving us advice, giving Bethi dreams, created us to help stop them from coming here. Why do that if she isn't in some way responsible for us, too?"

He nodded slowly then frowned.

"These things only you can see want to possess us? As in control our bodies?"

"Yes. And our minds to a degree. That's how I was able to leave Blake's home. When your group announced your existence, I knew it was the perfect time for one of the Others to possess Blake. Erratic behavior wouldn't seem so out of place in such a chaotic situation. After I told the one possessing Blake what to do, he called Frank and several of his other men back into his office and started giving out orders. He went one way, I went another. Since he controls the movements of the Urbat, it meant the Urbat would be less likely to regroup."

"It was also how I managed to get a letter out to Isabelle after the Lady gave me her address."

"That doesn't make any sense. You say they want to possess us...that they already have possessed Blake even though it hurts them. Why aren't they just possessing everyone, then?"

"They can't. There are rules. They have to be invited. Right now, I'm the only person who can do that."

"Why only you?"

"Because only I can see and hear them to understand their terms."

"Terms?"

I stood, turned, and lifted the back of my shirt, despite the pain, so he could see the bandages.

"What are you showing me?"

"Lift one of the bandages."

"I don't want to hurt you."

"Jim, this goes beyond one person's pain or another's discomfort. You need to understand. Lift a bandage." I didn't know why it mattered so much for him to see, but something told me he needed to. Maybe because, so far, he was the first one interested in listening to all of it, not just asking questions about Blake.

The first touch of his warm fingers on my cool skin almost sent a shiver through me. I hadn't even heard him move. He eased the tape from my skin and lifted the strip of gauze with care. He hissed an indrawn breath.

"They did this?" His voice vibrated with anger.

"They did. The Others. It was their payment for helping me. For possessing Blake. Inhabiting a body with a living soul hurts them. Weakens them. But a body without a soul is easy. Or would be if the Others actually were in this world."

His fingers stroked along the edge of the tape, all the way up to my shoulder. I stepped away, dislodging his touch, and dropped my shirt back into place. When I turned to face him, he already sat on the opposite bed in the same position as before.

"If we don't complete the Judgement, the veil separating our two worlds will disappear and the Others will come here. They have no form. Not even in their world. When they get here, they will find ways to kill every man, woman, and child so they can inhabit their bodies."

"How many of the Others are there?" he asked.

"Four times as many as there are humans on earth."

JIM...

W AS that why I felt the pull? So I would take the time to listen to what she knew?

I remained quiet for several moments, considering what she'd just shared. Bethi knew a lot about the Judgements and their history. She understood their gifts and Blake's consuming drive for power. Olivia understood a world that had stayed completely hidden to us until now. Other creatures who wanted to not just rule earth but use its people as playthings.

The Elders had always taken what Bethi said as truth, yet I knew they'd always thought some of her desperation was due to the repetition of vividly dreamed deaths. Her warning that the world would burn had seemed very literal at the time, and we'd wondered if the Urbat's drive for power would cause a world war if we didn't stop it. Now, I doubted that. These Others that Olivia saw would be the cause of our destruction if they escaped their world into ours.

"And the Judgement will stop them from coming?" I asked.

"Yes."

"So Judge, now. Why wait?"

"I don't know how to make the Judgement. Bethi does. The Lady is giving her the dreams with the answer, she's just not seeing it yet."

I could hear the frustration in her voice but not a drop of it touched her scent.

"Before, you said the Lady knows I was testing you. You made it sound like she talks to you."

"She does."

"Then why not ask her what we need to do?"

She shook her head slowly.

"You aren't the only one who liked to ask why while growing up. Every time I did, she told me that she was helping us as much as she could. She has rules she needs to follow, just like we do. She can't give us the answers. She can't sway the Judgement in favor of one over the other. She can only show Bethi the past and give Michelle access to our futures."

How do Michelle's premonitions work? I sent Emmitt. *Not the stock market ones, but the other ones.*

Mostly they just pop into her head, unless she touches Mom. Then, she sees a room full of premonitions. Why are you asking?

Just trying to figure things out.

Don't hurt yourself, he sent back.

I ignored him and focused on Olivia.

"If she can't sway the Judgement, why does it feel like she's stacking the deck in our favor?" I asked.

"I honestly don't know."

My gaze swept over her serene expression, her loosely folded hands on her lap, and her perfect posture. Her words, body language, and scent never matched. She maintained a calm and beautiful exterior, her scent even and pleasant. Her voice, when she spoke, carried soft, pleasant tones. Her words seemed to carry the true message.

She waited for me to speak again. In that silence, I noticed a small scar on the back of her hand. My gut clenched at the sight of it and thoughts of the fresh injuries on her back. I hadn't smelled her blood until I'd lifted the bandages. I wouldn't have thought that possible. Just additional proof that something more was at work here.

"How many times have you asked them to help you?" I asked, remembering her comment about a letter to Isabelle.

To answer me, she lifted her shirt, showing her stomach. The smooth, pale perfection made my mouth water and my chest squeeze with a warning pain. I swallowed hard and focused on the real reason she'd lifted her shirt. The lengthy pale scars of old wounds healed long ago.

"Whenever I needed to," she said softly.

"If what you're saying is true, then you've been helping us for a long time. What was it like growing up attached to Blake?"

She sighed and sat, her shirt falling back into place, which was both a disappointment and a relief.

"Cold, guarded, miserable. You've seen what he's capable of. I'm sure Michelle has told you stories of her time with him. How do you think it was for me?"

I hadn't meant to upset her. Yet, despite her undisturbed scent, I was certain I had.

Where are you? Winifred's thoughts cut into mine.

With Olivia, I sent back.

You're going to kill yourself. Leave.

I'm fine. There's something going on here, Winifred. According to Bethi, these women have lived and died countless times in previous lives. They've never all been together. The Urbat always hunted them down. Why did they all fall into our lives before we even knew what they were? My Mom is one, Emmitt's a Mate of one, and now I feel the pull for one? That's beyond coincidence, don't you think? We need to figure this out.

She remained quiet for so long, I thought she wouldn't answer.

If you start hurting, you reach out to Sam or me immediately.

I understand, I sent back.

But, I knew I wouldn't reach out to either of them. If I started hurting, I'd think of how I was helping the pack.

"Do you believe me?" Olivia asked.

"Yes."

"Then help me."

"How?"

"I don't know."

I thought about the things I knew and everything she'd just told me. We needed answers. Specifically, what the sisters needed to do to hand down their Judgement and end Blake's chance for control as well as end any chance of the Others coming to this world. Supposedly, Bethi had the answer. However, given the girl's constant agitated state of mind, it made sense that she might not understand whatever answer she'd been given. That left Michelle and her prophecies and

Mom. I hated asking them to try. I knew what would happen to Mom. But, if Olivia was right about the Others, it was a risk we needed them to take.

Can you and Michelle meet me in Mom's room? I sent Emmitt.

Sure. Something wrong? he sent back immediately.

Other than the humans knowing about us and the Urbat trying to kill our women? No.

We'll be right there.

I stood and held out my hand to Olivia. Her sightless gaze shifted to it. The offer had nothing to do with helping her stand and everything with my need to touch her. She seemed to sense that too because, instead of taking it, she lifted her gaze to me.

"I don't think that would be wise," she said.

"Much wiser than what every instinct is telling me to do. Why did she pair us? Did she tell you that?"

"She didn't tell me about you specifically, Jim. But, I knew I would find my Mate with this group. It's about stacking the deck, after all."

"So this attraction is just to influence you to make the Judgement on behalf of the werewolves?" I could live with that.

"No. This attraction is to influence you to help me complete the Judgement this time around."

Her scent shifted, a wisp of sadness and longing escaping before she stood and it vanished. I wondered why. I didn't mind being influenced by her. Hell, I'd like a lot more influencing.

"It's dangerous being around you, Jim. If I upset Blake, he will make his move before we're ready."

Tucking my hands into my pockets to keep from reaching for her, I sighed regretfully.

"You're right. We don't want that. I think we should talk to Mom and Michelle about how to get this Judgement going."

She followed me into the hallway and stood behind me as I knocked on Mom's door. Dad opened it a second later.

"Just the boy we wanted to see," he said.

He motioned me in. I stepped aside and let Olivia lead. Dad's brows rose to his hairline as she entered, but he didn't comment. At least not until the door closed.

"Why are you with her?"

Olivia stopped walking and turned to face us. Mom stood from her perched position on the bed and moved toward Olivia.

"Cut it out, Thomas," she said. "Now isn't the time." She wrapped her hand around Olivia's and led her to the chair.

Before I could object, Olivia sat carefully on the edge of the seat. Her back had to hurt.

"Emmitt and Michelle are coming, too. Mom, do you have any pain relievers?"

"Yes."

"Get two for Olivia. I'll get some water."

"That's not necessary," Olivia said to both of us.

"It is. I think you've suffered in silence long enough."

I turned and left the room. The vending machine halfway down the hall had a selection of drinks. I bought three waters. One for now and two for later. She had a lot of healing to do.

When I returned to the room, Olivia still sat in the chair but now held two pills in her open palm. I opened a bottle and handed it to her just as I heard Michelle and Emmitt in the hallway.

"They're coming," I said.

Olivia took the pills with the water and said a quiet thank

you. Mom watched her with a sad expression. She caught me watching her and gave me a small smile, but that smile faded when she looked back at Olivia.

Dad moved to the door and let Emmitt and Michelle in before I could respond.

"What's this about?" Dad asked, shutting the door softly behind them.

"It's about the Judgement Bethi and Olivia keep talking about. Olivia says that the Lady has already given Bethi the dream with the answer. Bethi just hasn't figured it out yet. After talking to Olivia, I realized Bethi might not be the only one with the answers." I looked directly at Michelle. "I think you need to tell us what you can see in that room of yours when you touch Mom."

"Jim, your mother can't—"

"Thomas, I can and will," Mom said, giving him a hard look. "We're all making sacrifices and taking risks to secure a better future. Isabelle, Mary, Gregory, Clay, Carlos…"

Dad sighed and ran his hand through his hair. A hint of desperation flavored his scent.

"At least this time, I'm close to a bed," she said with a small smile.

He didn't look reassured.

CHAPTER TWELVE

MICHELLE...

I GLANCED AT EMMITT, NERVES TWISTING IN MY STOMACH. THE last time I'd touched his mom, she'd passed out. It had taken her a long time to regain color and stand on her own.

"I don't think this is a good idea," I said.

Charlene looked at me and smiled wider.

"You are so sweet for worrying about me, Michelle. But we need to think about the people depending on us to stop Blake."

My thoughts immediately turned to my brothers. I'd managed a quick call to them once we'd gotten here. Aden had cried while telling me that Aunt Mary had died. Liam hadn't, and that scared me more than Aden's tears. Blake had almost stolen his childhood from him once. I wouldn't let him do it again.

"You're right," I said. "You can pull away when it gets to be too much, right?"

She nodded.

"There's no need to pull away," Olivia said.

I glanced at her, trying not to shudder at the sight of her eyes. If she had irises, I couldn't tell because her black pupils seemed to consume them. How was no one else bothered by her stare?

Emmitt's thumb smoothed over the back of my hand, and a gentle nudge in my mind brought a wave of comfort.

"Why is there no need?" Charlene asked.

"If Thomas holds you, you won't feel as drained."

"Really?" Charlene asked in surprise.

"Really. That's the purpose of our Mates. To anchor us."

Jim, who still stood near Olivia, frowned slightly as he continued to watch her. A surge of worry and pity welled up inside me. I loved him like a brother. The knowledge that he'd given up any chance of a family of his own to go after my brothers made me want to cry.

What's going on in that head of yours? Emmitt's thought interrupted my own.

Jim and Olivia. The way he looks at her. The way he fell to the floor the first time he saw her. It's just like your dad and Grey. History repeating itself. I thought that was what we didn't want.

It's not exactly repeating itself. Grey never saw a potential Mate.

You're not helping me feel any less guilty that he gave up his chance for a family to save mine.

Those boys are his family. He wouldn't like to hear you thinking otherwise.

"So if Thomas holds me when I touch Michelle, I'll be fine?" Charlene asked, unaware of our conversation.

"I believe so. The Lady's not exactly clear with all of her answers," Olivia said.

That didn't help my nerves.

Charlene glanced at me then the bed.

"Thomas, you should sit behind me. Michelle, why don't you sit next to me?"

The four of us got into position with Emmitt sitting behind me. Charlene took a deep breath then held out her hand.

"Promise you'll pull away when it gets to be too much," I said.

"I promise."

With that, I clasped her hand.

The black void swallowed me. The feel of Emmitt's arms wrapped around me or Charlene's reassuring hold no longer existed. Turning slowly, I watched for the pinprick of white light. It came from the right, zooming toward me like the last time, until I stood within its blinding brightness.

I blinked, trying to force my eyes to adjust. After a few moments, they did, and what I saw shocked me. I floated, suspended in the center of the vacant space surrounded by images of the future. Before, there had been layers upon layers. Images stacked so thickly I had no hope of going through them all. Now, there were less than a quarter of what there had been before. Why? What had changed?

I focused on one at random. The reflection of Gabby and Clay resting on a hotel bed came toward me. While she slept with her head on his shoulder, he lay beside her, very much awake. His facial hair made it hard to tell his expression, but a glisten in his eyes hinted at tears. Uncomfortable with the private moment, I focused on a different scene to the right of it. The image of Clay and Gabby flew behind me to the other side of the room.

This one showed Isabelle and Carlos mid-spar. Bruises covered her arms and calves. Her capris probably hid more. I began to wonder how far into the future these images portrayed. They all seemed like something that could be happening now.

I flipped through more images, trying to hurry and study them at the same time. Many of them were of different members of the group together. Bethi sleeping while Luke lay beside her, eating chips. Olivia and Jim lying in separate beds, facing each other like they were talking. Another of Isabelle and Carlos sparring in an exercise room. Her bruises looked darker in this one, though. Clay and Gabby under the covers together, which I flipped past really quickly. Olivia and Jim in a restaurant, seated near a window. The way he looked at her, the intensity of his gaze a blend of anger and devotion, gave me pause. Her hand lay on a cell phone on the surface of the table. The paleness of her face and worried shock of her expression hinted at something wrong. Something important. As much as I wanted to study the image to figure out what, I knew I needed to hurry.

Between the images of our group, several desertscape scenes left me worried. While the images clearly displayed the towering pillars of brown-red rocks and barren expanses of long-dry valleys, the main part of the scene remained blurred. Almost as if someone had taken a picture with the camera out of focus.

An array of varying colors made up the center. Only after staring for several moments did I place what I was seeing. A large-scale fight. Why were the people in the image blurred, though?

I shuffled through the images until I reached the bottom layer. On the final screen, swirls of grey covered the pastels of what seemed to be a sunset or sunrise. That was it. There'd been nothing helpful. Nothing that would give me a clue about what we needed to do to make the Judgement. I had to have missed something.

Frowning, I started back through the images again, slower this time. Most of them were of us here at the hotel or in our vehicles. The rest were unfocused stills of a lot of people in a desert setting. Was that it, then? Did that mean we would go from this hotel to the final fight? That we only had a few days, or maybe hours, until the Judgement?

I reached the last image once more. My stomach twisted with fear as I studied the grey swirls. Olivia and Bethi's warnings rang in my ears. The world would burn, and I was seeing the smoke.

CHARLENE...

IT HURT TO BREATHE. To think. I blinked slowly but refused to let go. We needed answers.

Beside me, Michelle leaned back against Emmitt. She seemed to be looking at Jim, but I knew better. Though her body remained in this room, her mind had fled to her white room, searching for the answer to end Blake's desperate reach for control. And each minute she stayed in there, I could feel my life draining further, just like I could feel Thomas's concern, his energy, pulsing through our connection. I could feel them all.

My gaze drifted to Olivia. She hadn't said anything since

we'd started. Had she known what I would need to do? What she was asking me to risk? No, she wasn't asking me to risk anything. I had a choice.

As soon as Michelle had touched her hand to mine, I'd understood why Thomas needed to hold me. Through him, I could pull the energy I needed to sustain the connection with Michelle. Not just his energy, but the energy of every man, woman, and child connected to the Elders through Thomas. A network of power. Of control.

My heart gave a fluttering thump, and I knew I needed to choose now. Take the energy I needed and risk exposing what I could do, or release Michelle and lose the chance for answers about the Judgement we needed to pass? The Judgement that would save the world. There was no real choice.

I opened myself to Thomas and let his energy flow into me. He exhaled suddenly, like I'd punched him, and I opened myself further to those energies that waited just beyond him. In two heartbeats, the ache and exhaustion vanished. I felt ready to run twenty miles and quickly closed myself off.

Thomas's fingers twitched on my arms, and I waited for the hate and the fear. Instead, love and warmth wrapped around me.

They'll think it was Isabelle again, he sent me.

I fought not to cry. He understood what I'd done and didn't care.

I don't fully understand, but you're right. I don't care. I love you, Charlene. And I'll never stop trying to prove how much. By the time I die, you won't doubt me.

My heart wanted to burst with what I felt for the man holding me.

Michelle's fingers twitched in mine before I could answer.

This time, she released me. Any lingering strain from keeping her in that white room faded as she looked around, aware of the present.

"What did you see?" Olivia asked.

"A disturbingly large decrease in images. Mostly scenes of us here at the hotel or on the road. Mixed in were scenes of a desertscape. A bunch of people were in those, all grouped close together. I could see the smallest detail of the desert, but everything about the people, who they were, what they were doing, all of it was blurry."

Our future was blurred? That didn't sound good.

"Maybe it was blurry because the future is not yet decided," Jim said.

I watched Olivia and her quietly thoughtful expression. She knew more than she let on, and that worried Winifred because she thought it meant Olivia was going to betray us. I didn't believe that, though. I knew what it was like to have a secret that couldn't be shared.

"I'm not sure," she said finally. "Did you see anything else?" Her gentle, dark gaze shifted to Michelle.

"Just that same desert location. It reminded me of pictures I saw in a magazine of Utah's desert."

"You saw nothing else?" she pressed.

"Nope. Just here, the vehicles, and the desert." She hesitated for a moment. "Wait, there was one other thing that stood out. It was a swirl of grey over the desert, like the whole thing was covered with smoke. A fire maybe."

Olivia closed her eyes for a brief moment.

"At least, we know we need to go to a desert," she said when she opened them again. "Just not what we need to do once we get there."

"Maybe we'll have the answer by that time," Jim said. "If you're only seeing this hotel and driving, it's clear we're meant to head to the desert from here. Clay should be well enough to travel in a few hours."

Michelle shook her head before he finished.

"I know we need to hurry, but we also need time to rest," she said.

"The longer we sit in one spot, the more we risk everyone. Everything," he said.

I understood what he was saying, but all we'd been doing was rush around, which hadn't gotten us any further ahead in this game we seemed to be playing.

"I agree with Michelle," I said. "Winifred is still stitching Clay, and I'm pretty sure Isabelle and Carlos took a beating to keep as many away from us as possible. If we rush into this without everyone healed…"

"We will fail," Olivia said with a sigh. "How long will it take for everyone to recover?"

"I'll check with Winifred," Jim said.

He didn't move to leave, though, and I knew he was using his new ability to communicate with the other Elders.

My heart broke for him all over again. My baby. My boy. I'd seen the way he'd looked at Olivia. She was meant to be his Mate, and fate had cruelly taken that chance from him. Just like Grey.

GABBY…

CLAY DIDN'T MOVE MUCH as Winifred continued her work. She, Henry, and Sam were the only ones still in the room with us.

Henry watched me from across the room, pity in his gaze. He understood what I was going through better than anyone else. The terror of the moment when I'd felt his pain still gripped me.

A wash of love swept through me, not as comforting as it should have been. If not for all those humans suddenly coming to our aid...

A shaky exhale escaped me.

"Clay will be fine, Gabby," Sam said.

"Will he?" I asked angrily. "Why are we doing this alone? There were werewolves not far from us. You could have called out to them and asked for help as soon as I told you the Urbat were coming."

"We don't want to risk more lives," Winifred said, not looking up from her work.

"But it's okay to risk mine and Clay's and everyone else's in the group? Why are we less important?"

"You're not less important," Sam said firmly.

I ignored him.

"If those humans wouldn't have shown up, we'd all be dead, and everything we have done would be for nothing. Is that how you want this to end? You expose the existence of werewolves and Urbat to the entire world then die and leave the werewolves without a single leader or Elder?"

Winifred's stitching paused.

"Because that almost happened. We can't fight this alone, Winifred," I said. "I know you heard Olivia say the same things Bethi's been saying. The world will burn, and humans and werewolves alike will all die anyway if we fail. Who are you really protecting?"

Clay squeezed my hand, and I felt his worry and love brush

my mind. He didn't like it when I talked back to the Elders. Whether they liked what I had to say or not, though, they needed to hear my words.

"How did you know how to call those humans to come to our aid?" Winifred asked when she resumed her stitching.

My frustration boiled. Instead of addressing the real issue, why she didn't call all the werewolves, she wanted to focus on that?

"I didn't know. It just happened. I was desperate." The scene played again in my mind, and I looked down at Clay's beautiful, furry face. He watched me closely, his warm brown eyes missing nothing. His fingers squeezed my leg gently.

With the last knot tied off, Winifred straightened with a sigh.

"That's more stitches than I would have liked to put in. But, given the uncertainty of what might happen next, a few extra will hold it better if you need to move."

My heart sank at her words. More? I didn't want any more. I wanted to leave and never look back. I wanted a place where Clay and I could hide from the world and just be us.

"Thank you, Winifred," Clay said. "I'll be fine."

"I'm sure you will. If you do need anything, either of you, let me know."

I nodded numbly and watched her leave. Sam gave us a long look and picked up his bag.

"Henry, grab those pizza boxes. These two could use some quiet time."

The door closed behind them, and Clay and I found ourselves alone for the first time in a very long time.

"What you're feeling is killing me," he said softly.

"I'm sorry."

"No. I am. I'm sorry you're suffering because of me."

"Because of? No. We're a team. We suffer together." I leaned over him and gently brushed my lips to his. He tilted his head, giving me better access, and I deepened the kiss.

My heart thrummed excitedly, like it did every time he touched me. Only this time, I understood how close I'd come to never being able to kiss him again. To touch him. To make him mine in every way.

Reaching over him, I gently trailed my fingers down his bare, muscled chest. The hair tickled my fingertips. He groaned and lifted his hands to cup my face, turning a heartfelt kiss into a passionate one that curled my toes.

Clay owned me. He'd wormed his way into my life until he'd become such a part of it I wasn't sure I'd ever be able to live without him again. I poured all that feeling, all the desperation, into our kiss. He growled softly, and I knew he understood.

My head spun when I finally pulled away.

"I don't want to wait any more," I whispered. "Life is too short to hesitate."

He groaned and tried to sit up. The effort ended with a grunt and him on his back next to me.

"Five hours," he said. "The stitches will be set, then you're mine."

I grinned sadly and lay next to him, resting my head on his shoulder. I doubted five hours would be enough to heal what they'd done to him. Not when he'd been holding his insides in with his arm on the way here. His lips were hidden, but I didn't doubt they were pale, like his exposed arms. He'd lost a lot of blood.

I closed my eyes and sighed.

"Don't leave me. If something happens where you think you won't make it, take me with you," I whispered. "I don't want to live without you."

"I love you, Gabrielle Winters. More than you can possibly know."

CHAPTER THIRTEEN

JIM...

Everyone watched me as they waited for the decision of the Elders.

"Winifred just finished stitching Clay up. She thinks he will need at least two days to fully heal. She hasn't yet checked on Isabelle," I said.

"I think Isabelle is pretty badly bruised and will need a few days, too," Michelle said. "I'll use that time to see if I can figure out which desert I saw in those images."

"That also gives Bethi time to keep dreaming of her answers. Let's hope it's enough," Olivia said.

I glanced at Mom's pale, worried face again. Dad still held her tight. Remembering the last time Michelle had touched her, I knew she probably wanted to rest. Michelle looked like she could use some time alone with Emmitt, too. At least, that's what I told myself as I tried to ignore the burning need I had to touch Olivia. To spend time alone with her again.

"I'll walk Olivia back to our room," I said, holding out my hand.

Olivia glanced at it for a long moment before hesitantly reaching for it. Her cool fingers felt so fragile in mine. I carefully wrapped my hand around hers and gave a light reassuring squeeze. She'd just stood when Winifred walked into the room.

Winifred took one look at us and scowled.

"I don't think that's a wise idea."

"Why not?" I asked. "I'm fine, now, aren't I?"

Olivia made a small sound almost like a laugh, and I realized that I'd just asked why again. I almost grinned, but Winifred looked anything but amused as she continued to study me.

"At this moment, perhaps," Winifred said, angering me. "But I'm worried you'll make a mistake. We can't afford to lose you to your stubbornness."

Mom reached up to clasp Dad's hand, and I wanted to growl in frustration at Winifred. I understood her concern; but I wasn't Sam and Olivia wasn't Winifred. We were different. Thrown together because of a different set of circumstances. Winifred knew that. But it didn't change why she worried. She cared because she loved me. She loved all of us. How could I argue with that?

"Winifred, I saw them in the white room," Michelle said, coming to my rescue. "He is going to spend time with her. They'll even stay together in the same room overnight. Those images weren't blurry."

A surge of joy tried surfacing, and my chest cramped with pain. I quickly told myself my joy was because I'd have more time to learn about Olivia which would only help assure the safety of my people. That thought helped suppress the blossoming pain.

Olivia wasn't as quick to stifle her reaction. Her fingers twitched in mine. I glanced at her, noting the flush rising to her cheeks.

"Excuse me," she said softly. "I need to lay down for a bit."

She pulled her hand from mine and started for the door. It opened before she reached it. Sam and Henry stood in the hall. Winifred went to Henry and took the pizza boxes he held.

"Thought we'd bring some of these here since this is where most of you are," Sam said.

"Henry, can you walk Olivia to her room?" Winifred asked.

A growl almost rose at the idea of the pup around her. The pain in my chest hit me hard. Winifred noticed my wince because her gaze had never left me, not even when talking to Henry.

"Yes, Nana," Henry said. Olivia moved toward him. He politely held out his arm and wrapped Olivia's hand around it.

Everyone in the room watched me as they left.

"Are you hungry, Jim?" Winifred asked, holding out a box.

Hungry? Yes. But not for the pizza. Another pain hit me between the ribs.

"You're not being smart about this," Winifred said. "I don't care what Michelle said. You shouldn't spend any more time with Olivia than necessary."

"I think we'll just take that box and run," Emmitt said, sliding out from behind Michelle. She stood, took the box from Winifred, and led the way out.

Just Winifred, Sam, Mom, Dad, and I remained in the room. They all watched me with varying degrees of concern.

I absently scratched my chest and sighed. At what point

would they stop looking at me like a run-away pup? At what point would they trust that I truly did have the best interest of the pack and our people at heart?

"You told me to listen to my heart, and I am. With both ears. There's a reason fate made her my Mate. We just don't know why, yet. If I don't spend time with her, how will we ever learn?"

"And, it has to be something important if Michelle saw him staying in the same room with her," Mom added.

I winked at Mom. She might not be happy that I'd found Olivia after taking the oath, but she had wanted me to find a Mate since the first time I stole Dad's car to hang out in town with human girls.

Winifred sighed.

"Just be careful." She stepped aside and waved me out of the room. I quickly left and caught up with Henry just as he left Olivia's room.

He took one look at me and shook his head.

"You look like you want to cuff me when I didn't even do anything. I thought 'be nice, but don't trust' was meant for her, not me," he said.

"Sorry, Henry. I'm trying."

I put my hand on the door, impatient to join her.

"I know. Good luck. And don't forget what you told me," he said before he walked away.

Don't trust. I didn't. Not blindly anyway. But I was starting to believe that Olivia was telling the truth. If Blake saw her as a tool like the rest of the girls and there was no true caring between the pair of them, she would have every reason to keep her emotions buried. Other than hiding those, she didn't seem to be hiding anything else.

I opened the door and stepped inside.

OLIVIA...

MY HEART still wanted to race when Jim walked with purpose into the room. That Michelle had seen the two of us spending time together shouldn't have shocked me. That was the reason for my time here, after all. Yet, hearing we would spend the night together did worry me. Everything rode on how carefully I proceeded, now. I couldn't fail. Not now. Not this close.

I continued looking through my bag, as if I didn't notice him, and struggled to maintain my breathing and pulse. He was dangerous. So very dangerous.

As much as I wanted to push him away, to tell him to leave, I knew I couldn't. I needed him. Only not as a Mate, no matter what he felt for me. No matter what I was starting to feel for him.

When I found a clean pair of leggings and a loose t-shirt, I turned toward the bathroom.

"You can change the bandages after I'm done," I said in an even tone.

"Me?"

"Yes. That's why you're here, isn't it? To take care of me?" I held my breath, waiting for his answer.

"I don't know. Is it?" he said softly.

His purpose was so much more, and the question made my heart thump harder for a beat. I was sure he heard it. Instead of cringing, I met his gaze, or what I thought might be his gaze given the shape of his head, with a steady stare.

"Only if you want to," I said.

I stepped into the bathroom without waiting for his answer and closed the door. I watched him through the wall as he ran a hand over his chest then wandered around the room. His broad shoulders looked like they could easily take on any weight in the world. They would have to.

A stab of regret hit me before I could stop it. Blake's impatience immediately followed. This time, I did cringe. I'd slipped too many times in just a few hours. I would need to call him before I went to bed, and I dreaded it.

Someone walking in the hall stopped to knock on our door, distracting me from my suppressed misery. Jim crossed the room to answer. The person's shape looked familiar, but I hadn't been with the group long enough to easily identify each of them yet.

I watched Jim accept something as I carefully removed my shirt. The open wounds twinged, but Winifred's bandages held firm. Quickly changing with a back flayed by the Others proved impossible. Every move I executed, I did slowly and with purpose. It took a few tries to get the new shirt back on. By the time I finished, Jim had closed the door and resumed his wandering.

The bra, which had ridden high on my back prior to the Others taking their due, lay on the floor. My brow already glistened from the effort of putting a shirt on. The thought of the bra accidently rubbing the top of my wounds had me turning away. I wouldn't be wearing it again for a long while.

Holding out my hand, I felt for the handle and opened the door. Jim turned from his position near the room's work table and faced me.

My back ached with each step as I walked toward him. It needed to be checked to ensure I hadn't made the wounds bleed again with all my moving around. I knew that. However, I honestly just wanted to lay on my stomach and sleep while the world worried about its own problems for a while. The thought made the deeply hidden part of me want to cry. As much as I wanted to hide from my fate, I couldn't.

I was so wrapped up in my thoughts, I didn't immediately recognize the silence or the tense way Jim held himself as he faced me. Stopping, I glanced around the room at the Others, trying to understand what might be wrong. They seemed to be swirling around normally.

Shifting my attention back to Jim, I suppressed my apprehension.

"What's wrong?" I asked.

"Your shirt." His rough words didn't help ease my nervousness.

I smoothed my hand over the front of it, feeling the soft material. The softest shirt I owned. I'd packed it knowing what would happen, knowing I'd need something comfortable. It was one of my favorite sleep shirts.

"Is it stained?" I asked. I always washed my own clothes, making it difficult to know if I'd ruined something until Blake commented on it, which he hadn't.

"No." That single word came out in a whoosh like I'd hit him.

"Is it an ugly color? Tell me."

He reached out and trailed the knuckle of his first finger along my collar bone.

"I can see through it. Every beautiful detail. And I want—" He groaned, clutched at his chest, and collapsed to his knees.

I barely paid him attention as understanding, followed immediately by disgust, filled me. Jim could see through my shirt. He could see my breasts. I didn't care about Jim seeing. I cared about how many times I'd worn this shirt before this moment. Blake had always complimented me on it when he'd come to lock me in my room for the night. I'd worn it often because he would be less cold.

Bile rose in my throat, and I staggered a step to sit on the bed. He would touch my cheek gently and kiss me good night. I'd never felt lust. But, deep down, I knew it had been there.

Jim's choking noise drew my attention. The Others swirled around him in excitement. I moved quickly, hurting my back, and knelt beside him.

"Jim." I reached out and placed my hand against his cheek. Sweat wet my palm. "This was my favorite shirt to wear to bed."

"Not helping," he panted between pained grunts.

"Blake saw me in it every time he locked me in my room for the night. He never said anything when he looked at me. But I would always feel...something from him. I ignored it. Pretended it wasn't there. You need to do the same. Ignore what you feel for me. You can't die now, Jim. I can't do this alone."

His hand gripped mine, pressing my fingers more firmly into his cheek. Gradually, his breathing slowed, and he turned his face, brushing his lips against the palm of my hand. My heart thumped heavily in my chest at the sensation. Dangerous. I swallowed hard and pushed what I wanted to feel aside.

The tickling warmth of his breath against the skin of my hand made my insides go hot and cold.

I tried to stand, but he didn't release my hand.

"Go lay on the bed," he said. "On your stomach."

That just made my insides act crazier. He inhaled deeply and gave another choked groan.

"You smell so good."

"Not helping," I said nervously, repeating his words. "My insides are going crazy, and I don't know how well I'm holding it all back from Blake. If he suspects I'm with an interested male—"

"He'll send everyone he has at us," Jim said. He released me, his reluctance shown in the drag of his fingers against the back of my hand.

"Lay down," he said again. "I'll look at your back."

I stood with care and went to the bed. Getting onto my stomach hurt, but once I was there, I could relax. Until I felt his fingers on my shirt. I struggled not to go all hot and cold again. The material slowly inched its way up under his gentle touch. When he had the bottom above the top of the cuts, he stopped. Then he started peeling off the taped gauze.

"How does it look?" I asked when he did nothing for a moment.

"Not good."

"It started bleeding again?"

"No. It's oozing clear, but not bleeding."

"Oh. That's good then."

He didn't comment as he spread some ointment on and covered the area with clean gauze again.

"I'll be right back," he said after gently tugging my shirt back into place.

The door softly opened and closed. I didn't bother to track his progress. Instead, I reached for the cell phone that rested on the nightstand between the beds and dialed Blake's number. He picked up on the first ring.

"They tried using the Provider to see if she could get a premonition of what we need to do," I said without preamble. "It didn't work. They seem to have no set plan regarding what they will do with or without the answer."

"Stop telling me useless information," Blake said into the phone. "What is happening? I'm feeling things from you."

"I didn't want to worry you, but the bruises on my face aren't my worst injuries. I have three gashes on my back. They hurt. And I've also been trying to encourage interest in the males here, thinking it would put me in a favorable position of influence."

The soft brush of something on my back told me I wasn't alone anymore.

"I don't like it."

"I don't either, but you told me to use their kindness to gain answers. That's what I'm trying to do."

"I don't like your tone," he said softly. I shivered despite trying not to.

"I'm sorry, Father," I said as contritely as I could manage.

"I'll see you soon, Olivia. When we're together again, I'll keep you safe. Perhaps we'll finally finish what you started."

I let my mind go blank at his words. *Don't think about it. Don't feel. Don't react.*

"Yes, Father," I said.

"Goodnight, Olivia."

The line went dead, and I lifted the phone for whoever was there to take it. Tears leaked from my eyes. The only physical sign that I really did feel something after that phone call.

"There's no happy ending for me," I said, mostly to myself. "If we don't make the Judgement or if we Judge in favor of the humans, the Others will come. If we make the Judgement…"

I swallowed hard and refused to think about what would happen then as well.

Large, warm fingers gently brushed away the tears.

"If you make the Judgement, there will always be a place for you with us. With me," Jim said.

I swallowed hard. His words painted a picture I would hold onto when the time for Judgement came.

"I have some ice for your back," he said.

A moment later, a slight weight settled over my wounds. The cool felt so good.

"You can only keep it on for a short time. Slowing blood flow slows the healing, but I thought it might feel good after changing."

"Why are you doing this?" I asked. He'd heard the call with Blake. He knew I hadn't lied about any of it, even the part about encouraging his interest. His continued kindness confused me.

His fingers brushed the hair away from my face.

"Because I believe you," he said simply.

CHAPTER FOURTEEN

JIM...

MY CHEST CONTINUED TO ACHE DULLY FROM WHEN SHE'D FIRST stepped out of the bathroom in her white, threadbare t-shirt. I hadn't given a single thought to the Urbat or saving my kind. A goddess had stood before me, and all I'd wanted to do was worship her. Still did. Hearing her call with Blake and seeing her expression had removed any remaining doubt. She'd been his prisoner, too. And continued to be one because of their link.

She hid her pain well. It didn't touch her scent or her features, yet I felt every ounce of it in each tear that trailed down her pale cheek. I wanted to pick her up, hold her in my arms, and comfort her. But both of us would suffer for that. While I was willing to endure anything, I couldn't be the cause of any further pain for her. Yet, I had to offer her something.

"You've had a lifetime of being used and mistreated. I want to give you a lifetime of being cherished for who you are, instead of what you are."

"You don't even know me," she said.

"I feel the pull. That's enough for me to trust that I'll like what I discover when you finally let me in." I'd seen too many happy couples not to believe that.

"Let you in?"

I smiled and removed the ice. Then, I took the comforter from my bed and covered her so she wouldn't need to get up again.

"You don't lie and are honest in every word you say. It's a skill only people with deep secrets learn."

Her gaze stayed on me as I laid on the opposite bed and faced her.

"Deep secrets," she said with a sigh. "I'm tired of them."

"Would you like to tell me?"

"No. I'd like to pretend that the future I know is coming isn't our future. If I wasn't a Judgement and you weren't an Elder, what would tonight be like?"

My first thought sent a shock of immediate pain through me. I set aside the mental image of her perfect breasts under that shirt and focused on a different version of our future.

"I suppose, if you weren't a Judgement, you'd be a regular human, and I wouldn't feel the pull for you. But I think I'd still notice you. I'd buy you a drink or two, and we'd spend the night talking about you."

"Why not you?"

"Because I'm a werewolf and that's the deepest, darkest secret we need to keep from humans. Especially now that they know we exist."

"Do you think it's pointless to wish for a future you can't have?" she asked after a quiet moment.

"No. That would be like saying dreaming is pointless, and Bethi's proven just how important dreams can be."

"Then I'm going to wish for that future. A future where you'd buy me a drink, and we'd get to know one another because I know I would like you very much, Jim."

She closed her eyes, and her tears eventually stopped.

I'd heard what Blake had said to her and knew that, as an Elder and her Mate, I could never let him have her back. But to what lengths would I go to keep that from happening?

Long after her breathing evened out, I lay on the bed watching her. Every time my mind wandered back to the moment she'd stepped out of the bathroom and walked toward me with the hint of her nipples showing through her shirt, the pain in my chest spiked. Why? Winifred said to listen to my heart. My heart was telling me the fragile, nearly broken woman before me was meant to be mine. Any guilt I felt over being lucky enough to have found her came from my damn head.

She sighed slightly in her sleep, drawing my attention to her mouth. A different kind of ache grew inside me. Longing. To hold her in comfort. To protect her. To show her kindness. Was this how Emmitt felt every time he looked at Michelle and saw fear in her eyes? I remembered my advice to wait and give her time. Olivia didn't need time. She'd experienced too much of it already. She needed an escape now.

How are things with you? Winifred sent me, cutting into my thoughts.

We're alive and breathing. She called Blake before she fell asleep. She thinks she's keeping him at bay and buying us time by giving him updates.

Do you think it's working?

I considered her question for a moment.

I don't think it's Blake we need to stall. Bethi and Olivia are both sure our time is running short. I think our clock is ticking no matter what Olivia tells him.

I agree.

How is everyone else? I sent back.

Good. Resting and healing. Isabelle and Carlos are with Grey. Sam is giving Gabby and Clay some space and staying with Bethi, Luke, and Henry. I'll stay with Michelle and Emmitt for tonight. Sam, Grey, and I will keep watch while everyone rests. Reach out if you need anything.

The only thing I needed was answers. Why me? Why now? Why with Olivia? Deep down, I knew there had to be a reason. Once I figured that out, I'd know what to do about my feelings for Olivia.

I closed my eyes and briefly dozed. When I woke, I knew sunrise still remained hours away and got out of bed.

"Leaving?" Her soft voice surprised me.

"Only so I didn't wake you," I said, settling back into my spot. "Does your back hurt?"

"Yes, but only because I move in my sleep. Tell me your favorite memory."

Her request made me frown. She hurt more than she let on if she wanted a distraction. I quickly reached out to Winifred.

Can you bring some more pain relievers? Olivia is awake, and I don't want to leave her alone.

Yes.

"Favorite?" I said, addressing Olivia. "Not sure I have a single favorite. There are a lot of really good ones."

"Tell me all of them."

"Where we grew up, there weren't always many cubs. Most of the time, it was just me, Emmitt, and Carlos. Carlos didn't want to play too often, though. It bugged me that he preferred to be alone, and I decided he needed to have as much fun as Emmitt and I did." I grinned, remembering the type of fun I'd gravitated toward. "What Emmitt and I did usually got us into trouble, and my young self was smart enough to know that if I wanted to pull Carlos into our fun, I'd need to do it when my parents and Grey wouldn't stop me. So, one night, I woke up after everyone else was asleep. My parents never heard me sneak from my room, and Uncle Grey slept through me sneaking into their rooms, too. Carlos heard me, though. As soon as I opened the door to his room, he flew at me, a ball of shaking fur. At the time, I thought he was finally ready to play and shifted so we could wrestle on the floor. But, Carlos wasn't playing. He was fighting like I was there to kill him. Uncle Grey had to pull him off of me. My nose bled, and I had a few bruised ribs."

"That sounds awful. How is that a good memory?"

"After that, Carlos started talking. I'll never forget Uncle Grey's face when he sat us both down at his table to ask what had happened, and Carlos turned to me and called me an idiot. Not the best first word, but Uncle Grey had looked like Carlos said the smartest thing ever."

She frowned slightly.

"Still don't think it's a good memory?"

She shrugged slightly and winced. I stood and went to her side, lightly running my fingers over her hair, the only way I could think to sooth her pain.

"That was the first time I realized good can still come from what might seem like a bad situation."

Her pulse stuttered slightly.

"Don't write off your life yet," I said. "Something really good is going to happen."

She tilted her head to look at me.

"Someone's at the door," she said.

I went to open the door for Winifred. Her long braid trailed over one night-gowned shoulder. Without a word, she handed me a small white bottle then started back to her room. I closed the door and went to the bathroom for a glass of water. Olivia sat up as I shook out two pills for her. I kept my gaze locked on her face. Looking lower wouldn't do either of us any good.

"Thank you," she said, accepting the medicine and the water.

She swallowed the pills down and handed me the empty glass. I returned the glass to the bathroom.

"Tell me another one," she said when I sat on the bed across from her.

"No, it's your turn. Tell me your favorite memory."

Any trace of tired contentment previously on her face disappeared from her expression. Instead of answering, she lay down on the bed and pulled the cover up to her chin.

I rubbed the ache in my chest and lay down on the other bed so I faced her again.

"I'm sorry," I said.

"Why?"

"For bringing up something that upset you."

She took a long deep breath.

"It's upsetting for so many reasons. My best memory is also the worst."

"Tell me about it."

"There's not much to tell. It's the moment I saw you."

She closed her eyes, signaling she didn't want to talk anymore. Yet, with those words, I couldn't keep quiet.

"It's the same for me."

To see something I wanted so much and know I couldn't have? It created a perfect balance of heaven and hell.

It didn't take long for Olivia's breathing to even out again. I closed my eyes and tried to sleep. It took a long time before my mind let me.

OLIVIA...

THE RUMBLE of Jim's snores woke me. The volume rather surprised me as did the fact I'd apparently slept through quite a bit of it.

I eased from the covers and sat up, taking my time and gauging how my back felt. A night's rest had helped. Oh, it still hurt, but it didn't quite burn with pain like it had the day before. Standing, I made my way to the bathroom and closed myself in.

The Others swirled around me, outlining the toilet, sink, and shower. I used the toilet then washed my hands and brushed my teeth. Although I tried to move quietly, I still disturbed Jim's sleep. While I rinsed my mouth, I saw him sit up and run a hand over his face.

Opening the door, I stepped out with an apology ready.

"You are so beautiful," he breathed.

I felt my cheeks begin to heat and crossed my arms over my chest.

He stood and walked toward me before gently coaxing my arms away. He made a pained sound, and I knew he was looking where he shouldn't. And, heaven help me, I wanted him to keep doing it. My pulse dipped then jumped dangerously.

"Don't hide from me. Don't feel embarrassed about what I feel for you." He smoothed his fingers over my cheek. "When I think you feel shame, it starts to hurt. I can't stop what I feel. Please don't make me hurt more because of it."

I exhaled heavily. Hurting him was the last thing I wanted. Yet, I knew before this ended, he would be very hurt. The knowledge of what we both still needed to endure had me stepping forward. The need to wrap my arms around his waist and hug him warred with logic. My back wouldn't take that kind of stretching. Instead, I set my hands on his sides and leaned against him.

Jim tensed then placed his hands on my shoulders and rested his chin on top of my head. Closing my eyes, I let myself enjoy the simple physical contact. The shadowy memory of the last hug I'd received paled in comparison to this moment.

A shudder went through Jim. Then another. I didn't move or try to pull away. Breathing deeply, I tried to memorize his scent.

"If I weren't a Judgement or hurt, what would happen next?" I asked, craving a glimpse of what my life could be like if things were different.

His pulse spiked under my ear, and he grunted. Still, he didn't release me.

"I'd try to get you to say yes." His rough, pained words brought more despair than comfort.

"Yes to what?"

"To me."

I pulled back, and he let me go.

"If I weren't a Judgement or connected to Blake, I would say yes," I said sadly.

He stopped breathing and pressed his hand to his chest. The

Others started to swirl around him in a frenzy, and he slowly sank to a knee.

Panic gripped me. I'd said too much. I'd opened up too much.

"Jim, don't leave me. I can't do this without you."

Just as I reached for him, the door burst open. Whoever strode in, moved too fast for me to identify them by their walk or shape.

One came toward me. The other went toward Jim. In seconds, I was up in someone's arms and being taken from the room. The pressure on my back brought tears to my eyes.

"He needs to be okay," I said desperately. "Make sure he's okay."

"We will," Winifred said. "He just needs a little space to calm down."

"Please let me walk," I begged, unable to hold back a moan of pain.

I immediately found myself on my feet.

"I'm so sorry, Olivia. I wasn't thinking."

"No, it's okay. Jim first. I understand."

"I can see why he was having trouble," she said. "Your shirt is slightly see through."

I blushed.

"I didn't know when I packed it."

"I imagine not."

"Do you have one I could borrow? Is it morning yet? I had a watch that told me the time, but Frank took it."

"It's after six. Close enough to morning. Let's get you a shirt."

I followed her the rest of the way to her room, and saw two

other people laying snuggled in bed before she opened the door.

"I'll wait out here," I said.

"Nonsense. Come in. Michelle's up already, anyway."

As soon as I stepped into the room, I noticed one of the pair held an object. The shape had me thinking it might be some kind of tablet.

"Morning, Olivia. It's Michelle," Michelle said.

Surprise shot through me. No one ever announced themselves, leaving me to guess based on their voices and movement. Her consideration warmed me.

"Good morning, Michelle. Couldn't sleep?" I asked as Winifred went to look through the bags in her room.

"Not really. I kept thinking about the desert I saw in the white room. I think I might have found it."

"Don't tell me," I said quickly. "Not yet. The less I know about where we are going, the safer we are while we wait for the answers."

"Uh...okay."

"This one should work," Winifred said, straightening.

I accepted the shirt and went into the bathroom to change. It took some effort, and I ached by the time I finished. Wanting to lay down again, I left the bathroom and turned toward Winifred.

"Is Jim all right enough for me to return?"

"What happened to Jim?" Michelle asked, concern lacing her voice.

"He saw Olivia in the shirt she was just wearing," Winifred answered.

"Oh."

Emmitt suddenly got out of bed and strode toward the door.

"Where are you going?" Winifred asked.

"Don't worry; I'm going to help. I have some advice to give Jim about cookies."

He left, closing the door behind him and leaving me confused.

"Emmitt is Jim's brother," Michelle said. "Jim gave Emmitt a hard time when I first moved in with them."

"So he's going to give Jim a hard time? Now?"

"Probably."

"But, Jim's hurting," I said.

Michelle sighed. "I know. So does Emmitt. He's been more than a little worried since Jim saw you and recognized you as a potential Mate. We all have. No one wants Jim to suffer or die because of what he feels for you."

I swallowed hard and said nothing. Fate was too cruel.

CHAPTER FIFTEEN

GABBY...

Something tickled my nose. I brushed at it and heard a rumbling laugh. Opening my eyes, I lifted my head to look up at Clay.

"How do you feel?" I asked, tiredly. I'd set my phone alarm to wake me every hour so I could check the Urbat movement. Once I verified they hadn't moved, I'd gone back to sleep. Now, though, it felt like I hadn't slept at all.

"Good. You look tired."

"I am. But it's nothing I can't handle."

"I'm sorry I woke you. I need to use the bathroom." He hadn't been able to get out of bed because I liked to use him as a human pillow. He loved it, too.

I smiled slightly and rolled away from him. He moved to the side and sat up while he was still partially bent over.

"You don't look good," I commented, eyeing the broad, muscled expanse of his back as he stood. "I mean, you do look good. Really good from here, but your stomach..."

He turned toward me, tilting his head and giving me his full attention. I saw his whiskers twitch near his mouth and knew he was smiling at me.

"I'm just being extra careful, in the hopes you haven't changed your mind."

"I haven't changed my mind," I said, ignoring the blush creeping onto my face. "I won't. I'm done waiting."

He groaned and took a step toward me.

I grinned and quickly pointed in the direction he'd originally intended.

"Focus," I said.

"I'm very focused." He leaned over and brushed his lips against mine.

I shivered at the contact. Overtired, wanting Clay, and not thinking clearly, I lifted my hand to clutch at him. Instead of gripping him, I hit him in the stitches.

Clay grunted and pulled back.

"Saying stop would have worked."

"I'm so sorry! I didn't mean to do that. I meant to pull you closer."

His lips twitched again.

"I'll do closer in just a minute."

"I don't think that's a good idea. You were stitched together just hours ago."

"If I were human, that might be a problem. It's not. Are you changing your mind?"

"I'm not. I just don't want you to hurt yourself."

He straightened away from me then met my gaze.

"I feel like I've waited forever for a yes. I'll wait longer if you're not ready. But if you're ready, I don't want to wait another minute."

He kissed my cheek then strode to the bathroom. Watching him, my heart beat rapidly. Were we really doing this? I brought my hands to my flushing cheeks in a slight panic. I hadn't lied. I was ready. However, I was also nervous as hell.

I heard running water in the bathroom, and I scrambled out of bed. I still wore yesterday's clothes. Should I change? Should I just strip? My hands shook as I reached for my shirt and chickened out. I'd look stupid standing out here in my bra and underwear.

The water shut off. I all-out panicked and froze like a deer in headlights when the door opened. He took a single step out, froze, and inhaled deeply.

"Gabby..."

Busted.

"You're not ready."

"I am," I insisted. He took another step toward me, and my pulse spiked. "I'm just freaking out big time because I don't know what to do."

He came toward me, wrapping me in his arms as soon as he reached me.

"I love you so much it hurts. You don't need to do anything but let me love you."

I nodded jerkily, looking up at him.

He lowered his head slowly. My heart felt like it was making every attempt to hammer its way out of my chest. My insides got hot then cold then hot again. Everything felt wrong and right at the same time. Yep, I was panicked and turned on and didn't know which to let take over.

Just before his lips touched mine, I turned my head away.

"I need to brush my teeth."

Before he could say anything, I darted from his arms and closed myself into the bathroom.

Come on, Gabby, I scolded myself in the mirror. *You'd kissed the hell out of him after Isabelle got you high, and you'd enjoyed every minute of it.*

I put some paste on my toothbrush and started scrubbing.

You just need to pretend this is another make out session where he's going to say no. You can do this.

I ended my pep talk with a rinse then faced the door.

When I opened it, I found Clay right where I'd left him. He had both hands in the pockets of his jeans and looked completely relaxed. I took a step toward him and another. Before I knew it, we stood toe to toe. I shook. Why was I being such a baby?

He watched me for a minute, then turned away and went to the bed. Taking his time, he eased himself down to the mattress. I could tell he hurt.

Lifting his hand, he silently tapped his lips. The gesture made my heart squeeze with bittersweet memories.

Clay was my world, and I'd almost lost him.

"I'm tired of hesitating," I whispered, moving toward him.

When I reached the bed, I eyed his position and the room on both sides of him. Perfect. It reminded me of our time in that farm house. Taking care, I climbed up and over him, straddling his waist. He didn't make a sound or move as I settled my weight on his hips.

"Don't let me hurt you again," I said.

"You won't."

His rough voice made my stomach go wild, and I leaned over to give him a light, teasing kiss. My intention to go slow flew out the window the moment he opened his mouth and his tongue touched mine. This was Clay. My heart. My soul. My Mate.

Careful to keep my weight on his hips and not his chest, I threaded my fingers through his hair and lost myself to the feel of him. Memories of the farm invaded. The way I'd pressed him for more. His desperation to take what I'd offered. I wanted that again.

Slowly, I rotated my hips against his. The friction sent a jolt of need through me. I did it again, making a little sound into our kiss.

He growled, and suddenly I found our positions changed. Hooking my hands around his shoulders, I arched up, giving into the fire that burned me from the inside.

Clay's mouth left mine, and he nibbled his way down the side of my neck. I shivered at the sensation. When his hand slid under my shirt, my breath caught. He hesitated.

"Don't stop," I whispered, giving the side of his head a kiss.

The slow drag of my shirt up over my ribs made me tremble. My skin burned where a finger teased the edge of my bra. The touch of his mouth on my stomach set me on fire, and I burned for more. When he hooked his fingers in the cups and pulled them down, a desperate sound escaped me. The bed shook, but I barely noticed. I wanted more.

Cool air brushed my exposed skin for too long, and I opened my eyes, which I hadn't realized I'd closed. I met his hungry gaze. Without looking away from me, he slowly lowered his mouth to the valley between my breasts. I could barely breathe at the soft touch of his lips.

His tongue darted out, licking where he'd kissed. He moved just a bit to the right, pressing his lips to the curve of my breast. An ache grew. I knew what he intended as he slowly worked his way to the side toward a part of me that demanded to feel the heat of his mouth. I nearly screamed when he gave me what I craved. His lips grazed the sensitive skin a moment before they closed over the peak. I gripped his hair, needing him to stay there. He obliged. My hips involuntarily bucked with need.

He groaned, and his hands went to my waist while his tongue continue to lick and tease my breast. I quivered when his fingers trailed to the tops of my jeans and stopped at my button. Waves of needs swept through me. I wanted this… him…so much. I lifted my hips again, rubbing against him, encouraging him to keep going.

His fingers fumbled at the fastening for too long, and I reached down to help him, impatient for more. My hand slid wetly against the bared skin of my stomach. Wet?

Jerking my hand back in surprise, I stared at my red fingers.

The button finally released, and Clay began to tug my jeans from my hips. My gaze flew to his head as he slowly started to kiss his way to my other breast. I ached for him to continue, but fear for him had me opening my mouth.

"Clay, wait."

He growled low and continued to lick his way to my other breast. I gasped as his mouth closed over me and grabbed the sheets for an anchor. The bed shook violently and fur lined Clay's arms.

I swallowed hard at the signs of his slipping control. We needed to stop, and I knew what to say to make him listen.

"Do I still have a choice?" I asked, hating myself for saying the words.

He stopped and jerked as if I'd slapped him. Lifting his

head, he met my gaze. His pupils had fully dilated with his need for me.

"Always." The rough word and the concern in his gaze almost broke me.

"Clay, I want you. Now and forever. But not like this."

I lifted my hand to show him the blood. He closed his eyes against the sight and maybe against what he knew I would say next.

"I love you, Clay. And I don't want you hurt by it."

I leaned up and kissed him gently to take the sting from my words.

"Reach out to Winifred so she can fix you again. It's not sexy to bleed all over your partner."

He fell to the side with a groan.

WINIFRED...

CLAY'S MIND touched mine as I watched Olivia slowly sit on the bed across from Michelle.

Winifred, I'm bleeding again. I may have torn a few of the stitches.
What happened?
Gabby was finally ready.

Ah. I didn't say anything further. Instead, I picked up my supply bag.

"I need to check on Clay. Perhaps the two of you would like to see if the hotel offers a breakfast?"

"Sure," Michelle said, getting out of bed. "I'll just use the bathroom real quick."

While Michelle walked to the bathroom, I slipped out the door and hurried down the hall. Gabby opened the door on the first knock. Blood painted the hem of her shirt. She stepped aside and let me in without a word of explanation.

Clay lay on the bed, slightly at an angle. The scent of arousal clogged the air.

"Gabby, honey, Michelle and Olivia are going to check our breakfast options. Perhaps you'd like to go with them?" I said.

"Yeah. Sure. I'm just going to wash up and change real quick." She hurried to shut herself in the bathroom.

"How many stitches do you think you tore?" I asked Clay, approaching the bed.

"I can't really feel it."

I tilted my head in concern until he clarified.

"Other parts hurt worse."

I patted his shoulder and peeled back the first bandage. Several of the stitches had torn into the skin, but not completely out. The bathroom door opened, and Gabby left with a soft farewell.

Clay sighed but held still as I checked the other gashes, which seemed about the same.

"No more stitches needed. But you need to keep your distance from Gabby for the rest of today. Sam should probably stay with you two tonight, too."

"You're killing me."

I chuckled.

"You've been patient for so long. Hold on for a few more days. Try to rest. And avoid cold showers. They're not good for the stitches."

He closed his eyes and threw his arms over his face. I left the room and my humor quickly vanished. Clay wasn't the only male suffering because of a Mate. I walked a few doors down to Jim and Olivia's room.

When I knocked, Sam answered the door.

"How is he?" I asked, not stepping in.

"He's fine," Sam said.

"You need to get it through your thick skull," Emmitt said from inside. "When you took the oath, you gave up your right to cookies. You can't think of cookies. You can't smell cookies. And you sure as hell can't eat cookies."

"Are you enjoying yourself?" Jim asked in a bored tone.

"Yes. The only thing that could top this is if you could do something that would get her to kick you in the balls so I can throw a bag of peas at you."

"Emmitt's helping distract him," Sam said.

I nodded and stepped back so he could join me in the hall. His scent tickled my nose as it always did when we were close. An ache started in my chest, and I quickly thought of Jim, Clay, and everyone else under our care.

"Clay ripped a few of his stitches. I think it would be best if you stayed in their room tonight to prevent any further damage. We need him to heal as quickly as possible."

"I'll move my things back before breakfast," Sam said, walking with me toward my room.

When we reached the door, we both stopped.

"What are we doing, Winifred?"

"What do you mean?"

He shook his head slightly.

"All of this. Another werewolf race, six women with irrefutable gifts, two of whom claim they need to do something to maintain a balance between races we didn't even know existed six months ago, exposing our race to humans…what are we doing? Is this really the best course for us?"

I calmed my mind and listened to my heart.

"It is. You know as well as I do that even with Charlene's help, our people were barely existing. We couldn't have continued like that for another fifty years, not when Blake and his kind have been secretly killing families and taking female cubs.

"All those years ago, we needed change and change was forced upon us. I don't believe that was a coincidence, just like I don't believe the events of the past year have been a coincidence. I'll never admit this to Jim," I said with a half-smile, "but he's right. There's a reason for all of this. We just need to figure out what."

He frowned and looked away, absently rubbing his chest right where mine ached, too. It hurt both of us to be this close; yet, I would change nothing. My heart belonged to my people. The oath demanded that. But we both knew it only beat for Sam.

"I'll see you at breakfast," he said before turning away.

Exhaling shakily, I went inside my room to compose myself before joining the others for breakfast. Sam's question continued to echo in my mind. What were we doing? We weren't just saving our people; we were saving the world from a threat greater than any we'd knowingly faced before, and these girls were the keys to our survival.

"Don't doubt yourself now, Sam. I can't bear the thought of losing you."

CHAPTER SIXTEEN

JIM...

"Don't you have something better to do?" I asked Emmitt after Sam left with Winifred.

"Not really," he said, lounging on the bed. He wore his sleep shorts and nothing else. The idea of Olivia walking in with him dressed like that set my teeth on edge. And the ass knew it. I could tell by the way he folded his hands behind his head and grinned at me.

I could play his game.

"Christmas is only a few days away, and the boys are in a strange hotel without their family. Are you having gifts sent over to them so they have something to open Christmas morning?" I asked.

Emmitt frowned, and I almost grinned. He was too easy to read and distract.

"That's below the belt," he said.

"I hear that's where you like being hit."

He sat up and ran a hand through his hair.

"I'm hoping we'll be done with this before then. I miss the cubs. Michelle goes into the bathroom and cries at night. She thinks I don't know, but I can feel it."

"Is she calling them?"

"Yes. They're having a blast with Paul. They swim and eat whatever they want and watch cartoons."

"They're safe. That's the most important thing, even if this does take a while. Olivia keeps saying that Bethi has the answer. I'll talk to Carlos and Isabelle and see if Isabelle can help Bethi figure out what that answer might be."

Emmitt nodded and stood.

"I was being serious, you know," he said.

"I know."

"It would be better if you stayed away from Olivia. Sam told me he avoided being near Winifred for ten years after he saw her. Feeling her in his head was a comfort, but seeing her caused pain."

I sighed.

"Maybe if things were different, that would be an option." But we both knew I couldn't avoid Olivia. Not with what Bethi and Olivia said was coming.

"Yeah. Just be careful. The boys need their Uncle Jim."

After Emmitt left, I showered and changed. The pain in my chest had eased enough that I could breathe normally. It was getting harder to convince myself that what I felt for Olivia in some way benefited the pack. The way she'd touched me, what she'd said, the burst of interest in her scent, the way she'd leaned in and sighed like she'd found home...it had all pushed me too far. I wanted her and knew that want had nothing to do with helping the pack. And, I'd almost died because of it.

But now, I couldn't get a new thought out of my head.

Olivia said the Lady stacked the deck. Wouldn't that then mean everything that was happening was supposed to happen? Not just with the girls, but with each of us, individually.

I frowned as I left the room and made my way to Isabelle's. My mind circled back to the same questions. Why me? Why now?

Isabelle opened the door on the first knock.

"Do you have to be so damn loud with your emotion? Turn it off or I'm stealing it then kicking your ass."

I grinned and immediately closed myself off.

"Sorry, Isabelle. Could I talk to you for a minute?"

"Sure. Come in."

I stepped just inside the door but didn't follow her as she walked further into the room and slid back into bed next to Carlos. The man watched me intently as he slid his arms around Isabelle.

"Olivia said Bethi's dreamed the answer. Bethi's saying all she's dreaming is about death. I think she's focusing on the wrong parts of the dreams because they are so upsetting. Could you talk to her? Calm her enough that she can maybe see past the death?" I asked.

"Yep," she said, not even hesitating. "Carlos and I will need to take her somewhere else, though. I can't spar for a while." She lifted her arms to show the colorful array of bruises lining her forearms.

Taking Bethi somewhere else meant a remote location where Isabelle could release the emotions she pulled in, without risking hurting anyone else. It almost meant separating the group. They'd need an Elder to go with them.

"All right. Let me know, and I'll go, too. The sooner the better," I said.

She was already shaking her head before I finished.

"Not you. Grey's better at blocking. We'll take him. Probably Luke, too." She grinned slightly. "He likes it when I hit him."

"I doubt that," Carlos said. "I've reached out to Grey. He'll talk to Bethi and Luke. If they agree, we'll leave in a bit."

"Thank you."

As soon as I stepped into the hall, I smelled muffins. My stomach growled, a reminder that I hadn't eaten since before seeing Olivia.

Following my nose, I discovered most of the group in the breakfast area. Olivia, Michelle, and Gabby sat at a table of four near the window. The morning sun glinted off Olivia's hair, a blonde so pale it almost seemed white. A small smile tugged at her lips as she listened to whatever Gabby was saying. If not for my heart thundering in my ears, I would have heard every word.

Thoughts of eating vanished. Like a man in a dream, I moved toward their table, seeing nothing else but my Mate.

Olivia turned, her gaze falling on me.

"Jim, are you all right now?"

"Yes." I pulled out the open chair and sat across from her.

"I was just telling Olivia about the time you got me drunk in a bar," Michelle said.

"That technically happened twice, didn't it?" Gabby added.

"I was more careful the second time. I think most of that was Isabelle," Michelle said.

The pair grinned at me. I smiled and leaned back in my chair.

"I'm pretty sure Emmitt's on your tablet ordering Christmas gifts for the boys right now," I said.

Michelle frowned, pushed her half-finished plate at me, then quickly left.

Gabby watched me with a hint of amusement.

"How are you going to get rid of me?" she asked.

I laughed.

"I'm going to ask you nicely. Can I please have a moment with Olivia?"

"I could use a nap anyway." She stood, picking up her plate. "I know it'll be hard for you, but be good, Jim."

She walked away with her plate, heading back toward the rooms. From a table near the hall, Sam stood to follow her, giving me a parting look of warning. I noticed Henry sitting with Mom, Dad, and Uncle Grey. Grey winked at me and went back to his waffle.

"I'm sorry I hurt you," Olivia said, drawing my attention again.

"You didn't. The oath I took hurt me."

Saying those words brought me back to the moment that I took the oath and the voice.

Power is granted until worthiness is lost. Death rewards self-interest.

The words hadn't come from Winifred. I hadn't given who the voice belonged to any thought at the time. The need to get to Mary's family and the boys had consumed me. Yet, now, after everything that had happened and everything Olivia had said, I began to wonder. Had it been the Lady?

If so, what did it mean that she granted a few of our race the power and strength to guide our people?

"I'm still sorry you were hurt," Olivia said.

I stared at her.

Death rewards self-interest.

My interest in Olivia was fated, orchestrated by a being that seemed to influence all. How then, could it be self-interest? It couldn't.

I grinned widely.

OLIVIA...

GUILT WANTED to nibble its way into my mind. I hated that what Jim felt for me had hurt him and that my connection with him would only bring him more pain. I wished I could see his face to know how he was looking at me right then. Was he angry? Frustrated? I couldn't tell based off of his movements.

"We need to work on your memories," Jim said, sounding different from how he had a moment ago.

I studied the shadows around him. They seemed the same, not giving me any clue as to the cause for Jim's sudden change.

"What do you mean?"

"Your happy ones. You need more of them. Let's do something fun today."

Fun? We didn't have time for fun.

"We need to—"

"Have fun," he said. "Isabelle is going to try to help Bethi figure out what she's missing in her dreams. We can't do anything about the Judgement without that, right? And everyone else is doing their own thing while we wait. Emmitt and Michelle will be busy with Christmas shopping. Clay needs rest and Gabby."

"We're going to go see a movie," Charlene said from across the room.

"We are?" Henry asked, sounding confused.

I smiled slightly as I understood what Jim and his family were doing. Giving me a chance to do something more than worry about what the next few days would bring. Would it be so terrible for me to take some time for myself? To experience a fun moment that I could hold onto during what would come next? I couldn't recall a single fun moment in my life. Not one. And, I wanted one.

My heart gave an excited beat at the idea.

"What did you have in mind?" I asked Jim.

"Everything you're doing is to save the world. Do you know what you're saving?"

"No. I don't. I didn't leave Blake's property until I came to find the other Judgements."

"Would you like to see more? Let's go downtown. It will be safe with all of the people around us. You can walk on crowded streets, shop, and eat dinner with me. What do you say?"

"Yes."

Jim's hand closed over mine, and he lifted it to his mouth. The brush of his lips against my fingers set my heart racing. I struggled to suppress what I felt and waited for Blake's irritation. None came. I relaxed and let myself enjoy the moment.

"Finish eating, and I'll walk you back to the room so you can change."

He released my hand and set my fingers on my fork. My heart warmed at his consideration. While he finished what was left on Michelle's plate, I finished my breakfast. It had to be the first meal I'd ever consumed to the last crumb.

He took our plates, threw them away, then came back to walk with me. As soon as we reached the hall, his fingers laced through mine. My pulse jumped again.

"Jim, you really shouldn't do that."

"I don't mind sticky fingers," he said. He surprised me by lifting my hand again. This time his lips didn't brush my knuckles. His tongue swiped across the pads of my fingers. I shivered at the sensation.

"Please," I said. "I'm having a hard time holding my reactions back. Blake will notice."

"Good." He kissed my fingers then started walking again, still holding my hand.

"Not good. If he grows suspicious, he'll come here."

"Let him."

I let my anger free and tugged my hand from his grip. Jim stopped and inhaled deeply.

"Mmm, our first fight," he said, stepping closer. "You smell delicious even when you're angry. Let's hurry through this part so we can get to the making up part."

My mouth dropped open, and thoughts of lecturing about what would happen if Blake chose to come too soon evaporated.

"Why are you acting like this?" I said finally. "This isn't you."

He reached up and ran a finger down my cheek.

"Actually, this is the real me. I choose not to let serious situations rob life of its fun and beauty. Of its potential to be more than the current moments make us believe it will be. You're right that we don't know each other yet. But we will. Come on. Let's get you changed."

Embrace this moment, daughter, the Lady whispered.

He gently tugged on my hand, and with the Lady's encouragement, I let him have his way.

In our room, he led me to my bag. Instead of letting me feel my way through the clothes, he took charge.

"What would you like to wear today?" he asked. "There's a pretty pink sweater in here that feels soft." He held up the sweater, looking at it. "It should be thick enough to hide the fact you're not wearing a bra, too."

A small noise escaped me.

"It's okay. I like that you're not wearing one." His voice took on a husky tone. "A lot." His fingers brushed over my collarbone and down a few inches, making my heart hammer. Before I could tell him to stop, he removed his hand.

"But, I don't want all the other males to know."

He turned away and pulled something else from the bag while I stood there with my mouth still hanging open.

"And these white leggings would look nice with it. Do you need help changing?"

"No."

"You sure? With the cuts on your back, it must be hard lifting the shirt over your head. I could do that for you. With your back to me, of course."

I breathed through my nose, trying to calm myself and collect my thoughts.

"You're making my head spin," I said.

"In a good way, I hope."

"I'm not sure yet. I'm not used to this level of attention. You're a bit overwhelming."

"Overwhelming is better than underwhelming."

I could hear the amusement in his words and smiled despite myself.

"I'm serious about the shirt. I don't want you to hurt yourself changing," he said.

"But, I don't want you to hurt yourself by helping. You saw through my shirt and fell to the ground. I hugged you, and you fell to the ground. All of this time you're spending at my feet is going to give me a complex."

He laughed, a sound so full of humor that I couldn't help but join in.

"I won't fall down this time," he promised as he gently turned me away from him.

He took the sweater from my hands and set it on the bed. Then, standing so close that I could feel the heat of him at my back, he gently eased my borrowed shirt up. His fingers skimmed my ribs, making me tremble again.

Not believing I was doing this, I carefully raised my arms and let him work the shirt over my head. With his help, I'd barely felt a twinge on my back. Yet, now I stood before him, bare from the waist up. Facing away, sure, but still in the same room. Still within reach. What would it feel like to have his fingers explore my skin now? I struggled to keep any hint of excitement from my mind and tried to think of something else. Something less dangerous.

"Here comes the new top," he said. His voice seemed more growl than words.

"Are you okay?"

"I've never been better. You are so beautiful, Olivia. And, I'm grateful you're mine."

The last comment made me swallow hard. I couldn't be his. Not the way he wanted. Pushing that thought aside, I focused on the first part he'd said.

"You're staring at my scratched back and think I'm beautiful? You might need to get out more than I do."

He chuckled.

"Lift your arms again."

My heart skipped a beat when I did as he asked. His fingers drifted lightly up my sides, tracing the outside of my arms until he reached my hands. I fought not to let myself feel.

We were playing a dangerous game. Not just with the emotions I was struggling to keep at bay so Blake wouldn't know, but with Jim's safety. I didn't understand how he wasn't already on his knees gasping for air.

With care, he eased the sweater on. The soft, fuzzy material skimmed over my skin as he slowly drew it down. Unable to stop it, a shiver coursed through me. Everything felt too heightened and sensitive now. And I craved more.

When he finished, he eased my hair from the back of the sweater and set it over my shoulder. He moved closer, his legs brushing against my butt as the weight of his hands settled on my shoulders. I barely breathed, waiting for what he'd do next.

His lips grazed the exposed skin at the back of my neck just above the sweater.

I gasped.

He placed a lingering kiss there before moving to a new spot, just an inch above the first one.

With a strangled moan, I stepped forward, away from him and his tempting touch.

"If you keep doing that, I'm going to ask to stay with Winifred tonight and not go anywhere with you." I couldn't help the way my voice shook as I spoke. I was struggling.

He sighed heavily behind me.

"You're right. Too soon."

CHAPTER SEVENTEEN

JIM...

It took every ounce of willpower to remove my hands from Olivia's shoulders. I watched her in the mirror above the desk, as I had from the moment I'd turned her away from me. Her flushed cheeks and slightly parted lips increased the ache that had grown much further south than my pain-free chest.

I didn't feel a twinge of guilt for looking at her shirtless or for touching her or for kissing her soft skin. I'd needed to test my theory. Doing everything I'd done and seeing her bare without feeling a bit of pain proved I was right. The oath and my connection to the pack kept me from doing anything that might be self-serving. The key to being with Olivia was believing it wasn't in my interest but in the pack's interest.

Winifred had told me time and again to listen to my heart. My heart told me that the voice I'd heard when speaking the oath belonged to the Lady. The same mysterious being who, according to Olivia, had been stacking the deck to ensure the Judgement happened this time around.

If the Lady had been guiding not only the pack through our Elders and our oaths, but the Judgements as well, then there was only one logical conclusion. For the sake of the pack and the Judgement, Olivia and I were meant to be together.

I wasn't sure why the Lady had chosen me, but I wasn't going to let that stop me from enjoying the gift she'd given me.

"Let's go make some memories that will compete for favorite," I said.

"I think we already have," she said softly, then quickly held up her hand before I could take her comment as an okay to go back to what we were doing a moment ago.

"If I go with you today, do you promise to behave?" she asked.

"Nope. But I promise to listen if you tell me to cut it out."

She sighed and shook her head. I reached out to Winifred over our private link.

Can we borrow someone's car?

Why? she sent back.

Olivia has no good memories. None. Her whole life has been mistreatment and pain. I need to show her something good.

I don't think—

Can you imagine dying tomorrow without one good memory to hold onto in your final moments?

There was a moment of silence.

Come get the keys.

I grinned and laced my fingers through Olivia's.

"Winifred is going to let me drive her car. This should be fun."

"I'm starting to believe your idea of fun is different from everyone else's."

I chuckled.

"You might be right."

We left our room and walked down the hall. Winifred stood in her open door, waiting for us.

"Are you sure this is wise?" she asked, looking at my hand linked with Olivia's. "I could go with you two."

"We'll be fine on our own. I promise," I said.

"Olivia?" Winifred asked, shifting her gaze to my Mate.

"I'll be careful with him," Olivia said. "If anything happens, I can call you if you want to give me your number."

Winifred rattled off her number, and Olivia repeated it back. With reluctance, Winifred handed over her keys.

"Thank you, Nana," I said with a grin.

Stay in touch, she sent me. *I love you like my own, Jim. I'll worry the whole time you're gone.*

I leaned forward and kissed her cheek.

"I love you too, Nana."

She sighed and said nothing more as I led Olivia away.

"You're so lucky to have her," Olivia said. "To have all of them."

"You have them now, too." I gave her hand a gentle squeeze and held the lobby door for her. Everyone had cleared out of the breakfast area already.

After wrapping her hand around my arm, I led her across the parking lot and helped her into the car.

"What should we do first? Shop or walk around?" I asked.

"Walk around. I'm not sure shopping will be much fun when I can't see."

"Who shopped for your clothes?" I pulled out onto the road, and followed the flow of traffic toward the downtown area.

"Blake did."

The thought of him picking out her clothes made my

hackles rise, especially when I recalled what she'd said about her nightshirt.

"He shopped for me because it gave him satisfaction to provide for me and to see me dressed the way he liked me dressed. The Mated females hated me even more because of his consideration. Their males never shopped for them. They told me it wasn't something males liked to do."

"Emmitt shops with Michelle every chance she gives him." I didn't add that he spent most of the time trying to talk her into another little black dress or more swim suits. My mouth watered at the idea of Olivia in either.

"Don't write shopping off until you try it, all right?" I said.

"Okay. I could use a new nightshirt."

"No way. The one you have is perfect. Just don't open the door with it on."

She turned her head to look at me instead of out the window.

"I think continuing to wear it would be a little dangerous for us both. If I say yes to shopping today and want a nightshirt, can I trust you to help me buy something more appropriate than what Blake did?"

I wanted to squirm with guilt like I was a cub caught stealing food from the kitchen again.

"Yes. You can trust me." We'd have plenty of time to shop for less appropriate things after the Judgement. After she Claimed me.

Pleasant thoughts of what those items might be partially occupied my mind while I navigated the roads to the shopping district and pulled into the first parking spot I found downtown.

"Ready?" I asked.

She nodded, her attention on the buildings and people surrounding us. I got out and jogged around the front of the car to open the door for her. People already going about their day crowded the sidewalks.

Olivia got out slowly, her head turning left and right as she took in the busy street.

"I've never seen so many people. The ones at Blake's complex tended to avoid me. And on the way to your home, Frank had stuck to the highways and mostly avoided the cities."

The expression on her face didn't quite look like wonder, though.

"And what do you think of it?" I asked.

"It's so loud."

I grinned.

"It is. But, sometimes loud is good."

I threaded my fingers through hers and led her along the busy sidewalk. At the first coffee shop, I pulled her in and ordered us drinks to help keep her hand warm. Her first tentative sip and the surprise on her face made me ache to wrap her in my arms. Only the wounds on her back, not her warning to behave, stopped me.

"You like it?" I asked.

"I love it."

"Come on. Let's find out what else we can try." We walked further and found a bakery. The smells coming from that place made my mouth water and reminded me of Olivia's sweet scent. I led her inside and studied all the treats.

"There's a lot here," I said. "This one has a name I can't say. It looks like a tiny pie, but not the kind with the slanted sides. This one's sides go straight up and down. It has a fancy swirl of whipped cream on it and something stuck into it that looks like a cookie. It looks good. The one next to it…I have no idea what the card says, but it looks like someone had trouble with a layered biscuit and kind of balled it up in frustration. I'd still eat it, though."

Olivia's hand jerked in mine, and I glanced at her. She had her other hand over her mouth to stop from laughing aloud. The kid on the other side of the glass display case was looking at me with a mix of hesitation and mirth. I grinned and kept going, describing every pastry I saw inside the case to Olivia.

When I finished, I ordered a bear claw, the only thing I could pronounce without sounding like an idiot, then turned to Olivia.

"What do you want to try?" I asked.

"You pick for me. But not a bear claw. I'll try yours."

I liked that she knew I'd share with her.

"Do you like sweet or savory?" I asked.

"Both."

I turned to the man waiting on us.

"Can you choose three more for us? Whatever you would recommend."

When we had our four pastries, I led her to a free table. Instead of setting her plate in front of her, I kept it by me and lifted the first pastry.

"Ready?" I asked.

She leaned forward and took a bite of what I offered.

"Mmm. That's good."

I turned the pastry and bit where she had, eating half the concoction. The subtle hint of her taste coated my tongue and hit me hard. I nearly groaned on the spot and gripped the table with my free hand, trying to control my need to toss the pastry aside and pull Olivia into my lap.

Struggling, I reached out to the only person likely to understand.

What did it feel like the first time you drank out of Michelle's glass? I sent Emmitt.

Heaven. Like I was finally close to her, even if only for a second. Why are you asking?

Just took a bite out of Olivia's pastry.

Are you okay? The worry he felt came through with the message.

No. My pants feel ten sizes too small, and I'm fighting not to jump across the table and bring her to the ground. It's so intense I don't think I can speak out loud. I'm sitting here with a wad of food in my mouth, claws jabbing the underside of the table, and a throbbing—

But no pain? Emmitt sent.

Yes, there's pain. Do I need to clarify the pants feeling too small?

I mean the pain you felt as an Elder.

None.

"Do I get another bite?" Olivia asked, smiling slightly.

With a shaking hand, I extended the pastry toward her and hoped no one would notice my nails. She took another dainty bite and licked her lips. A soft whoosh of air escaped me like I'd been hit.

I'm asking because this doesn't feel right. I was there when you were struggling with Michelle. I smelled your desperation and your interest. This is more. A lot more. Like I'd die if I tried walking away from her just then; but I didn't tell Emmitt that.

Maybe your feelings are more intense because you're an Elder, he sent back.

Maybe.

"Don't you want any more?" Olivia asked.

I forced myself to chew twice before I tried swallowing. The food barely went down.

"Yes. More you."

She blushed, a pretty pink to match her sweater and reached out to steal the pastry from my hand.

"You can't have me," she said. "I thought we'd established that."

"That's what you say, but I think your Lady has different ideas."

She froze, her hand partway to her mouth. All the color drained from her face. Her scent soured with panic and fear. The combination killed the swell of desire riding me.

"Why does that scare you?" I asked. "I thought you felt the pull toward me, too."

"I do." This time it was her hand shaking as she put the pastry down.

"I don't understand, then. Did I misread something? The way you hugged me, I thought…"

OLIVIA…

MY HEART WAS BREAKING. No, not breaking. That had happened the moment Jim had gotten ice for me. The moment I'd realized how kind and amazing he really was.

He sat across from me now, waiting for an answer.

"You're not wrong, Jim. I do feel the pull, and I am interested in you. I only misunderstood what you meant."

He tilted his head. I'd confused him further, now.

"What did you think I meant?" he asked.

"Remember those deep dark secrets? You know I have them. What I thought you meant relates to those secrets, and I'm not ready to talk about them yet." I sat still waiting for his response, hoping I hadn't just said too much.

Jim exhaled a long breath and relaxed in his chair.

"Fair enough."

The Others swirled around him as he split the pastries in half. He didn't seem mad, but I couldn't help but wonder why else he no longer wanted to feed me from the whole pastry.

"We're not sharing?" I asked.

"Oh, I want to. Too much. But maintaining control is difficult with the taste of you on my tongue."

The way he said it sent a thrill of need and sorrow through me. Making a choice, I focused on the need. I wanted the good memories he'd promised. Reaching across the table, I offered my hand. He took it, his warm touch a comfort as he gave my hand a brief squeeze then fed me another bite of pastry. While I chewed, he took a bite from his own half.

We finished the rest of our treats in silence. Every bite another memory to hold onto. And I would hold them. Forever.

Once we finished, he threw away our trash then offered me his hand again. We left the bakery and walked together down the busy sidewalk.

For the next several hours we wandered, he described the buildings, the people, and city life to me. His words painted a wonderful picture. He gave definition to the vague shapes I'd seen my whole life. He wasn't just giving me a few favorite moments; he was giving me thousands because each moment spent with him was a new favorite. I drank in his attention, wishing it could be like this forever. But, I knew reality waited and wouldn't be denied for much longer.

"Should we go back?" I asked after he finished describing an outfit on a window mannequin.

"Are you afraid I'll drag you inside?"

"No. I'm worried we're spending too much time having fun and not enough trying to help Bethi figure out—"

The finger he set on my mouth invited trouble. I opened my mouth and nipped him. He grunted and tugged me closer. My insides heated as his fingers swept over my cheek and down the sides of my neck, a gentle, fond caress.

"Grey says that Bethi and Isabelle drove closer to the mountains. They're spending some time getting rid of Bethi's fear and just talking. When they're on their way back, we'll head back, too.

"And, since you're not afraid, let's go inside. I think you need some new clothes."

I half-laughed, because I knew I didn't, but let him lead me in anyway. Racks of clothes filled the large space. The Others didn't spend too much time swirling around the clothes but did move around the people. Several shoppers moved in the main space. Another person stood off to the side near a counter. One stood near the door where we'd entered.

"There's nothing interesting in the front. Let's go to the back," Jim said, uncharacteristically non-descriptive as he tugged me forward.

"What do you see?" I asked.

"Dresses, but not good ones."

The person near the door clicked her tongue in annoyance.

"Since you're a man, I doubt you'd find any dress good enough," I said to mollify her.

"Not true," Jim answered, ruining my attempt. "This one is perfect for you."

He plucked something from a rack and held it up, calling the attention of the Others. They swirled around it, outlining the dress. There were no sleeves, just thick straps, and the front seemed to dip low.

"What color is it?" I asked. My fingers brushed over the silky material. When I felt around to the back, Jim pulled it out of my reach.

"You should try it on," he said.

"I don't think that's a good idea. My back is still sore."

"Oh. Right. We'll just get it then. And a swim suit. I'll pick that out for you, too."

I smothered my amusement.

"When do you think I'm going to wear either?"

"As soon as your back is healed. I'll take you on a real date."

"And a real date involves swimming?" I asked.

"If I'm extremely lucky, it does."

I snorted and followed him as he looked at swim suits. The Others followed him, also, and outlined the suits enough to let me know the one he finally picked didn't have much material to it. I'd never wear it, but I kept that to myself. He was having too much fun shopping for me to ruin it.

When we finished and paid, I thought he would say it was time to go back. Instead of calling it a day, he tugged me into another building.

The Others danced around the people in the restaurant, creating a mesmerizing display of movement to go with the mouthwatering smells coming from the kitchen.

"Table for two, please," Jim said.

"Of course. It's about a thirty-minute wait," the host said.

"That's fine." Jim gave his name.

"If you'd like to go to the bar area, I'll call you when your table's ready."

Jim took my hand and led me toward the long, curved bar off to one side of the dining area. The Others outlined the chair he held out for me. Not that I needed them. Jim gently guided me into the seat then ordered us both a beer.

"I'm guessing you've never had one before," he said.

"You'd be correct. I've had wine, but no beer."

"Yeah, Michelle described Blake's dinners to us after a while. Beer's better."

When the bartender returned with a chilled glass, I took it, ready for my first sip. The beer bubbled on my tongue slightly. A hint of bitterness hit me. I swallowed, and the bitterness faded followed by a smooth aftertaste.

"Not bad," I said.

"Not bad? Beer is the nectar of life."

"I thought water was the nectar of life."

"Whoever told you that lied and wanted you to suffer a life of sobriety."

I snorted a laugh.

"You're ridiculous."

"Says the person who's never been tipsy. Drink up, buttercup."

I arched a playful brow and drank deeply, draining half my glass.

"And what will you do when I'm drunk, and you have to take me back to the hotel? Michelle told me this is your favorite way to get into trouble."

"Nah, it's my favorite way to show girls there's more to life than what they thought."

He leaned toward me. I held my glass and kept my focus forward.

"You're already flushing from what you've drunk," he said softly, near my ear. "A pretty pink that draws my eyes to your lips and makes me wonder what it would feel like to kiss you. What you'd taste like. You say I'm not supposed to think like this, but I can't seem to think about anything else."

I turned my head and found his face inches from mine.

"You promised," I whispered.

"I did."

He leaned back with a sigh and rubbed his chest.

"Are you hurting?"

"Yes. But not the way you mean."

I blushed further and took another big drink from my glass, trying to ignore him and the insistent fluttering in my stomach. Several deep breaths calmed everything. Just in time, too, because we heard Jim's name called from the side of the room. He helped me from my chair and held my hand, leading me while I carried my glass.

"Your server will be right with you," the man said after he'd seated us at our table.

Not a moment later, another shape approached.

"Can I interest you in a new…"

I tilted my head and waited for more, unsure why he'd trailed off like that.

"Her pupils don't work. She's blind," Jim said.

I blushed, understanding, and ducked my head in embarrassment.

"But she can hear just fine," I whispered, annoyed with myself. How could I have forgotten? Because being with Jim, I felt normal. Whole.

"I'm sorry. It wasn't your eyes, ma'am," the man said. "I don't think I've ever seen anyone as pretty as you."

I grinned but didn't lift my eyes.

"Just tell us the specials," Jim said impatiently, making me smile even wider.

The man rattled off several things then gave me a few recommendations from the menu. After we ordered and he went away, I focused on Jim.

"Are you frowning?" I asked.

"Maybe."

"Pouting?"

"Yep."

I laughed, feeling such pure happiness, I couldn't contain it.

A sudden stab of rage right between my eyes made me wince and my stomach sink to my toes with dread. I stilled and turned my head, trying to sense Blake. He wasn't as far away anymore.

I swore and reached for my phone, but Jim covered my hand.

"Leave it. Whatever you're feeling from him can wait. This is supposed to be a fun afternoon just for you."

The phone chirped. I frowned, confused.

"That can't be Blake. He wouldn't text. He knows I wouldn't be able to read it."

CHAPTER EIGHTEEN

JIM...

I REACHED FOR THE PHONE, WONDERING WHO WOULD MESSAGE Gabby's phone when everyone in the group knew Olivia was using it.

The text was from an unknown contact. I opened it, and my gut clenched at the three images she'd received.

One of Olivia and me at the bakery. One of us outside the store where we'd purchased her dress and swim suit. And one of us sitting at this table, taken from just outside the window. I stared out at the people moving along the sidewalk.

Sam, are there any Urbat near us?

None. Gabby's been keeping an eye on you.

The phone chirped with a new message.

I'm coming for what's mine. Blake.

I swore under my breath.

Blake sent three pictures of me with Olivia, I sent Sam. *His men have to be near us.*

"What is it, Jim? What's wrong?" Olivia asked.

There aren't any near you. Gabby checked, Sam sent back.

That didn't make any sense. We hadn't been at our table long. There still should have been an Urbat nearby.

"How close is Blake?" I asked Olivia.

She turned toward the east as if looking for him.

"Closer than he was, but still hours if not a day away."

"He sent three pictures of us, and a message. He said he's coming for what's his."

All trace of color left her face.

"No. No," she whispered slowly. "It's too soon." She gripped the table, her panic rising as she turned her head to look around.

"Gabby said there aren't any Urbat near us."

She turned and pinned me with her dark gaze.

"They are all around us. Warn the rest."

Olivia thinks they're all around us, I sent Sam.

The message had barely formed when Olivia's head whipped to the side, and her eyes widened slightly. I followed her gaze to see a man shove his way through the restaurant's door. He reached across his body for something hidden under his shirt. The shape of the object was unmistakable.

Rage clawed at me, and I stood as he began to pull the gun free.

"Die werewolf!" he screamed.

I launched myself over the table, wrapping my arms around Olivia as the idiot fired. The momentum of my collision tipped her back into her chair. Her gasp of pain enraged me further. As did the bite of the bullet into my calf, where my chest had been a moment before.

Twisting mid-air, I tried to position us so I took the brunt of the impact. With a light kiss on her forehead, I left Olivia on the floor and sped toward the gunman before he could fire another shot. The man never saw me coming. Closing one hand around his throat, I ripped the gun from his hand with the other then tossed him into the nearest wall before he could hurt anyone else. He sailed through the air, his scream echoing throughout the bar.

Without slowing, I turned and rushed for Olivia, not forgetting that she'd said they were all around us. She lay where I left her, her eyes open and watching for me. I scooped her into my arms and didn't slow on my way through the window.

Curled protectively around Olivia, I blocked the shower of glass that fell around us. My feet hit the ground, and I used every ounce of speed to clear the city block within seconds. Any humans who saw us would wonder if they'd imagined our blur.

"Tell the others," Olivia said against my chest. "Blake's using his humans."

I growled at our blindness.

Sam, we were just attacked in the restaurant. Tell Gabby it's not the Urbat; it's the humans. Blake's using them.

Are you all right? he sent back.

Yes. We're moving to the car now.

We reached Winifred's vehicle a moment later, and I carefully set Olivia in her seat.

She was shaking and pale. I desperately wanted to stop and make sure she was okay, but there wasn't time. Sirens already wailed in the not too far off distance. I closed her door and sprinted around the hood.

As soon as I slipped behind the wheel, I started the engine and took off. Traffic honked behind me, but I didn't slow down.

Humans. Blake was using humans. They were everywhere. Crossing sidewalks. Driving cars. There was no easy way to tell whose side they were on. No way to know if they had a connection to Blake.

My claws scratched the steering wheel as I took the first turn.

"Find out from Michelle where we need to go," Olivia said, her voice strained. She gripped her seat with white knuckles.

"What do you mean?" I asked.

"He said he's coming for what's his, right? I'm not the only one of us he thinks belongs to him. If he's attacking here, he's attacking at the hotel, too. We can't go back."

I thought of Michelle and reached out to Sam once more.

Is everything quiet there? Olivia thinks Blake will try for the rest of the girls.

I took a sharp corner, and the tires protested.

Everything's quiet here, but I've warned the others. We're packing up.

"Slow down. Don't call attention to us," Olivia cautioned.

I slowed and took the next turn onto a road that would lead us in the general direction of the hotel.

Ask Michelle where we need to go, I sent Winifred. *Olivia wants to know.*

She didn't answer, but that didn't worry me. It took Michelle and Gabby time to decide the next safe stop. If they were in a hurry to leave, it would take a few minutes.

I hadn't made it more than two blocks when Sam's words touched my mind.

Don't come back to the hotel.

Why, what's happening? I sent back.

When I didn't immediately receive an answer, I started to worry.

"I think you're right. I think Blake's men are already at the hotel," I said to Olivia.

GABBY...

HENRY LAUGHED and threw another piece of popcorn into his mouth. Beside me, Clay sighed heavily. I kept my eyes on the TV, grateful for our chaperons.

Sam jerked forward, sitting up from his position on the bed.

"Gabby, check Jim and Olivia."

I kept my sonar open all the time so I easily answered.

"They're fine. No Urbat nearby. They're waiting in the distance, just like before."

Sam didn't relax, though. While he silently communicated with someone, most likely Jim, I studied the Urbat. The clustered groups hadn't moved much. The groups spread around Salt Lake in a half circle to the north. Nothing too close. Heavier groups waited far to the south near the Mexican border, which made sense. They didn't want us to escape that way. We didn't want to run, though. We wanted to make the Judgement and end the war that Blake had declared on the werewolves.

While the group to the south didn't really matter to us. The others did. The larger groups that had lingered far to the east had moved. As I watched, they covered hundreds of miles. How was that possible? I'd never seen any Urbat move that fast before. I opened my mouth to say something when Sam swore.

"Jim and Olivia were just attacked," Sam said. "It's the humans. Blake's using them."

"Are Jim and Olivia okay?" Henry asked.

"They're okay. Pack," he said. "We need to leave as soon as Jim's back."

Henry got off his bed and started putting things away, not that we had much out. Clay rolled to his side and eased off the bed. I changed my focus and tried to make sense of the human sparks. There were so many.

I barely paid Clay and Henry any attention as I slowly walked toward my bag. My mind wasn't on packing but on the human sparks. They moved along the roads, walked short distances before turning around, or stayed in place, all seemingly going about their daily business. However, I frowned as I noticed a different, consistent advancement amidst the otherwise chaotic movement.

A swarm of yellow with green converged on our location from every direction. There had to be hundreds of humans closing in around us.

"Tell Jim not to come back here," I said quickly. "Humans are on their way here, too."

I turned to look at Clay. He had an arm over his middle again, probably hurting it just getting out of bed.

"No shifting," I warned him. "Remember you're staying unMated until you're healed, so no setbacks."

Henry snorted a laugh. I ignored it and focused on Henry.

"There are hundreds, Henry." Something about my expression sobered him. "They're not going to show up with empty hands. You know what humans with guns can do."

The sparks surrounded the hotel.

"I can't see a way out," I whispered, the crushing weight of panic tightening in my chest.

A wave of love caressed my mind, and Clay's hand brushed against mine.

"Henry, Gabby, you two carry the bags. Clay, listen to Gabby. No shifting unless it's life or death," Sam said.

He put his hand on the door as the first human entered the building.

MICHELLE...

I TURNED OFF THE SHOWER, wiped the water from my face, and put a hand over my churning stomach. Something on my plate at breakfast hadn't agreed with me. I considered asking Jim if he felt okay, but he could eat anything and feel fine.

"You were too fast," Emmitt said from just outside the curtain.

I pulled the material aside and found him standing there naked. My stomach heaved, and I barely made it to the toilet without slipping and falling.

Emmitt wrapped an arm around my waist to steady me, but that just made the nausea worse.

"Stop. Please."

The arm disappeared, and I clung to the toilet as I continued to empty my stomach.

"Honey, what's wrong?" His hand very briefly touched my forehead.

I stood weakly and went to the sink to rinse my mouth out. He watched me the entire time, worry and love touching my mind.

"Breakfast, I think," I said after spitting out my mouthful of water.

"I'll have Mom check with the other girls," he said, wrapping me in a towel. "Let's dry you off before you get cold."

The gentle swipe of the towel against my back soothed me. I leaned against his chest and let him do the work.

"Winifred is sending Mom in to take a look at you," he said after a moment.

I smiled slightly, knowing Charlene probably just wanted to mother me a bit. By Mating Emmitt, I'd gained a full family. A Mom, Dad, and even Grandma. I loved all of them and didn't mind moments like this when they wanted to take care of me.

A knock sounded at the door. Emmitt grabbed a towel to wrap around his own waist and called out "just a minute" as he helped me from the bathroom to our bed. With a towel securely around my torso and my stomach still trying to talk me back into the bathroom, I willingly laid back.

He strode across the room and pulled open the door. A man stepped forward and hit Emmitt in the face with the butt of his rifle, driving him back a step. I screamed. More men pushed into the room.

Emmitt burst into his fur, snarling and growling. He went after the first man while the second leveled his gun at Emmitt.

"No!" I wailed.

"Stop!"

The shout echoed into the room from the hallway. The men froze, only their panicked eyes moving.

Emmitt snarled and stalked closer. I shook, too afraid to leave my place on the bed.

CHARLENE...

THOMAS KEPT a hand on my shoulder, but I barely felt it as the attackers' wills became my own. I could feel Blake's influence. No one here had been coerced or threatened. These were Blake's men, bought and paid for. They understood what they were doing. They liked it. I read their intentions through their wills. They meant to kill them all. My family. But they would spare the women and take them safely to Blake at the airport.

I boiled with rage. It would be so easy to end them. Such a move would save us from worrying they would ever come back. But I couldn't. Something bad would happen if I started making those kinds of choices. I knew that in my bones.

Sam called out from down the hall.

"We're pinned in but okay."

"Is anyone hurt?" Winifred asked.

"No." The word came from Sam and was echoed by Michelle inside the room.

Taking a deep breath, I focused my will on the humans in the hall.

"Step aside to let them through," I said.

The humans shuffled their positions just enough so I could see Sam, Gabby, Henry, and Clay.

Sam nodded at me. "We'll get the cars ready."

"It looks clear outside the hotel," Gabby added.

"We'll be right behind you," Winifred said. "Charlene, should I get our things?"

"Yes. I have control of them all."

I focused on the men crowding the doorway of Emmitt's room.

"Step aside to let us through."

My son stood in his fur between Michelle and the attackers. When he saw me, he shifted back to his skin. I stayed in the hall, feeling every connection.

"You don't belong here," I said. "You don't hate werewolves. You understand they are being hunted. You want to leave."

"Not good enough, Mom. After they leave, they call Blake and tell him to go fuck himself. Have each one take a turn so Blake's getting calls for the next hour."

I pushed that into their wills as well.

"Done." The men set their guns in the hall and walked away slowly.

Hurrying into the room, I looked at Emmitt and then Michelle.

"Are you two sure you're okay?"

Michelle nodded shakily and moved toward Emmitt.

"I might throw up again," she said.

I reached for her will, not to control, but to touch it to gain a better understanding of how she felt. My reach brushed her will and another. Stunned, I stared at her for a moment.

What is it, Thomas sent me. *Your emotions are all over the place.*

I mentally shook myself and glanced at him.

She's pregnant. I don't think they know. And now isn't the time to tell them.

Agreed.

"We need to leave," I said instead, focusing on Michelle. "I'll help you get dressed."

ISABELLE...

224

I SMOOTHED BACK Bethi's hair. The weight of her head in my lap brought out motherly type instincts I didn't think I had.

"You high enough yet?" I asked, pulling just a bit more.

"Not nearly," she slurred. "We should have brought some beer."

I grinned down at her.

"Next time, we'll get you high for fun and bring beer. You can torment Luke with it until you pass out."

"He won't care so much once I turn eighteen."

I doubted her age was the driving factor for his protectiveness. Instead of saying so, I glanced up at Carlos, Luke, and Grey who all waited in the car a healthy distance away. They'd been sitting in the car for hours while Bethi and I talked, not that I'd gotten much out of her other than vivid descriptions of her numerous deaths.

Exhaling slowly, I took in the view. She and I sat on an overlook bench on some random mountain road. The cold air helped keep her awake, and the surrounding vista was as beautiful as it was peaceful. I'd hoped both, along with my gift, would calm her down enough to talk about her dreams. It had, but I still didn't see an answer in anything she'd shared.

"Is there anything else you can remember about your dreams since Olivia joined us?" I asked.

"Nope."

A brush of worry touched my mind right before the sudden blast of the horn made me jump. I looked up in time to watch Luke climb out and sprint our way.

"Asshats," Bethi mumbled, snuggling in.

"We need to go, luv," he said, scooting Bethi up without acknowledging her choice word.

"Fine. Next time we're bringing beer, though."

"What's wrong?" I asked, standing and jogging with him.

"Jim and Olivia were attacked at a restaurant. Humans. The rest just got attacked at the hotel. Humans again. Charlene stopped them. Gabby said we're free of humans out here, but there are a group of Urbat heading toward us."

I stopped jogging.

"How many?" I asked.

"About twenty." Carlos got out and opened the back door for Luke, who quickly slid in with Bethi.

"I call front," I said, already sliding into Carlos's warm seat.

The car dipped as Carlos got in back. Grey had the car in gear as soon as the door closed.

"How close are they?" I asked.

"Close. We'll be there in two minutes," Grey said.

"You mean you're going toward them?"

"Yes. Gabby says the Urbat are closing in around Salt Lake City now. The rest of our group is heading south toward Canyonlands National Park. They'll make it through without running into any Urbat. We wouldn't if we tried going back that way. Instead, we're going over the mountain and punching through the band heading our way. Once through, we'll go around the long way."

"Isabelle likes punching," Bethi said from the back. She leaned forward suddenly and grabbed my hand. Her cold fingers wrapped around mine.

"This is just like the dreams," Bethi said sleepily. "Holding hands while we die."

My mouth dropped open. Not once in all her rambling recounting of deaths had she mentioned anyone holding hands. That had to be it. After Charlene's display of power in New York, I'd asked more questions about our gifts, and Michelle had mentioned something about her powers changing when she touched Charlene.

I looked at Grey, and he winked at me.

"It's about damn time, Bethi. And, we're not dying; we're running."

"Toward our deaths. Just remember your promise," she said, her eyes pleading with me.

"I remember," I said. If things looked bad, I'd promised to steal everything from her, so she died high as a kite. I wouldn't just ease her passing, though. I'd do that for all of them. And then kill the fuckers who caused me to do it.

"But, there's only twenty," I added. "I don't think we need to worry about anything."

"I've let the others know we have our answer," Grey said. "And that we'll meet them in the desert."

CHAPTER NINETEEN

OLIVIA...

MY BACK BURNED FIERCELY. LANDING ON THE FLOOR, HAVING JIM run with me, and then his wild driving had ripped some of Winifred's bandaging loose. I could feel something tickling down my lower back. It was only a matter of time before Jim noticed the scent of my blood.

"Blake's people tried to attack the hotel, but Mom stopped them," he said.

"Was anyone hurt? Are all the Judgments okay?"

"Gabby, Mom, and Michelle are fine. Isabelle and Bethi are still on the mountain."

He paused for a moment.

"According to Gabby, the Urbat were in clusters to the north before the attack. Now the Urbat are moving south. Isabelle and Bethi will need to go through a cluster before they're in the clear. Gabby also thinks Blake's flying into Salt Lake City."

I exhaled slowly and focused on Blake's location. That feeling of close, yet still far away, now made more sense. As soon as his plane started to descend, I'd feel his presence grow stronger.

"The rest of our group's heading to the national park that Michelle saw in her dreams."

"Is it getting dark out, yet?" I asked. We'd eaten breakfast and those pastries, but I wasn't sure if that had been a snack or lunch and if the restaurant would have counted as dinner.

"Yes, the sun's just starting to set."

"Ask Michelle if it was day or night in her images."

The noise of the tires filled the car in his silence.

"Day. She said the sun looked like it was right overhead in most of the images."

I felt a bit of relief at knowing we still had more time. I wasn't yet ready.

Jim inhaled deeply.

"You're bleeding."

"Yes."

"Why didn't you tell me?" The car started to slow.

"Don't stop, Jim. We need to get as close as possible to that park. I'll be fine until then."

"I'll just stop to get—"

"You will die, they will take me back, and the Judgement will fail. We cannot stop."

He was quiet for a moment.

"We have four hours until we reach the park."

"Look for somewhere for us to stay when we're an hour away. Make sure we're not close to the rest of our group." I leaned my head back and closed my eyes, not that it did any good. The Others continued to swirl around, filling my vision with the passing cars, passing trees, and the man beside me.

Have courage, daughter. You will not be alone.

No, I wouldn't. But I didn't want to think about that. I focused on today and my time with Jim. In my mind, I could still see the shops and the people he'd described. If I concentrated, I could recall the taste of the pastries and the way his husky voice had made my insides flutter. The attention and consideration he'd given me would never fade.

"Thank you for today and the memories," I said.

"Just the first of many. I'm sorry you were hurt again."

Those words made me ache to tell him the truth. That this would be the end of my fun days. That this wouldn't be the last hurt I would suffer before we completed the Judgement.

Instead, I concentrated on the sound of the tires and Blake's increasing nearness and anger, neither of which worried me any longer. The end was near, and he knew it. He still wanted the Judgements under his control. Now, instead of catching us like he'd hoped, we'd scattered.

Blake was growing desperate, too. More dangerous. It was time to control him like he'd tried to control the rest of us. I knew what to do and glanced toward Jim. The Others moved around him, only giving his shape a general outline.

How would he react to what was coming? To what I would soon ask of him?

Noticing my attention, Jim reached over and held my hand. The feel of his thumb smoothing over my skin gave me a measure of peace. I treasured each quiet moment as the tires slowly covered the miles to our destination.

As soon as I felt Blake grow closer, I released Jim's hand and dialed Blake's number. It immediately went to voice mail. On the second try, he picked up.

"Olivia."

"Hello, Father." I clasped Jim's hand again.

"Where are you?"

"South of you, as you know. Michelle's visions show that we'll meet tomorrow at noon in the Canyonlands National Park."

"That no longer matters."

I laughed, ignoring the anger filling my mind.

"Of course it matters. I'm not with the others, Father. They know when and where to show. Without them, without me, there will be no Judgement."

He growled.

"Then I'll settle for you," he said with soft menace.

"No, you won't. You'll wait and meet all of us there. Gabby is watching. If you or any other Urbat gets close to me, I'll—"

This time he laughed.

"You'll do nothing. You're useless and blind."

I exhaled slowly, knowing it was time to prove just how smart and useful I could be. Heart hammering, I turned my hand in Jim's and lifted his hand to my breast. He jerked and turned his head toward me.

"I do have a use, Father. A use you've been saving for yourself."

Jim growled, his fingers twitching around my breast. I let myself feel. Not just his hot palm covering my bare breast through my sweater, but the flutter of anticipation he created in my stomach and the sudden jolt of desire that crept lower because of his touch.

Blake roared in my ear.

"What are you doing? Who is with you?"

Jim tried to remove his hand, and his thumb brushed over my nipple. I shivered and held his hand in place.

"A male willing to take everything you think you own," I said, slightly breathless.

"You Claimed me," Blake yelled. "You're mine."

"We both know a Claim wouldn't stop me from having sex with someone else. You'll just experience every moment of another male taking what belongs to you. Stay away, and so will he. Make a move in our direction, and he'll have me on my back before you can howl."

I hung up the phone, released Jim's hand, and set the phone on the seat between us. It immediately began ringing, but I ignored it and the guilt that wanted to surge forward as I watched Jim's shape.

"I'm sorry," I said quietly. Blake's anger still boiled in my mind. "Tell Gabby she'll need to watch the Urbat. If any start moving toward us, she should let you know."

Jim rubbed his chest.

"You know, we'd be safer if you just broke your Claim with Blake," he said, his voice rough and with an angry edge.

I shook my head, thinking of the next twenty-four hours and what lay ahead. Fear threaded its way through my heart.

"No. I can't. No matter what, I can't release my hold on him. With it, he's the one under our control."

"Is that really the reason? Without it, he can't find you."

"Please, trust me," I said. "This is the safest way."

He didn't say anything more, and I wondered what he thought about the threat I'd just delivered to Blake. Would the pull be enough to gain Jim's willingness to help me, or had I just lost any hope of having his support?

JIM...

THE IDEA of that monster crawling around inside Olivia's head, feeling her emotions when I couldn't, was killing me. I wanted him out. Now. But I refused to push her like he had.

Fisting my hand and setting it in my lap, I struggled for calm and control. Once I had a small measure of both, I reached out to Sam, the least likely to overreact at the latest news.

Sam, Olivia's bleeding again. We need to find somewhere to stop and clean her up. If any Urbat start moving toward us, let me know.

Will do. Gabby's watching everything now. We'll meet you at Canyonlands in an hour.

No. According to Michelle's visions, we don't meet the Urbat there until the sun's high. That means we should be fine for the rest of tonight. And, because of Olivia's Claim on Blake, he knows right where she is. So, it's safer if we stay separate until tomorrow.

It's not smart to stop. There's nothing to prevent Blake from taking her back.

There is. He doesn't just want her as a Judgement to control; he wants her as a Mate. She's already let him know that I would mate her if he took a step in our direction.

I could feel Sam's panic before he even sent his message.

You can't.

I didn't try to explain that I thought I could. It would have only panicked him more.

Blake doesn't know Olivia's with an Elder, I sent back instead.

It's just a bluff?

Let's hope Blake doesn't test it.

In the silence that followed, Olivia shifted slightly in her seat. The movement drew my attention to the lingering scent of her interest and the feel and shape of her breast that seemed burned into my palm.

Keep heading south till you hit Richfield, Sam sent, interrupting my fixation. *There's a hotel there and stores for whatever you might need. Gabby says it's clear of Urbat.*

He gave directions to the hotel after I promised to stay in contact throughout the night. Not long after that, Winifred's message touched my mind. It felt larger and more open, and I knew she was communicating with all the Elders at once.

Gabby and Bethi have convinced me that we cannot face Blake's numbers alone. I think it's time we put out a call for help.

No one disagreed, and I listened to her message to all of our kind.

The time for shedding our shadowed existence is at hand. No longer can we hide in the eclipse of the humans' numbers. We must step forward as one and face our true enemy, the Urbat, and their zealot leader, Blake. All werewolves should come to Canyonlands National Park at noon tomorrow.

"Everyone is stopping for the night. Michelle's made arrangements for us."

The scent of Olivia's nervousness filled the car. I glanced at her and saw that pretty pink blush back on her cheeks.

"Are you all right?" I asked.

"Yes. It's probably for the best we stop for the night." She opened her mouth, like she wanted to say more, then closed it again. After a second, she reached over and took my fisted hand.

"I'm sorry for what I did," she said quietly. "It was the only thing that would have made Blake hesitate."

I turned my hand to grip hers.

"You gave me a favorite memory to beat all the rest."

She blushed harder.

"If he does start toward us. We might need to…touch again. Will you be okay?"

The image of her standing naked in front of me clouded my mind for a moment. She thought I still suffered when she touched me. She didn't know I could touch her all night long if she wanted me to.

"I'll find a way to pull through," I managed to say, not setting her straight.

"Thank you."

I was an ass and completely unashamed of it.

Lifting Olivia's hand to my lips, I kissed her knuckles then just held her hand as I let my mind wander to what would likely happen tonight. Blake had too much at stake to just sit back and wait. He'd try for Olivia. What would she be willing to do to keep him at bay? My blood ran hot at the thought, and I impatiently followed Sam's directions to where we'd be staying.

I pulled into the parking lot a few minutes later.

"We're at the hotel," I said. "Three stories, painted blue, well-lit from the outside. The place looks clean. There's some spare clothes in the trunk. I'll get them then come around to help you out."

"Thank you."

She waited for me, and I eagerly held her hand to help her from the car. Her pale fingers trembled in mine, increasing my excitement. With Winifred's bag on my shoulder and Olivia beside me, I successfully navigated us through the doors and got us checked in.

She remained quiet as we walked down the hall to our room where I used the key card and held the door for her.

As she stepped past me and entered the room, I breathed deeply. The scent of her fresh blood slashed through my fantasies. What the hell was wrong with me? She's bleeding like crazy, and I was imagining all the ways I could prove how much I loved her.

"Are you hungry?" she asked.

"Not really." I followed her into the room. The door clicked shut behind me.

She stopped near the bathroom door, her back to me. I stepped close and helped her ease the jacket off her shoulders.

"Does this hotel have room service?" she asked. "I think I'd like to eat a big meal after I clean up. Could you order for me?"

I tossed the jacket aside.

"Yes. I'll get us something to eat." I gingerly lifted her shirt. "First, let me see what happened."

The sight of her back had me growling at myself.

Several of Winifred's butterfly bandages had come loose. Where the rest held together, the wound looked scabbed over already. Taking the sweater off the normal way would pull at the areas still holding.

"How much do you like this sweater?" I asked.

"The sweater doesn't matter to me."

"Good." I shifted just enough for claws to form and split the sweater down her back. When she lifted her arms to start reaching for it, the wounds gaped.

"Stop. Let it fall," I said. "You're making things worse back here."

She let the sweater fall to the floor, and I went to the bathroom to wet a washcloth. I hesitated then filled a glass of water and retrieved some pain relievers from Winifred's bag.

Standing behind Olivia, I held out two pills over her shoulder. She surprised me by eating them from my hand. A bolt of heat shot from my palm, where her lips had brushed my skin, to my groin. Ignoring my response to her, I lifted the cup over her other shoulder. She turned her head and drank from the glass, not lifting her arms at all, an indicator of her pain. Her scent remained clear of it, though. Guilt ate at me.

For the next few minutes, I worked in silence, cleaning away the blood, disinfecting, stopping the bleeding and then finally reapplying the bandages like Winifred had.

"That should hold you," I said, stepping back.

She started to turn, and I set my hands on her shoulders to stop her. The soft texture of her skin under my fingertips sent my mind down a tempting, dangerous path. I cleared my throat and removed my hands.

"Let me dig in the bag to see if I can come up with some fresh clothes for you. Stay right where you're at."

I turned my back to her and looked through the bag. Jeans and shirts. Probably my mom's stuff. I grabbed out a clean shirt and underwear and put everything in the bathroom.

"You change, and I'll order your feast," I said, keeping my back to her. "And if it hurts to do something, don't do it. Ask for help."

Olivia disappeared into the bathroom, and I exhaled heavily before searching for the room service menu. It didn't list much, but I ordered two of everything they had.

When I hung up, I watched the bathroom door with a mixture of hope and uncertainty. Blake would make a move tonight. Although I dreamed of touching Olivia, I didn't want to do it when she was so hurt or as a game to stop Blake.

CHAPTER TWENTY

OLIVIA...

CHANGING SOUNDED LIKE A GOOD IDEA UNTIL I TRIED LIFTING MY arms while leaning forward. The fire that lit my back helped me decide the pain wasn't worth the effort of putting on a shirt. I considered changing my pants because the waist stuck to my skin. However, clean clothes wouldn't fix that problem entirely. I needed to wash.

How many days had it been since I left Blake's home? Since my last shower? I gingerly lifted my hand, felt my greasy hair, and wrinkled my nose. Bloody, half-starved, and stinky, I wanted a shower. I wanted to show Jim I could be more than the waif he likely saw. I wanted the freedom to choose my own destiny. I wanted a lot that I wouldn't get. Showering was as out of the question as putting on a shirt. Both would hurt me more than I cared to endure.

I ran my fingers over the pile of clean clothes then turned from them, grabbed a towel, and held it against my front. There, I hesitated and watched Jim.

He stood by the desk with the hotel phone to his ear. The Others seemed to like him. Too much. An ache started in my middle for all the things that might have been in my life had I not been born a Judgement. Normalcy. Dating. A first kiss that meant something.

Jim hung up the phone and turned to face the bathroom. Taking a deep breath, I held the towel with one hand and opened the door with the other while trying my hardest not to stretch the skin on my back.

He didn't say anything when I stepped out. The awkward silence grew, and I felt the need to break it.

"I'm sorry about the towel," I said. "It hurt too much to try to be respectable. I just want to lay down."

"That's fine. The food will be here in an hour."

"Thank you."

I walked toward him since he stood between the two beds. He remained quietly watchful as I sat on the mattress then eased onto my stomach.

"What did you order?" I asked.

"One of everything they had. A feast. Would you like some ice for your back?"

His endless consideration never failed to send a jolt of pleasure through me. This close to the end, I didn't bother trying to suppress it.

"That would be wonderful. Thank you."

He left the room while I waited on the bed. I could feel Blake in my mind and pictured him pacing in his room. He, too, knew how little time we now had. The fight for the Judgements would happen tomorrow. Blake would try to make his move tonight. Would I be enough to stop him? Something would, I knew. Michelle's premonitions wouldn't lie and wouldn't change.

I lifted my head and spotted Jim's familiar form down the hall.

"Mother, is there no other way?" I asked.

Have courage, daughter. Her whispered words came with a gentle touch that tingled over the top of my head and stroked down the length of my back. I shivered at the contact and almost shouted in joy. Her rare touches infused me with whatever I needed most at the time. Now, I felt the absolute certainty and determination to complete what still lay before me, as well as a relief from the pain that had heated my back.

"Thank you, Mother."

You are not alone, loved one. Never forget.

The door opened and closed gently.

"I have some ice." The brush of Jim's feet against the carpet announced his approach.

Instead of setting the ice on my back, I felt the light touch of a fingertip trace my skin from shoulder to spine.

"It's less red," he said, surprise lacing his words. "Less swollen, too. How?"

"It was the Lady," I said. "She came and eased my pain."

The mattress dipped as he sat beside me. He used the loose end of the towel to lie over my wounds then set the ice on top. In the absence of relief, I only felt a slight chill.

"I don't think I need the ice anymore," I said.

"That's bullshit," he said.

The calm way he spoke confused me, and I lifted my head, wishing I could see his expression.

"What's bullshit? I honestly feel better now."

"You shouldn't have suffered in the first place. She helps

when it's convenient for her to help. Not because she can't, but because she won't."

I set my head down and smiled slightly.

"I fail to find the humor in that," he said.

"I'm not laughing at how you feel. The humor is because I spent most of my early teenage years feeling the same way. And then, she began to explain things to me. My purpose. My place in this world and what would happen if I don't fulfill my purpose." I breathed deeply and noticed the complete lack of pain.

"How does it look?" I asked.

"Your back?"

"Yes."

"Well on its way to being healed. Do you want to try sitting up?"

He stood and offered his hand. I cautiously sat up while clutching the towel. The skin on my back pulled but remained pain free.

"Tell me what she told you," he said, releasing me and sitting on the bed across from mine. "Help me understand."

I considered his request for a moment. He needed to know, eventually. I just wasn't yet ready to tell him everything. Would he sense it if I told him half the story? I hoped not.

"The Lady told me the story of the four races. In the beginning, we existed together. She described a lush, beautiful world full of food. A world abundant with animals. The four races were equal in numbers, tens of thousands of each. In a world so large, that left vast unoccupied spaces. For a long time, each race lived in ignorance of the existence of any race but its own. However, while humans struggled to survive in a world so filled with harsh, primitive life, the Urbat and werewolves thrived.

"Urbat were the first to find humans. To them, humans had no use beyond another possible food source. However, because of their intelligence, humans were not as easy to kill as a deer or an ox, and the Urbat left the humans in a tentative peace, harrying them only for fun. Humans retreated further to safety, into caves and other places clogged with pungent scents that the Urbat preferred to leave alone.

"The werewolves discovered the Urbat next. The two races, so closely made, bonded. Pairs coupled. Life for the werewolves and Urbat remained peaceful only a short period of time before the Others found them.

"The Others were stronger and faster but had no form to interact with the world in which they'd been born. Years of seeing the beauty and the abundance without partaking left them craving more than just an observatory view of the world. Then, the Others discovered the werewolves and Urbat. They saw how both races could touch, taste, and smell everything around them; and the Others knew they'd found a way to get what they wanted.

"In order to interact with the world, they needed the three races that did have form. They needed flesh. Not to eat, but to wear. The first few tricked a handful of Urbat and werewolves into giving them their skin. Imagine your skin is just a jacket someone can steal. But without it you would no longer exist and your stolen jacket would start to fall apart at the seams.

"I'm sure you can imagine what happened next. Those with tattered jackets, threw them aside to steal nicer ones. The werewolf and Urbat numbers declined.

"Some of the Others realized very quickly what would

happen if all of the other races died. The Others would be without skin forever. Without any chance to ever again interact with this world. So a veil was created, a separation from the Others and the rest of the races.

"Once again the Others found themselves watching what they considered paradise from afar and fought to find a way back. To prevent that and pacify the Others, a system was set in place. So long as the three races could exist together in balance, the existence of the veil and the decision to separate the Others from this world would remain in place. However, if any of the three races ever started to dominate the remaining two races to the point of an imbalance, that decision would come under review. Not by any of the four races but by an impartial fifth. The Judgments.

"Without the need for balance, the Judgements wouldn't even exist. I'm not human. I'm not werewolf. I'm not Urbat. The Judgements are children born of the Lady and the strongest of the three races. We are not one race but a combination of two. Unnatural. Born of necessity and given a single purpose. My sisters don't understand. I do. The Lady helped me see that I have no place here without my purpose. So I embraced it. And whatever comes once Judgement is made, I accept because you've shown me there is so much in this world we need to save."

He remained quiet for so long after I stopped talking that I began to wonder if my story had put him to sleep. When he finally spoke, I jumped a little.

"I'm still calling bullshit on her."

I knew he meant the Lady.

"In what way?"

"Her help is given when it suits her. What was the point of

even letting the Others take your flesh? Yes, you made a deal. So what? She could have stepped in if she wanted to."

He is right. I chose not to save you that pain. The pain that will—

"Stop," I nearly shouted, cutting her off. I didn't want to hear more. I already knew.

"I didn't mean to upset you," Jim said tenderly.

He stood and came over to offer me a hand again. I took it and stood.

"I wasn't yelling at you. She could have helped me and acknowledges that. There are reasons she doesn't and times she takes pity on me despite those reasons. She is not bad or good. She just is. Just like the rest of her kind. They exist. They want to enjoy our world. They don't think ahead of what their unbridled enjoyment will mean to the three other races or to the planet. That's why they need to stay where they are. That's why we need to pass Judgement and bring the three races back into balance.

"Do you understand? This isn't about me or about you. This is about every creature that lives and breathes. This is about preserving this world for another tomorrow instead of blindly believing there will be another tomorrow regardless of our choices today. We are not the Others. We are more. So much more."

JIM...

I COULDN'T ARGUE with Olivia's passionate words. From the way she spoke, she believed them to her core. So did I. The Judgement needed to be made and those Others needed to stay where they were. That didn't mean I believed or trusted this Lady's role in everything, though.

"She told you all that? The history, the future of this world, just so you would understand your purpose?"

"Yes."

"Then ask her about mine. They have to be connected, right? Because we are."

She turned her head away from me and nibbled at her bottom lip.

"I don't need to ask her. I already know," she said softly. "Will you trust me a little longer? Just long enough to put a shirt on and eat a meal and maybe talk about something that doesn't involve Blake or the Others or my sisters?"

When she turned her head to look at me, I couldn't say no.

"All right. Do you need help with your shirt?"

"No. Thank you. There's no pain now." She turned her back to me and walked to the bathroom.

She'd destroyed and recreated my world with my first glimpse of her. In less than a heartbeat, everything, yet nothing, had changed. The pack still needed to come first, and everything I wished for as I stared at the pale, soft line of her back came second.

The door closed quietly, and I rubbed a hand over my face. The fact she didn't want to talk about her big secret, yet, worried me.

If this Lady knew everything, she knew my tie to the pack. No other reason made sense when I asked myself, "Why me?" But, how was my tie to the pack important? As my first glimpse of Olivia had proven, I couldn't make a choice that I felt wasn't in the best interest of the pack. If the Lady thought otherwise, she would be in for a surprise; and I would probably end up dead because a deep, cynical part of me believed that the Lady wanted Olivia to ask me to do something that would put Olivia first.

The shower turned on. I sat on the bed with a sigh and reached out to Winifred. I hoped that relating the story would distract me from thoughts of Olivia completely bare on the other side of the insubstantial wood panel. However, the conversation didn't last nearly long enough.

Alone, with nothing to do, I waited and listened.

Olivia swore softly, and I quickly moved to the door.

"Is everything all right?" I asked, hand already gripping the knob.

"No. I need your help."

The panic and urgency in her voice had me thrusting the door open. A single step took me to the shower where I yanked the curtain aside. I'd expected blood, open wounds, Olivia with soap in her eyes...anything but the trembling, sexy, wet, woman staring at me.

I tried to focus on her unusually pale face or the way she shivered in the steamy shower or the scent of her fear. I really tried. My damn eyes wouldn't cooperate as I took a sweeping glance at the length of her, searching for the source of the problem. All I saw was curve after delicious curve.

Need pooled in my gut. With my gaze fixed on the trail of water cascading from her belly button, I tried to speak.

"What's wrong?" The words came out a raw rasp.

"I'm sorry," she said, a moment before she lifted her arms and wrapped them around my neck.

In the next second, she touched her lips to mine. The contact seared me. I could barely breathe, let alone think. The taste of her, sweetness like I'd never before experienced, had blood rushing to every cell in my body. I wanted. I needed. Her taste. Her touch. Her teeth sinking into my skin.

I shuddered. Driven by that primal need, my hands rose to grip her arms and pull her flush to my chest. The feel of her breasts crushed against me almost made my knees buckle. I growled, needing more. So much more.

Without breaking our contact, I stooped and gently lifted her out of the warm spray. Her wet, slick skin filled my palms. My heart pounded in my chest. She slowly brushed her lips against mine, letting me memorize the feel of them as I turned and walked us back into the bedroom. I didn't try to lay her on the bed. Instead, I sat on the edge of it and kept her in my arms.

She ran her hands from the back of my head to my shoulders while her mouth teased and tested mine. Another shudder ran through me when she kissed my bottom lip. I desperately wanted her to open for me, but didn't try to rush her exploration.

Her lips abruptly left mine.

"Take your shirt off, Jim." I didn't need to be told twice. Some of the seams ripped in my hurry to remove it. Before it fell to the floor, she set her hands on my shoulders and nudged me back.

Blood pounded in my ears. We were in a hotel, alone. No one to stop what might happen. Honestly, I didn't care if making love to Olivia would kill me. It would be the best half a second of my life.

"Jim, you're shaking," Olivia said softly.

"I know. I'll be all right." But, I wouldn't. The sight of her naked and straddling my jean clad hips was seconds from destroying me.

She leaned forward, her breasts skimming against my chest.

My shaking grew worse, and I closed my eyes, losing coherent thought as I focused on the feel of her softness. Her fingers trailed over my chest and toyed with my neck. I growled and fisted my hands.

"I'm sorry, Jim," she said.

I shook my head, not wanting her apology. I'd be patient. I liked that she wanted to play.

Her lips pressed on the skin over my heart, followed by her tongue, then her weight settled more firmly on my hips. She moved a little. I struggled to hold still. Need pounded through me.

A moment later, I heard beeping. I shook my head, trying to understand and place the noise, but I didn't open my eyes. I didn't think I could look at her and not have her under me in the next second.

"He needs to know what I'm doing to you," she said. "Tell him. Everything. If you stop talking, I stop doing."

I frowned, not understanding. Before I could ask what she meant, she leaned over me again, nuzzling my neck in the sweet spot. I groaned.

"Talk, Jim, and I promise you won't be disappointed."

She nipped my neck.

"Do it again," I begged.

"Do what? Say what you want."

"Bite my neck again. Harder."

She did. I growled in response and almost lost control when she trailed her tongue down to the hollow of my neck.

"Yes," I panted as she licked her way down my sternum. When she pulled back, I knew she wanted me to beg some more. I didn't mind.

"Keep licking me. Every inch of my chest. Then, it's my turn."

"And after that?" she breathed.

"After that, you're mine."

A howl penetrated the fog she'd created in my mind. The tinny, faint echo of it seemed wrong.

She slid off me and started talking.

"I warned you. Decide now. Push and lose everything, or wait and see what tomorrow will bring."

Reality came crashing down on me. She'd used me to stop Blake, just as she'd promised she would. I sat up with a sick feeling in my stomach.

CHAPTER TWENTY-ONE

OLIVIA...

"Tomorrow, your games end," Blake growled before he hung up.

The phone fell from my shaking hand and hit the floor with a thud. The Others danced around Jim in a frenzy while I trembled from head to toe. In the shower, it had been fear. On the bed, it had turned into something so much more. At first, I'd only hoped that Jim wouldn't laugh at my attempts. I didn't know the first thing about real kissing or foreplay, only the bits I'd overheard the Urbat women say in the center while they watched their young torment me.

I continued to watch Jim and the Others with uncertainty.

"Was that my purpose?" he said, his voice so soft, low, and filled with anger that my shaking intensified. "To be used?"

"Blake was moving toward us. I had to do something to stop him."

"I understand," he said. He stood and moved to step around me. I caught his arm and stopped him.

"I don't think you do. You feel used. I understand that too well. That's my whole life."

"And you think being used allows you to use me?" There was no accusation in his tone, but plenty in his words.

"No. Being used has taught me to understand the difference between what I want for myself and what I need to want for a higher purpose. I thought you wanted me for yourself as much as I wanted you. I didn't mean to use you. "

He turned and tilted his head as if maybe looking down at me.

"So not just to hurt Blake?"

My chest tightened with guilt.

"No. There were many reasons for what I did. The best one was because I really wanted to touch you and let myself enjoy it just for me."

He reached up and slipped his hand through the tangle of wet hair hanging from the back of my head. A reminder that I stood in front of him with no clothes.

"Then, thank you," he said. "For taking what you wanted and for helping me understand."

He bent his head and brushed his lips against mine, sending a tingle of awareness rushing over my skin. I suppressed my joy at the feel of him. At the feel of his tongue licking the seam of my lips. Of the way my heart pounded as I opened my mouth and experienced the first real kiss of my life.

Just when my control started to break, someone knocked on the door.

Jim pulled back with a groan.

"Under the covers," he said. "So I can answer the door without killing someone."

I quickly got under the covers and listened to him accept a tray from the hotel staff.

As soon as the door closed, I left my protection and started for the bathroom.

"Where are you going?" he asked as he set the tray on the table.

"To the bathroom to finish drying off and to get dressed."

"You don't have to." The husky note in his voice sent a shiver through me.

"I do. If we continue, it'll bring Blake. I'm not ready to face that fight, yet."

He sighed and went back to laying out the food from the tray.

I SMILED and ran the brush through my hair. Dinner with Jim and our time "watching" T.V. still ran through my mind. He never seemed to object to describing things to me. Or just talking. He liked being with me. My stomach did an odd flip at that thought, and I struggled not to feel any guilt over it.

Setting the brush aside, I opened the door. Jim already lay in the bed closest to the exit. The bed we'd used to kiss and I'd used to hide, remained empty. My bed. An empty, lonely one. I sat on the edge of the mattress and looked at him. He had his head turned as if watching me.

"What's wrong?" he asked. "Still hungry?"

I shook my head with a small laugh. I'd eaten everything he'd set in front of me. My stomach hurt, but I didn't care. After all the times I'd gone hungry, I'd glutted myself.

"I won't be hungry for days."

Any humor I felt faded as the words brought what would happen tomorrow back into focus. I moved closer to him.

"I don't want to sleep by myself. We both know Blake will likely try something, again, and it makes more sense to sleep beside you because of that. But, that's not why I'm asking. I'm tired of feeling so alone."

"You'll never feel that way again. I meant what I said before. You're mine. We're just waiting until you decide the time is right."

He lifted the covers, a silent invitation I didn't hesitate to accept. I burrowed into his warmth, setting my cheek on his bare chest. His fingers stroked over my hair, a tender comfort as I closed my eyes.

Well done, daughter. You have his heart. Now ask for the rest.

I couldn't. Instead, I held him close, wanting this last night to be about me.

JIM...

OLIVIA'S HAIR tickled my chin and my chest. I didn't move to scratch the itch, though. I didn't want to wake her while I basked in our closeness. Five times during the night, she'd woken abruptly to claim my lips in a searing kiss. Twice, she'd climbed on top of me, hip to hip. The last time, she'd moved and nearly killed me.

I hadn't let her apologize for any of those moments together. She'd explained herself, and I understood. It wouldn't be long until she and the girls made the Judgement and her need to control Blake would end. I could wait.

Yet, part of me worried about waiting. I understood well

enough that my ability to touch her and be with her like this only stemmed from my heartfelt belief that I was meant to help her in some way. Fate, the Lady, whatever, threw us together for a reason. But once the Judgement finished, that reason would be done. Then what? Would I have lost my chance to make Olivia mine? Would I feel crippling pain once more?

Are you awake? Winifred sent me.

I grinned up at the dimly lit ceiling, not missing the irony of thinking of crippling pain while receiving a message from Winifred.

Yes. Olivia is still sleeping, though.

Any trouble?

No. I would have reached out immediately. You?

Everything has been quiet here, for the most part. Gabby woke Sam a few times because of Urbat movement but almost as soon as she spotted it, the movement stopped.

I smoothed my hand over Olivia's hair in appreciation. She stirred, nuzzling against my bare chest with her nose, mouth, and cheek while her hand roamed over my stomach.

Olivia is waking up now. Send Gabby to rest. Olivia will be able to sense when Blake's on the move.

Good. Let me know when you leave.

I will.

"Good morning," I said softly.

Olivia stilled then lifted her head.

"Good morning. Sorry about that."

I studied her face. She never showed much emotion, but something about her expression seemed more relaxed than I'd ever seen it.

"No apologies. Let's take what we want from life while we have the chance."

She nodded slowly, a slight frown pulling at her features. I regretted my words, and wished I could take them back.

"Ready for some breakfast?" I asked lightly.

She smiled and slid from the bed.

"I'll be ready in a bit."

While she closed herself in the bathroom, I searched the floor for my discarded shirt then changed into a clean set of clothes. Olivia stepped out with a hint of mint in her scent and a cascade of smooth hair hanging down her back.

I handed her a set of clean clothes, which she accepted with a word of thanks before disappearing into the bathroom again. By the time she reemerged, I had the bags packed and everything ready. I took a quick turn at the bathroom before we headed out.

Not wanting to bring more unhappiness to her expression, I didn't ask about her back as I helped her into the seat. Instead, I asked what she wanted to eat for breakfast.

"Do you like homemade waffles?" she asked in return. "They were too time consuming to make, so I've never had any. The freezer ones I tried were okay, but someone told me the really big ones were better."

"I love waffles."

I watched hopefully for signs for a waffle house but had to settle for a chain restaurant that I knew served breakfast food. They thankfully had waffles on the menu.

An hour later, we left with full stomachs and a smile on Olivia's face. A smile that quickly faded as I started the engine.

She stared out the window as I drove, and I let her have her silence.

We're on our way, I sent Winifred.

Good. We'll see you at the park just before noon.

"Blake's moving," Olivia said.

"Close? Do we need to stop?"

"No. I think he's moving toward the park like I said he should. Don't think for a moment he's given up, though. Michelle's visions will come true. He will fight for the Judgement to fall in his favor, likely by trying to kill all the werewolves."

A heavy weight settled just behind my sternum. We'd called them all to help.

"The Urbat have been looking for each of you in every one of Bethi's relived lifetimes. They've known you girls existed far longer than we have. If they know so much, Blake has to know what killing all the werewolves would mean. That it would bring imbalance and the Others."

She shook her head.

"The Urbat only care that we are the key to power. Blake and his predecessors have always believed the need for balance between the races was just a story told by desperate people. They're blind to the truth. And, men with blind ambition will sacrifice anything to achieve their goals."

The news wasn't overly surprising. Blake had been trying to reduce our numbers for years. However, I hadn't forgotten the way the group of Urbat had found and hunted down Mary and Gregory. Of all the werewolves hidden around the states, how had the Urbat found them first?

What if they hadn't? I opened my mind to feel the links of my people, searching for any that might be missing in the thousands of connections. All the connections were too new to tell, though.

WINIFRED…

EMMITT DROVE SO I could focus on communicating with all the wolves I'd called to our aid. They were coming from far and wide. Several of those who'd fled Europe just before I'd exposed our existence to the world while in New York had already arrived and had reported the park was quiet.

I was just about to communicate that to Sam when Jim interrupted my thoughts.

Winifred, Olivia thinks that Blake will try to kill us all to force the Judgement in his favor.

He's been trying to kill us all for years and has failed. He will fail again today, I sent.

I know. But humor me for a minute. You know our people. Have any gone missing?

I opened my mind, touching the familiar links. Some new. Some old. I frowned when I reached for one and found it missing. The first of many. Too many. How had this happened? I'd known Blake had quietly hunted Mated pairs in the past and killed families for the female cubs. Why had I assumed that genocidal brutality had ended since revealing ourselves to the world? How had I failed my people yet again? A fist of pain struck me in the chest. I gasped and leaned forward.

Winifred, what is it? Sam sent, more attuned to me than he should be. Yet, at the moment, I grasped his connection like a lifeline. He needed to know. They all did.

Over one hundred werewolves are gone, I sent them. *How did we not notice?*

If they don't reach out to us, we wouldn't know, Grey sent. *It's not your fault or theirs. We underestimated Blake. Warn the rest.*

He was right. My failing was in not being vigilant enough. It wouldn't happen again.

Blake's men are out there, human and Urbat, silencing our people in hopes of winning. If you see anything suspicious, reach out to us. Go nowhere alone. His attempt to decimate our race ends now.

GREY...

I REACHED out and touched Gregory's faint link. He was as much of a brother to me as Thomas. I mourned for him and for all the others I, now too, felt missing. So many links lost but not his. Not yet. Likely soon, though. Just like many more before the sun would set.

"Grey, if you don't tone it down, I'm going to have to hit someone in the face pretty soon," Isabelle said from her place in back.

Carlos glanced at me.

"What is it?" he asked.

"Blake's men have been quietly thinning our numbers. Families. Cubs. More than a hundred gone since we left New York."

"Bloody hell," Luke swore from the back.

"It won't end there. With the call for help we made, many more will die today." I turned to look back at Bethi.

She leaned against Luke. Because of her high emotions, we'd already had to stop once for Isabelle and Carlos to spar. I knew this news wouldn't help calm her, but they all needed to know.

"You can't let them win," I said.

Bethi snorted and sat up straight. "To save the world, yes

we can. We don't want to. We want to stop him. But, if he tries to wipe out all werewolves, there's no chance for balance; and the world will burn."

Isabelle reached over and grabbed Bethi's hand.

"We'll just need to make the Judgement before the Urbat get there. You keep visualizing your emotions trapped in a small steel box, and I'll keep visualizing all the ways I'm going to kick Luke's ass when we stop next."

Luke made an annoyed sound.

"Sounds good to me," Bethi said. She snuggled into Luke's side and closed her eyes. The scent of her worry immediately faded.

CHAPTER TWENTY-TWO

ISABELLE...

I ITCHED TO HIT SOMETHING. BETHI TRIED, BUT SHE SUCKED AT holding back everything just as much as I sucked at not soaking everything up like a sponge. Deep breathing didn't help. Focusing on Carlos in my head like a cute creeper didn't help.

"Do you think the trunk's air tight?" I asked after Bethi fell into one of her twitchy sleeps.

"You are not putting my Mate in the trunk," Luke said crisply.

"Well, I'm trying to think of something because I need to stop again and at this rate, we'll get there tomorrow."

The car immediately started to slow.

"You should have said something," Carlos said.

"Babe, I'm not going to whine every time I get the itch."

"Your nose is bleeding. It's not an itch."

I swiped at my nose and rolled my eyes at the blood there. As soon as the car came to a stop, I got out and started walking.

"Be back in a minute," I called over my shoulder.

Disappearing into the trees, I kept going until I thought I had walked far enough. Then I looked up into the branches.

"If there's any critters up there, you better run now."

A horn echoed faintly in the distance.

"Yeah, yeah. I know. We're on a schedule."

I closed my eyes and tried to stop worrying about the squirrels.

"Funny. We're on a schedule, too," a male voice said.

I opened my eyes and found myself surrounded by twelve grinning idiots.

"Looks like you ran into a door," one said.

I didn't mess around. I exhaled what I had, inhaled what they tried to keep and pushed it all out again in less than a second. The effect was like a mini nuclear explosion. The first wave started the Urbat falling to their knees, the second wave knocked them backward off their feet. They all lay in a circle around me, their sightless eyes staring up at the sun speckled canopy.

Branches broke behind me, and I spun around, ready to fight. Carlos looked at the bodies, then me.

"No hitting?" he said.

"None. I promised."

"Good."

He came toward me and hugged me gently, careful of the bruises covering my body.

"Are you empty?"

"Completely."

"We need to hurry back, now."

Without another word, he picked me up and ran back to the car.

JIM...

THE SILENCE in the car continued as we drove. The land stretched out flat in all directions around us. Sand, rock, and some occasional low-growing shrub like plants dotted the expanse. There wasn't much to see on our way toward Green River, just distant hazy mountains blended in with the light horizon.

The closer we drew, the more the distant mountains clarified into views of multicolored plateaus. I could see beauty in it, though. While I drove, I kept the rest of the group appraised of our location. They did the same for me.

Before long, I started seeing signs for the park.

"It's almost time," Olivia said. "It's not easy to have courage knowing what we face."

I opened my mouth to assure her that I would keep her safe, but she continued.

"Yes, I know I won't be alone. That still doesn't make this easier."

"The Lady?" I asked, understanding she wasn't talking to me.

"Yes."

"Does she have anything useful to say about us not dying?"

The scent of Olivia's fear and guilt filled the car. I inhaled deeply and glanced at her, unsure why she'd feel guilt.

"Want to talk about it?"

"No."

I hesitated. My gut said to keep quiet and wait it out. But, I thought back to Emmitt and Michelle's crazy courtship. He hadn't held back. He'd laid it all out for her and things had worked out fine. Yet, Michelle's initial terror...I would never forget the look in her eyes when she realized I was like Emmitt. Sure, this was a little different. Olivia knew what I was, just like I knew what she was.

I decided to go for it.

"I think I've figured it out already," I said. "My purpose."

"Oh?" Her voice was faint.

"I've been asking myself, 'why me,' since the moment I saw you. Not because I regret our connection, but because the timing and the likelihood felt too set up. Mom's a Judgement. Michelle's a Judgement. What are the chances of me feeling the pull for the last one? And why after I became an Elder? You've said the Lady influences things. I think she influenced this. And why else pair a Judgement with an Elder of the werewolves but because I need to decide something on behalf of my people? The question that remains is what decision is it that she wants me to make?"

Her black gaze swept over my face.

"No, Jim. The question that remains is how much do you love your people?"

I didn't answer, sensing it was rhetorical.

"You saw my back and understand what happened. I bargained with the Others. For their help, I paid with my flesh. That is my gift. I see what waits beyond the veil. I know what will come if the Judgement is not complete. And only I can complete it."

My grip on the wheel tightened as I listened. I had to be misunderstanding.

"What are you saying?"

"I am Courage. I know my purpose. I am the sacrifice. The payment to complete the Judgement."

I shook with rage. The road blurred as I fought the change.

Hair sprouted on my arms. Olivia said nothing as I braked and pulled over.

Olivia would die? No. She was mine. The Lady gave her to me. I didn't care if that meant an unfinished Judgement.

Pain shot through my chest. Gasping and struggling to breathe, I broke the steering wheel.

"Jim." Olivia's hands settled on my back and smoothed over my shoulders, leaving a chill under my shirt.

"I am yours. She chose you because only you have the strength and foresight to see what needs to be done. Do you love your people, your world, enough to help me fulfill my purpose? Because I can't do this without you."

In my mind, I railed at the Lady, hating her for placing Olivia in my care, for letting me touch her, taste her, love her. Why give her to me just to take her away? My throat closed with the increased pain. Grey crept in from the peripheral of my vision. None of that mattered as much as the possible absence of Olivia in my life after the Judgement. None of the pain hurt as much as that thought.

"Think of your mom. Of Emmitt and Michelle. Think of the two little boys you've left behind. Think of them, Jim," she said, reminding me of my responsibility.

I realized in that pain-filled moment, either way, I would lose Olivia. If I tried to prevent the Judgement, we would all die. The pain began to ease as I understood.

After a few moments, I drew an unsteady breath. A few more slow breaths removed the grey from my sight. Sitting up, I looked at Olivia. Tears wet her cheeks.

"I'm so sorry, Jim."

She was going to die, and she was trying to comfort me?

I pulled her into my arms and kissed her like there would be no tomorrow because there wouldn't. When we finally broke apart, she was gasping for air just as much as I had. I set my forehead against hers and let her scent wash over me.

"Tell me what I need to do to help."

"For now, just stay close. And don't tell the rest. I'm afraid they might try to stop it."

OLIVIA...

JIM STRAIGHTENED AWAY from me and focused on getting us back onto the road.

Resuming my silence, I waited and pretended each turn of the wheel wasn't bringing me one step closer to my death.

The Others raced outside the car. The barren landscape slowly changed, providing them with rock formations to swirl around and inspect. I wanted to ask Jim to talk to me, to describe what he could see. But I could still feel him shaking through the seat.

Since the day the Lady told me to bite Blake, she'd explained my purpose. I'd grown up knowing I would die, just like every other creature on the planet. The only difference was that I knew when and how.

As much as his shock and anger at hearing the news upset me, it also warmed me. He truly did care. I hoped it would be enough to see the Judgement through.

"The others are already there. We're close. But they're closing in," Jim said, his voice still low and raw.

"Who?"

"The Urbat."

"Will we make it before they do?" Blake felt closer, but not yet close enough for concern.

"We will but Isabelle's had to stop several times because of riding with Bethi. Winifred says that Isabelle ran into several Urbat groups already."

"The fighter," I said, mostly to myself. If any of us had to face a group of Urbat, she alone would survive.

"She'll make it through without our help."

"What about the rest?" he asked.

"Blake's too smart to risk any of us. Forcing Isabelle will mean that she uses her ability around Bethi. No Judgement can be made if any of us die."

The steering wheel groaned again.

"Except you," he said.

"Except me," I agreed. "But only at the right time."

Sweat coated my palms, and I casually wiped my hands on my thighs. The sweating had started the moment we'd walked out of the restaurant. The moment I'd realized I'd eaten my last meal, felt my last sunrise, and had my last drink. It was the only thing I couldn't seem to control. I could suppress my fear and keep my pulse steady, but I couldn't seem to stop sweating.

"How long until we get there?" I asked.

"We passed the sign for the park several minutes ago. Winifred said they parked their cars to the side and went in on foot. It shouldn't be far."

I watched the road ahead. The Others raced back and forth, swirling around the first car as soon as it came into view. My stomach flipped wildly as they stretched out to cover the long line of stationary vehicles.

As soon as Jim stopped, he told me to stay put then jogged around the front of the car to open the door for me.

"The ground's too rocky," he said. "I'll carry you."

Safely in the cradle of his arms, I traveled toward my end. The Others swirled in a dizzying frenzy, sensing their time was near. They outlined our path, the towering pillars that guarded it, and the men standing on top.

As we passed, the men jumped down from their perches.

"Are they werewolves?" I asked softly.

"Yes. They will follow us in to keep us safe. The first of the Urbat are here now and closing in."

He sped up, and I closed my eyes. With my ear pressed to his chest, I listened to his heartbeat and tried to enjoy each second.

Courage, the Lady said. *You've had it since the beginning and will keep it until the end. The world will know your sacrifice.*

I tried to let her words console me. I'd never doubted that the world was worth the sacrifice until I'd met Jim. Until I'd felt his lips on mine. I knew I had no choice, but I regretted we hadn't had more time together.

Jim ran into a vast canyon. People milled about in the center. Jim approached a group standing slightly apart from the rest and set me on my feet. He didn't let go, though. He threaded his fingers through mine and held me close.

"The Urbat will be here any minute," Gabby said. "Isabelle and Bethi are just behind the final wave coming from the north. There are more coming from the east who will arrive around the same time."

I could feel Blake drawing closer now that we'd stopped moving, and I turned my head in that direction. The direction from which we'd come.

"Bethi and Isabelle will arrive after Blake," I said. "He won't hurt them. He'll focus on us, on killing the werewolves, until they get here. When they do, he'll let them pass because he knows Isabelle will self-destruct if he tries something. Once she's with us, though, I don't know what he'll try. As soon as she's here, we need to make the Judgement as quickly as possible. Did Bethi and Isabelle discover the answer?"

"She thinks you only need to hold hands," Winifred said.

The answer has been given and understood, the Lady said. *This time, my daughters will not fail.*

The Others wailed their displeasure so loudly, I winced and brought my free hand to my ear, not that it helped.

"What's wrong?" Jim asked, pulling me protectively into his arms.

"The Others are upset that we have our answer."

CHAPTER TWENTY-THREE

JIM...

I DIDN'T GIVE A SHIT IF THE OTHERS WERE UPSET. SO WAS I. OLIVIA trembled in my arms. The idea of losing her tore at me.

Mom watched me with a critical eye.

"James Greyson Cole, I know that look. Every time I've seen it, something bad happens not long afterwards. What did you do?"

"I haven't done a thing, Mom." Just lost my heart to a girl meant to die.

Olivia sighed and lifted her head to look up at me. I brushed a loose piece of hair away from her face.

"Will you keep your promise?" she asked.

"I will." I would help her die to save the world.

She turned her head to look at my mom.

"He hasn't done anything. He now knows the price that needs to be paid to complete the Judgement."

Mom's eyes narrowed then widened with understanding.

"On the side of the road, when those things took your skin,

you said you had the courage to be the sacrifice. Courage to do what you must to save not just one race, but all of them. We thought you were talking about what had just happened."

Olivia shook her head slowly, and Mom's gaze pinned me. Tears welled.

"No," she breathed. Mom knew. She understood what losing Olivia would do to me. It would kill me.

With desperation in her eyes, Mom looked at Olivia.

"There has to be another way," she said. "Why you?"

"Why not Blake?" Michelle asked.

"This is what I was born for. We all have roles to play in this. Paying the price to change the future of this world is mine," Olivia said.

Mom opened her mouth to say more but was cut off by a chorus of distant howls.

"It begins," Olivia said.

"Defensive circle," Winifred called.

Mom grabbed Olivia's hand.

"You'll stick with me, Olivia."

I gave her hand a squeeze and released her. Together, Mom and Olivia moved toward the center of our group. Dad moved to my side, and the rest spread out around Mom, Gabby, Michelle, and Olivia. Wolves I hadn't seen in ages nodded to me and stepped around us, creating another barrier of protection. Henry stood in their midst. All were willing to give their lives to save our race.

I watched the various entrances to the canyon. Urbat, in their skin and in their fur, came pouring in. They greatly outnumbered us.

A hand touched my back.

"I need to be at the front, Jim, or too many will die."

"He'll try to take you."

The howls and snarls grew in volume. The ground vibrated beneath my feet.

"Where?" Olivia said, "There's nowhere to go. My sisters are here. He won't do anything to me."

I reached for her hand, and Dad grabbed my wrist.

"Is this a risk we can afford to take?" he asked.

"Endangering all these werewolves is a risk you cannot afford," Olivia said. "Blake wants this. He wants to thin your numbers. We need to prevent that until Isabelle and Bethi get here."

Dad released me, and I pulled Olivia forward.

Be careful. Winifred's worry touched my mind along with her message.

Always.

"They're coming from all directions," I warned Olivia as we wove our way through the hundreds gathered to protect us.

"This is the direction Blake's coming," she said. "Keep going."

The Urbat were less than one hundred feet away when we broke through the werewolves defending us.

Olivia immediately stepped in front of me. I set my hands on her shoulders, ready to toss her back to safety.

"Father!" she yelled. "Do you remember how it felt?"

All but one of the Urbat before us stopped abruptly.

From within the ranks, Blake continued to race forward, already in his fur. His enraged howl echoed through the canyon. The moment he cleared his men, Blake skidded to a halt while shifting to his skin. The sight of him made my hackles raise, and I knew he felt the same about me as he paced restlessly back and forth between us and his men. His gaze swept over Olivia before his eyes settled on my hands where I held her.

"Mutt. You'll die for what you did," he said, looking at me.

"Father, you're focused on the wrong thing. Like always," Olivia said. "I didn't mean what you felt last night. I meant what you felt days ago when the Others wore you like a coat."

He paled and stopped moving.

"What do you mean?" he half-growled.

"How do you think you ended up in Charlotte, North Carolina? You had no plans to go there. I needed you out of the way so I could accomplish what you never would have. The Judgements are finally all together. Well, almost. And, the time for the Judgement is near. Your attempt to manipulate the outcome has sealed the fate of it."

"You will suffer," he said softly.

A low growl escaped me.

"I will," she agreed. "But not by your hands."

"Then there's nothing left to say," he said.

Chaos erupted with his grin.

The Urbat behind him burst forward. Before the first of them placed more than a single step, I gripped Olivia's waist and heaved her up and back over my shoulders.

"Dad!" I yelled, not looking away from Blake.

"You're first," he snarled, already partially shifted.

I burst into my fur at the same time, ready to meet Blake head on.

MICHELLE...

IN THE CENTER of the silent sea of bodies, we stood on a slight rise. My left shoulder pressed against Charlene's and my right against Gabby's. Back to back, we watched the Urbat. My stomach twisted. Spotting familiar faces among their overwhelming numbers prodded the threatening nausea. All those dinners...

A wave of reassurance swept through my mind, and I glanced at Emmitt's strong back. I sent my love and gratitude in return and focused on the sound of Olivia's voice. Whether from anger, fear, or adrenaline, I shook at the first sound of Blake's. The way Olivia spoke to him didn't match the vision I'd seen or the way she'd acted since she'd found us. Something had given her courage to stand up for herself. Probably Jim. He was good at that.

The thought barely entered my mind when Jim yelled, and Olivia went sailing through the air at us.

After that, time seemed to slow.

Thomas jolted forward to catch Olivia. The surrounding Urbat lunged at the werewolves protectively encircling our defensive circle. Howls and snarls flooded the canyon, echoing and creating a frenzied din.

I tried not to let any of it distract me from my purpose.

"Urbat are climbing over the werewolves to the east," I yelled to be heard.

Thomas set Olivia near us, and I reached out to hold her hand as I continued to watch north, west, and east.

"More coming from the east," Gabby yelled. "Five minutes away. Heaviest concentration is to the north."

"The south is struggling," Charlene called.

"Sam, help the east," Winifred said as she burst into her fur and leapt over us to help those defending us to the south.

"How far away are Isabelle and Bethi?" Olivia asked.

"Ten minutes. Urbat climbing over the werewolves to the south," Gabby yelled.

One of the Urbat, jumping from head to head, caught my gaze and grinned. The grin disappeared when the owner of the current head on which he stood, gutted him from below. The Urbat fell into the mass of moving bodies.

My line of sight became clearer as more men shifted to their fur. Blood bathed both sides within minutes. The werewolves didn't give an inch, working together to maul, maim, or kill any Urbat that tried to go over or through them.

Despite their steadfast determination, our numbers began to thin. The Elders fought fiercely. Sam moved from place to place, killing any in his way. Jim struggled against Blake. Both sporting various cuts and slashes from the other.

The Urbat grew smarter and started pulling the werewolves from their positions and throwing them to those further back, clearing paths toward the center. To us.

I glanced at Emmitt's back again as he fought the first who'd already found their way close. We were losing.

GABBY...

LIKE LOCUSTS, the Urbat horde swarmed over the men attempting to protect us. The sight paralyzed me with fear and brought me back to that night in the field. The moonlight had hidden so much. Now, I saw everything. Blood everywhere.

One man turned, and I saw he had an empty eye socket and half of his face ripped off. I gagged and looked away, focusing on the sparks moving closer. Isabelle and Bethi were near. We needed them both desperately.

Clay backed toward me. His stitches had been removed last night. That didn't help me feel any better. A wolf, only three men away now, went down under a sudden wave of Urbat. How long until they reached us? Something wet hit the side of my face. I reached up and wiped my cheek, sparing a brief glance at the bit of tissue on my palm. Beside me, Michelle threw up, likely hit by the same thing.

We were going to die. No. Not us.

I looked at Clay's broad shoulders and fought not to cry.

I love you, I thought at him.

And I love you, he answered.

A sense of peace and warmth settled throughout my mind.

You are the best thing that has ever happened to me, I sent. *I'm sorry I didn't see that sooner.*

We'll be fine. You'll see.

A wolf leapt over the remaining men, aiming right for us.

"Wolf from the east," I shouted.

Sam jumped up, colliding with the beast in the air. The wolf he'd been fighting, lunged for him. I gasped. Clay dove forward, swiping his claws across the wolf's face. More gore. More blood. The air was thick with the smell of it.

"They're almost here," I shouted, still watching Isabelle and Bethi's sparks.

A hand touched my shoulder, and I glanced at Olivia. Dots of red painted her hair and face at an angle.

She wasn't looking at me, but at Jim who still fought Blake.

"They need to hurry."

I barely heard her over all the snarls and barking.

Pain erupted across my thigh. I gasped. My hands groped for whatever had hurt me but encountered nothing but unmarred jeans.

With horror, I looked up at Clay. He faced two Urbat. Saliva dripped from the elongated muzzle of one partially shifted man. The same man whose claw-tipped fingers of one hand were wrapped around Clay's throat. The claws of the other hand were buried deep in Clay's leg. The second man held Clay's straining arms.

"Sam!" I yelled.

Sam twisted and swung out, raking his own claws down the back of the one holding Clay. The distraction freed Clay but cost Sam.

I watched in disbelief as a hand suddenly emerged through Sam's front. His shocked gaze shifted to me.

"No," I breathed, heart pounding. This couldn't be happening again.

The hand pulled free, and I watched the man who'd raised me tip forward. I rushed to catch him, his weight bringing us both to the ground.

"No, Sam," I said, looking at the hole helplessly. I pressed my hand against it and started to cry as the blood continued to pool around my fingers.

His expression shifted to guilt as our gazes held.

"There were twelve just in your senior year," he rasped, his breathing labored.

"Twelve what?"

"Men I killed. They hid in the shadows, waiting for you to leave work."

Blood colored the corner of his mouth. I looked around, desperately seeking someone who could help me. Everyone fought, though.

Sam's hand touched my cheek, drawing my attention back to him.

"I waited, too. Every night. Made sure you got into your car safely. Made sure they never came back."

All those years...he'd protected me by doing more than just giving me a place to stay. Pain squeezed my insides, making it hard to breathe through my tears.

"Why are you telling me this now?"

"I don't want to die with you still doubting me. Seeing you Mated to one of ours was the best way to keep you safe. I never meant to hurt you, honey."

Tears streamed unchecked down my cheeks.

"Don't. I'm sorry. Don't go. Don't leave me. Please." I begged, and I sobbed.

"I love you, Gabby. You're the daughter I was lucky enough to find. Will you do something for me?"

I nodded, unable to speak.

"Comfort Winifred when I'm gone."

How could I when we'd all be dead soon?

I brought his hand to my lips and nodded anyway.

ISABELLE...

CARLOS SLAMMED ON THE BRAKES, opened the door, and pulled me out and up into his arms. We were running before I drew a breath. I looked over his shoulder and saw Grey carrying Bethi and Luke running beside them. The three of them let us get a fair lead, but not enough though. Not enough for what was waiting ahead. I could hear the fight echoing off the towering rock walls.

"Close yourselves off," I warned. "Bethi, we need you.

Don't let me take a thing, or I swear I'll never let you get high again."

"I'll be tighter than a virgin on prom night. Promise," she yelled back.

Despite the dire situation, I almost laughed.

"Keep your warped-self safe."

We came up from behind. Those Urbat pushing forward, wanting a piece of the fight, fell to their knees with my first pull.

I pushed out right away, not letting the emotions sit inside me for more than a heartbeat. There were too many. I glanced back at Bethi, who gave me a cool thumbs-up.

"I'm good," she yelled. "But our friends aren't. Start kicking some ass."

I looked at the fray and saw groups of werewolves dotted within the mass of Urbat. In the center of it all were Charlene, Olivia, and Michelle. Blood soaked their clothes. Michelle looked like she'd thrown up on herself. Around them, their Mates and the Elders fought frantically. Some of the outer mass of Urbat saw us and turned.

I patted Carlos's shoulder, and he set me down. Grey set Bethi down a distance to my right. She had her knife out and in her hand a second later.

"Bitches give stitches. Who's first?" Bethi yelled.

The Urbat snarled and charged toward us. I pulled and pushed, watching the Urbat fall like dominos. Those smart enough to block themselves off, Luke and Bethi finished. Carlos watched my left as we moved forward slowly. Grey protected us from any who attempted to go wide and circle around.

"Blake Torrin!" I yelled. "You took something from me. Now, I'm going to take everything from you."

The fighting slowed, and the Urbat backed up. Two wolves fought in the center, not far from where the rest stood.

"Shields," I yelled.

One of the wolves jumped away, shifting before he landed. The dark-haired man had cuts covering his bare body from head to toe. The other wolf shifted. Jim looked like shit. Pissed shit.

"Isabelle, so good to meet you at last," Blake said smoothly. "There's no need for you to use your powers, my dear. We both know what will happen. And despite what you think of me, I don't want any of you damaged."

"Then back off."

"Certainly."

He stepped away from Jim. The men around him took a few steps back, too.

I strode forward, pulling ever so slightly as I approached the group. I noticed Gabby sitting on the ground by Sam. Tears had washed clean paths down her cheeks. I couldn't look too closely, though. I didn't want to see why Sam's chest was so bloody. I couldn't afford to go back to that night.

Bethi and I joined the other Judgements. I could feel Carlos behind me. As I reached out with my right hand to take Bethi's, Carlos put his hands on my shoulders, giving me whatever support he could.

Bethi held her hand out to Gabby while I reached for Michelle with my left hand.

Sam nodded slightly to Gabby, who wiped her eyes and stood. She clasped Bethi's hand as Michelle clasped Olivia's.

"Oh," Blake said. "I forgot to mention, I invited a few more to our party. Wouldn't want this Judgement ending on the wrong note."

CHAPTER TWENTY-FOUR

OLIVIA...

BLAKE'S WORDS SENT A CHILL THROUGH ME.

The Others swirled around us in a frantic frenzy as a strip of weak darkness appeared in the center of our circle. I didn't know what it was, but it felt hungry. We needed to hurry. Ignoring Blake's ominous comment, I clasped Charlene's hand as Michelle did the same. Immediately, a string of light drifted from Charlene, the end floating toward the dark line, and Charlene's grasp tightened on mine.

"The Judgement can't be made alone. There's a reason we've Claimed mates. Thomas, hold Charlene," I said. "It's starting."

Thomas wrapped his hands around her from behind. Light ignited in the canyon. Strings from every werewolf floated from their centers to an Elder and from the Elders, a single thread floated to Thomas. I couldn't see what emerged from Thomas's chest, but I saw the thread from Charlene turn into a cable.

The rest of my sisters' chosen companions stepped forward and held them.

"Mimi!" a childlike voice screamed.

"Uncle Gregory," another voice yelled as a wolf howled.

Michelle jerked, as if hit, and tried releasing my hand.

"Do not let go!" I yelled. "Everyone will die if we fail." I was relieved when Isabelle and Emmitt both held tight to Michelle as well. She wailed and screamed as did the children.

Winifred, who still stood with the werewolves protecting us, snarled and leapt into the Urbat, the fighting starting anew.

Blake laughed. "I'll make this choice even easier for you, Michelle. I'll kill all the werewolves so there's only one way you can vote to save your brothers."

My heart hammered and my palms grew sweaty as the dark strip grew wider, and the Lady stepped out.

Bethi swore.

The Lady looked right at Charlene.

"Only you can bring balance. Feel your sister's connection, just as you can feel all the connections through Thomas. Use it."

Everyone around us stopped. Urbat and werewolf alike. I could feel Charlene's influence in my mind, touching my link to Blake because of her physical connection to me. I wanted to weep as I finally understood why the Lady said I must remain Blake's until the end.

"The time for Judgement is at hand," the Lady said. "How will you bring balance to the three races?"

Tears ran down my cheeks, and my hands trembled.

"I will give the werewolves courage to continue on until the next Judgement."

I turned my head toward Charlene.

"I will give them Strength," she said.

"I will give them Hope," Gabby said.

"I know you want me to say I'll give them Wisdom, but how? I don't feel wise. I feel bat-shit crazy, thanks to you."

The Lady stepped toward Bethi and smoothed her hand along her cheek.

"Daughter, you are more Wise than you know."

Bethi exhaled slowly.

"God, that feels good. I will give the werewolves my Wisdom. Thanks for giving me back my sanity."

"I will give them Peace," Isabelle said.

Michelle made a small sound between a sob and a hiccup.

"I will give them Prosperity. They deserve it."

The Lady turned to me and held out her hand. Behind her a shadow slipped from the darkness.

"What the hell is that?" Bethi asked. The Others moved around me, caressing my skin. I shivered.

"The Judgement has been heard. Payment must be made," the Lady said.

I nodded and turned to Jim.

JIM...

MY HEART ACHED as Olivia looked at me. I wasn't ready to say goodbye. Not yet. Not ever.

"I can't pay alone," she said.

The pale hand she held out trembled. Finally, I understood my purpose and why the Lady had chosen me. Because, I'd always had the courage to do what needed to be done.

"Good," I said. "I wasn't ready to let go of you."

I touched my hand to hers. The grey things that floated around her moved toward me.

CHARLENE...

"No!" I wailed as the grey things reached out toward Jim. At the same time I yelled, I grabbed my son's will.

His abrupt stop surprised Olivia. She turned toward him, obviously confused. But only for a moment.

"Charlene," she said, looking my direction. "Don't do this. If we don't fulfill our end of the agreement, the Judgement can't take place."

I looked at my baby boy. Then at Emmitt and Michelle and the rest of the people I loved.

"I understand. Just, not Jim." I exhaled slowly. "And, not you, either."

Thomas gave my shoulder a squeeze.

I am with you, he sent me. *Always.*

I knew he was. He always had been and always would be.

"Olivia, take care of our boy," I said.

"Mom, no," Jim managed to gasp out, a testament to his strength of will.

"Jim, honey, every Mom wants to stay and see their babies have babies. But, sometimes, we just can't. I have to go. I love you. I love all of you. This started with me; it should end with me."

Before either of them could protest, Thomas scooped me up in his arms and ran. Just like we did our first summer together. The memory held me as we sped into the void.

Through Olivia, I reached out and found the one will that had driven the werewolves to near extinction. As the void closed around us, I shattered Blake's will and Thomas kissed me hard.

OLIVIA...

THE OTHERS SWARMED around Thomas and Charlene and took their first payment. Jim yelled and rushed toward the void just as the veil sealed itself. A blast of something rippled outward and knocked all of us onto our backs.

Breathless and stunned, I stared up at the cloudless blue sky. Only a few wisps of grey floated there.

I blinked, and the grey disappeared. I blinked again as my skin prickled. Color. I could see color. How?

I sat up and looked around. Really looked. People. Their dust coated and bloody faces. Their expressions.

A man fell to his knees near me. His big, memorable shoulders shook. Not far from him, a girl rolled to her side then scrambled to a white-haired man lying next to her. The way she moved was familiar, too.

"Sam!" she yelled, shaking the man. "Sam!"

I knew that voice. Gabby. Further away, someone wailed, a keening sound the made the hair on the back of my neck stand up straight. A woman with white hair released two small boys and ran toward the fallen man. The way she moved. The power and control. I knew her.

Winifred cried so uncontrollably, I had to look away. In that glance, I saw the rest of the group I'd come to know in just a few short days.

Beside me, Isabelle stood and looked at the Urbat getting to their feet. Some of them growled at her. None of them made a move, though.

"Blake's dead," she said. "Judgement is over. Go home, assholes."

"And don't forget, the humans know you exist now. Good luck with that," Bethi said, sitting up.

I moved toward Jim, still on his knees, and reached out to set a hand on his shoulder.

He jerked at my touch then set a hand over mine. Two little boys came barreling his way. He caught them in his arms and held them tightly until they wiggled their way free to run toward Michelle.

"Dad! Paul!" Henry yelled. Like all the other werewolves, he was bleeding from different spots.

He rushed forward to another young man, who leaned over a still body.

"Gregory?" Jim surged to his feet and rushed forward, leaving me alone.

I looked around, studying this group of people I'd only known a few days. Gabby and Winifred cried over Sam. Michelle and Emmitt sat on the ground and hugged the two boys. All four of them cried. Luke had an arm wrapped around Bethi's shoulders while she gave the retreating Urbat an angry scowl. Isabelle leaned against Carlos, her nose bleeding.

"Let's go for a walk," he said, softly.

"No. I might need it."

"You won't," I said.

I glanced at the fallen middle-aged man near us. While the others cried, I wanted to smile. For the first time since as long as I could remember, he wasn't in my mind. Blake was gone. Dead. Finally.

"Without Blake, the Urbat have no clear leader. It will take them time to regroup. But it won't help. The werewolves will prosper this time around."

"You sure?" Isabelle asked.

I nodded, and she leaned closer to me.

"Holy shit. Your eyes are blue."

"Are they?" I asked, unable to stop my grin.

"What does that mean?"

I shrugged slightly, my grin fading.

"I'm not sure," I admitted. "I wasn't supposed to live. Do either of you feel different?"

Bethi looked at Luke then jumped up on him, wrapping her legs around his waist.

"I'm not tired!" she shouted. "Fuck, yeah!"

Isabelle chuckled and shook her head before looking at me.

"Nothing's seeping in. I can still feel your emotions. Bethi's joy. I can pull it if I want, but it's like I actually have control now."

I glanced at Michelle.

"Michelle, do you see anything?"

She glanced up over the head of a small boy, and her gaze grew unfocused.

"Stock market numbers. Tons of them. There's no pain with them, though."

"Jim?" Gabby called. "There are people coming. Humans. A small group."

I looked around at all the dead.

"What do we do?" she asked.

"We embrace our future," I said.

MICHELLE...

WE SAT in the front row. Winifred stood by Sam's closed casket, her hand resting on the wood. Lined around him were the boxes of ashes for every werewolf we'd lost. There were so many. Charlene and Thomas had neither a casket nor an urn. They had a large picture on a board. They stood together, smiling at the camera as two wolf cubs ran around their legs.

I felt Emmitt's pain and wrapped my arms around him.

"I'm so sorry."

"I know you are." He turned to pull me against his side and put a hand on my stomach.

"Are you feeling any better?"

"A little." Learning I was pregnant just after the fight had brought too many emotions. Mostly regret that Charlene and Thomas hadn't known.

"Good," he said. "I want this to be the first of many."

"Says the guy who isn't kissing the toilet every morning."

He kissed me softly.

"Excuse me," a man said, close by.

I pulled back, blushing. It probably looked horrible, kissing at a funeral. The man didn't look like he was judging, though. His face bore some new scars along his neck. He held out a hand to Emmitt.

"My name's Anton. I knew your mom and dad a long time ago. I'm sorry for your loss."

"Thank you for answering the call," Emmitt said.

"I made the mistake of not joining your father's pack years ago. I don't want to make the same mistake with you. If you'll have me, I'd be proud to belong."

That had been happening constantly since the fight ended.

Grey seemed surprised that Emmitt accepted each request. I didn't understand why. Emmitt had been groomed for a leadership role since the day he was born.

I moved away from them, as they took a moment to speak about the pack, and joined Isabelle and Bethi on the other side of the room.

"How's it going?" I asked.

"Not bad," Isabelle said. "Winifred is blocking the worst of it. When she lets it slip, though…" She shook her head.

"And Gabby?"

"I've been stealing," Isabelle admitted.

Paul and Henry entered. They held the door for a man I barely recognized. Gregory wore a patch over his missing right eye and had tucked an empty right sleeve into the front of his suit jacket.

I swallowed hard at the sight of him and still couldn't believe he'd survived what the Urbat had done to him in an attempt to discover where we were.

He walked right up to me and wrapped me in a partial hug. I gently returned it.

"I'm so sorry," I said, starting to cry again.

"Don't," Gregory said. "Mary had no regrets. You can't have any, either."

OLIVIA…

From the back, I listened to Michelle ask, "And you?"

"If I were a selfish man, I would regret not going with her. But I'm not. I'm looking forward to these two finding Mates and having some grandcubs for me. Speaking of that, I hear congratulations are in order."

I wondered if Jim had any regrets. He hadn't spoken to me since his mom and dad slipped into the void.

"The family would like to invite everyone downstairs for a light meal," an older lady announced from the arched opening.

My stomach rumbled at the thought of food. I felt someone nearby and looked up at Jim. He held out a hand to me.

"Let's get something to eat," he said.

I tentatively accepted his touch.

"I'm sorry," he whispered. "I wasn't sure."

"About what?"

"What would happen now that the Judgement was done. Now that I knew my purpose was to die with you."

"I don't understand."

"When I first saw you, the pain of the oath almost killed me. Something changed. My thinking. I knew we were meant to be together for a reason. After that reason disappeared..." He swallowed hard. "I wasn't sure what would happen if I thought of you as a Mate."

"And?"

He smiled slightly.

"I've acknowledged my interest and lived. I've thought of your teeth nipping my neck and lived. I think it's safe for me to say this now. Olivia, would you like to go on a date with me?"

I smiled and nodded.

HENRY...

289

I WALKED down the steps behind Dad. Something smelled amazing. What was it about grief that made a guy so hungry?

Dad cleared the doorway, and I looked ahead at the spread of food. A girl stood behind the table. She had sympathy in her eyes as she handed Aden a cookie. My heart skipped a beat. Then another. A tug started in my gut, and I inhaled deeply and stepped around Dad to get to her. She looked up at me with soft green eyes that reminded me of the forest.

"Hi," she said. "Would you like a plate?"

I inhaled deeply again. Human.

"Yes please."

"Henry?" Grey asked, standing close to me. I hadn't even noticed him in the room. "Is everything okay?"

"Things are...different," I said, unsure what else to say as she handed me a plate.

"Does anything smell good to you?"

"Oh, yeah. That's weird, though, right?"

Are you sure? he sent me.

Very. How can I feel the pull for a human? I sent back.

Grey glanced at the girl. I did, too.

I don't know. The girls said things changed for them with the Judgement. Maybe things changed for us, too.

A look of pity filled the girl's eyes, and she reached out to touch my hand. A small shiver raced up my spine.

"It's not weird," she said, unaware of the conversation I'd just had with Grey. "Grief affects people in different ways."

"Would you like to sit with me?" I asked.

"Sure," she said with a soft smile.

EPILOGUE

BETHI...

THE MIST FLOATED AROUND ME, AND I KNEW I DREAMED.

"Daughter, you have gained so much knowledge this life; yet, you and your sisters still know so little."

A gentle hand brushed my forehead.

"Enjoy this lifetime filled with love. You have earned it." Silent tears shook her words.

"What's wrong?" I asked.

"Dear one, I cry for the three races here. This Judgement did not end as it should have. Turmoil such as this world has never seen will result."

"I don't understand. We made the judgement and met the sacrifice."

"You sacrificed the leader who would have had the strength to hold the races together. Emmitt and Jim have some of her strength. We can only hope that will be enough. But, for now, the rules have changed as will the world. Only time will tell if it's a good change."

Fear gripped me.

"What happens now?"

"You finish this life as best you can, try to prepare those you love, and wait for the next Judgement. Every end is a new beginning."

Thank you for reading (Sur)real, book six of the Judgement of the Six and Judgement of the Six Companion series! It's hard to believe the Judgement is complete, and that chapter in their lives is over.

If you're ready to say goodbye to this world for good, be sure to read the alternate ending in the book extras on my website. It'll give you all the rainbows and fluffy kittens you're craving. If you're not ready to say goodbye, I've included a Bonus Scene at the end of Fury Frayed that will tie into this ominous epilogue and give you hints as to how the After Judgement world will develop.

Keep reading for more information!

AUTHOR'S NOTE

What a ride! If you're reading this, thank you so much for sticking with me on this journey. Writing the Judgement series was amazing fun. This was a longer series than I planned to write. Eleven books total, including the Companion Series!

For those of you who aren't ready to say goodbye to the Judgement world, don't worry...I already have more brewing in my head for the *After Judgement* world. Humans will still be the "dominant" race because of sheer numbers and technology. But, with the rules changed and humans now potential mates for werewolves, there's so much that can happen!

Want to see how I'm going to tie the *Judgement* series to the *After Judgement* series? Be sure to read the bonus scene at the end of *Fury Frayed* (keep reading for more info!).

If you loved reading the Judgement books, please consider leaving a review AND telling a friend about the books. You guys are helping put food on the table, which keeps the kiddos happy (and quiet) so I can write!

Watch for more books and keep up to date with new project

by following my newsletter at melissahaag.com/subscribe or joining my Facebook fan group, Haag's Howlers.

Happy reading! XOXO

Melissa

The hair on the back of my neck lifted with the sensation of being watched a moment before something darted through the trees to my right. The flash of light color low to the ground disappeared too quickly for me to see it clearly.

A soft growl came from behind me, and I twisted to look that direction. Another flash of movement, there and gone. A logical part of my brain said I should have been terrified. The growl had belonged to an animal. With trees this thick, who knew what roamed. Yet, I didn't feel fear, only impatience that whatever hid in the trees seemed to want to toy with me before attacking.

I waited.

A howl rose from within the trees, followed by another, and a third, until five voices blended into one mournful call.

"Just hurry up already," I said. "I have to get to Grandma's house."

A choked laugh came from behind me. I turned and found myself looking into an incredible pair of brown eyes that belonged to a tall boy close to my age. His longish shag of light brown hair fell around his amused face.

Surprisingly, he didn't annoy me at first glance. Not in the slightest.

"Wolves are howling, and the first thing you can think to say is that you need to get to Grandma's house?" A teasing smile played around his lips.

MORE BOOKS BY MELISSA HAAG

Judgement of the Six Series
(and Companion Books) in order:

Hope(less)

Clay's Hope*

(Mis)fortune

Emmitt's Treasure*

(Un)wise

Luke's Dream*

(Un)bidden

Thomas' Treasure*

(Dis)content

Carlos' Peace*

(Sur)real**

*optional companion book

**written in dual point of view

Of Fates and Furies Series

Fury Frayed

Fury Focused

Fury Freed

Other Titles

Touch
Moved
Warwolf
Nephilim

BOOKS BY M.J. HAAG

(MELISSA HAAG'S ADULT PEN NAME)

M.J. Haag books are not meant for readers under 18 or those who are offended by sex-loving tree nymphs, beasts who truly deserved to be cursed, or zombies (whaaaattt? Yeah, I know…).

Beastly Tales
(Beauty and the Beast retelling!)

Depravity

Deceit

Devastation

Tales of Cinder
Disowned (Prequel)

Defiant

*more to come!

Resurrection Chronicles
(zombies and hottie demons!)

Demon Ember

Demon Flames

Demon Ash

Demon Escape

Demon Deception

Demon Night

*More to come!

APPENDIX

The Judgements:

- Hope — Gabby, recently reluctant mate to Clay [*Book 1: Hope(less)*]
- Prosperity — Michelle, mate to Emmitt, son of Charlene [*Book 2: (Mis)fortune*]
- Wisdom — Bethi, mate to Luke [*Book 3: (Un)wise*]
- Strength — Charlene, Emmitt's mother, wife to the werewolf leader Thomas [*Book 4: (Un)bidden*]
- Peace — Isabelle, mate to Carlos [*Book 5: (Dis)content*]
- Courage — Olivia, mate to Jim [*Book 6: (Sur)real*]

The lights Gabby sees:

- Werewolf — Blue center with a green halo
- Urbat — Blue center with a grey halo
- Human — Yellow center with a green halo
- The Judgements:
- Charlene — Yellow with a red halo
- Gabby — Yellow with an orange halo
- Michelle — Yellow with a blue halo
- Bethi — Yellow with a purple halo
- Isabelle — Yellow with a white halo
- Olivia — Yellow with a brown halo

CPSIA information can be obtained
at www.ICGtesting.com
Printed in the USA
FSHW012004070220
66944FS